YOUR
NEXT-DOOR NEIGHBOR
IS A DRAGON

YOUR
NEXT-DOOR NEIGHBOR
IS A DRAGON

A Guided Tour of the Internet's
Strange Subcultures and Weird Realities

ZACK PARSONS

Illustrations by Dave Kelly

REBEL BASE

REBEL BASE BOOKS
Citadel Press
Kensington Publishing Corp.
www.kensingtonbooks.com

REBEL BASE BOOKS are published by

Kensington Publishing Corp.
119 West 40th Street
New York, NY 10018

All Kensington titles, imprints, and distributed lines are available at special quantity discounts for bulk purchases for sales promotions, premiums, fund-raising, educational, or institutional use. Special book excerpts or customized printings can also be created to fit specific needs. For details, write or phone the office of the Kensington special sales manager: Kensington Publishing Corp., 119 West 40th Street, New York, NY 10018, attn: Special Sales Department; phone 1-800-221-2647.

REBEL BASE and the R logo are trademarks of Kensington Publishing Corp.

First printing: August 2009

10 9 8 7 6 5 4 3 2 1

Printed in the United States of America

Library of Congress Control Number: 2009923867

ISBN-13: 978-0-8065-2759-8
ISBN-10: 0-8065-2759-5

I hereby announce this book is dedicated to my God, Super God.

The toughest God of all.

How many books the regular Lord got?

One less now, bitch.

Contents

Everything in this book is completely true.

And awesome.

Foreword: The Greatest Generation
by James Joyce

Hello! This is James Joyce, famous Irish novelist and maybe Nobel Prize winner. When my dear friend Zack Parsons asked me to write a foreword for his new book shortly before my death in 1941, I was flattered. Though the manuscript would not be completed within my lifetime, I left this world with the utmost confidence that it would be every bit the equal of my finest works, which include *Portrait of the Young Man* and *The Odyssey*. Now, some six decades later, his work is finally complete. Though I'm not alive to enjoy it—

This Joyce conceit is already running out of steam, so I'm just going to drop it before you throw the book down in disgust; save that for later, because this thing gets much worse. I was just trying to get my foot in the door by pretending to be someone respectable, but really I'm only David Thorpe, one of the author's detestable toadies.

Zack Parsons and I are members of the Greatest Generation (I'm stepping on the toes of some veterans here, but they're mostly dead anyway): we came of age before the rise of the Web, but got to it young enough to adapt. We now serve as an essential bridge between our parents' generation, which has no instinctive under-standing of the Internet, and the up-and-coming youth, who are so retarded by memes that they're practically incoherent. One day, we'll all have high-paying jobs as translators, explaining to the elderly what their young doctor means by "guy is p sick, idk wtf is wrong w/him, recommend can haz 2 aspirun and chillax, kthxbai."

Having lived in both worlds, we're the only ones who will ever see the Internet in its true context. Those who never lived without it take its weirdness for granted, and older people tend to view it with grouchy Luddite distrust, quaint ineptitude, or embarrassing, pony-tailed "look kids, I'm Twittering from my bicycle" techno-utopianism. Then there are those right-wing fringe loonies who, despite the fact that the Internet puts the totality of human wisdom at our fingertips, condemn it as a force of perversion and evil.

We of the Greatest Generation know the real story: the fringe loonies are absolutely right, and we love it. If the Internet is any kind of accurate representation of the human psyche, our species deserves swift extermination. It's a godless wasteland of insanity and grotes-querie, and in the time it takes you to read this sentence, a million children will be exposed to material more perverse than the Marquis de Sade could imagine in his ugliest fever dreams. It's terrifying to consider how it will warp their minds; it's a rootin'-tootin' Wild West of outlaw id, and it's horrifyingly reconditioning a generation's perceptions of what's normal.

The social consequences are already here: in just a couple of decades, the Internet has totally revolutionized the weirdo industry. In the olden days, sex weirdos had to indulge their seedy desires in shame and secrecy, delving into the George C. Scott *Hardcore* sub-culture of back-alley fetish clubs and underground mail-order cata-logs. Now there's Google Image Search, and a picture of a seven-foot Amazon shemale crushing a condor egg with her thighs is just a mouse-click away. What was once a risky, shameful pursuit is now fast, convenient, and anonymous.

And weirdo fetish porn isn't even the craziest part, or the part that will have the most profound effect on society. The weirdo intellect is also being reshaped, refined, and legitimized by the massive worldwide weirdo network that is the Web. Consider the following example:

Let's say you think you're a dragon.

Years ago, you'd probably bury your regal dragon shame deep inside, fearing that anyone who found out your terrible secret would think you were off your rocker. Desperate for answers, you might go see a therapist about it, and he would likely use words like "delusions of grandeur" and strongly urge you to reconsider your idea that you're a dragon. Through years of painful electroshock therapy and mind-numbing medication, you might kill the dragon inside you and begin a productive life as a drooling, ruined human being.

It's much easier nowadays. Just type the words "I am a dragon" into Google, and you'll instantly be dumped at the "Draconity FAQ," written by a dragon named Baxil, which explains everything you need to know about being a dragon. With a long list of convenient answers to common queries like "Are you crazy?" and "Isn't believing you're a dragon escapism?" the FAQ assures fledgling dragons that they're not alone, and that their perception of reality is just as valid as anyone else's. Instead of rejecting their draconity and trying to cure it through therapy, they can embrace it, and maybe even "come out" to their parents, friends, and bosses.

If you dig a little deeper, you can find one of the many online Dragonkin communities. Now you can hang out with your fellow dragons and reinforce your beliefs among a group of people who won't challenge you or call you crazy, because that would be a bummer. Instead of trying to adapt to your yucky human body, you can immerse yourself deeper and deeper into the dragon identity until it's so entrenched that you start hissing at people on the street.

Of course, the dragon thing is just one example among a thousand in the Internet's wide, wonderful weirdo rainbow. Deep inside, you might be an angel, an elf, a big sexy ostrich, a wizard, an anime character, a cannibal, a holocaust denier, or a Ron Paul supporter; whatever your wacky bent, there's a dozen communities out there where you can insulate yourself among like-minded freaks until you're convinced that you're normal and everyone else is just unfairly persecuting you, denying your God-given right to identify as an anime Nazi dragon.

The Greatest Generation knows that the Internet isn't just perverse and obscene: *it's actively creating crazy people*. Isn't it great? It is like Caligula's brain swimming around in a fish tank. We don't want to jump in, but holy shit, we sure do love to tap on the glass.

YOUR
NEXT-DOOR NEIGHBOR
IS A DRAGON

The Reluctant Anti-Hero

The finger bones of my right hand exploded like Chinese fun poppers stuffed into sausages. My experiment was a resounding success. I had proven that a car door *can* completely shut with a juicy human hand wedged between the frame and the door.

I heard the horrible crunch of the door closing an instant before I felt the pain. Then I screamed and bit down into the glazed doughnut I was carrying in my mouth. I exhaled a curse into the fried dough so terrible I have subsequently scrubbed it from my memory.

When I stub my toe I shout the f-word. I can only imagine the sort of twisted, high-yield, weapons-grade version of "fuck" that emerged from my mouth at that moment.

Things did not improve in the immediate aftermath of slamming my (motherfucking) hand in the car door. It was unfortunate, but my brain, the human brain, never evolved the ability to cope with that situation. My instinct when confronted with the explosive pain in my hand was to yank that hand in the opposite direction.

It's understandable. That instinct has served the hands of fifty generations of my forebears well, protecting their fragile digits from fire, explosions, rolling boulders, giant tusked tigers, and dinosaurs.

I'm sure that instinct will work just as well to protect my great-great-great-grandchildren's hands from vengeful robots and laser dinosaurs.

At that particular moment, with my hand shut into the door of my car, with a spit-covered doughnut tumbling in slow motion from my wailing mouth, I yanked my hand away. I yowled and I yanked my wounded hand from the door with all of my might.

That was my brain's rough draft at least.

The reality was a door that had somehow latched shut, securing my crushed hand in a vise. When I yanked with all my might my hand caught for a moment and then, with a unique ripping sound I will never forget, I freed my hand.

Or at least the inside part of it.

I looked at the bloody mass of my fingers, twisted and crimped and dripping blood, and I very nearly passed out. What I left behind between the door and the frame was a bloody glove bearing the fingerprints of four fingers and part of a thumb.

My doctors would later refer to this as a "degloving" or a "40 percent avulsion."

"You should have open door first, Dumb-Dumb," Dr. Lian, my Chinese doctor, would scold me in the coming days and weeks.

But that's jumping ahead. That's skipping the moment of horror as I realized I had just compounded a terrible injury.

I staggered back, my eyes flicking from the exposed pink and red insides of my right hand to the tattered cuff of bloodied skin dangling from the rim of my car door. I could barely even move my gory fingers, owing mostly to the severe fractures but also at least in part to the amount of pain I was experiencing.

Those people who tell you getting shot or breaking a leg barely hurts? Lying jerks. They're just saving the surprise for you.

Gentle reader, you probably bought this book, which means I owe you. I don't know you, but I like you. You have sound judgment. I sincerely hope a straight-shooter such as yourself never has your hand crushed and degloved. But, if such an accident befalls you, I feel you should be fully informed as to the degree of pain you might be expected to experience.

Allow me to go ahead and clear up any misconceptions on that subject.

It will hurt. A lot. How badly it hurts is difficult to say, but it will be measured in profane increments like "fuck loads" and "shit tons."

You may scream a great deal as a result of this pain. You might even urinate in your pants. Really. You don't think about that sort of thing, but when you experience a lot of pain, sometimes you lose control over other body functions. This may extend to defecating in your pants as well, although I was spared that level of indignity.

Don't worry about peeing. You won't even notice, what with the pain and most of the blood falling out of your body through the exposed meat of your hand. I didn't notice as I began to empty my bladder. I was yelling incoherently and rolling around in a puddle of blood and doing a good job of smashing my doughnut.

Taking the groceries home was right out. Forget it. That frozen food could go ahead and thaw itself out in the trunk. Those Klondike bars could go ahead and melt. I had some serious yelling and peeing and bleeding to do.

My cell phone began to ring.

"Say, baby, put down that pipe and get my pipe *up*," said Bill O'Reilly as his Robo the pimp character.

I was unable to stop yelling and bleeding, but I was able to reduce my crazed thrashing just enough to dig into the pocket of my blood-soaked jeans and grab my phone.

"Say, baby, put down that pipe and get my pipe *up*," Bill O'Reilly repeated.

I managed to flip the phone open with my left hand and hold it up to my ear. It was covered in blood and smelled like pee.

"Aaaaahhh!" I screamed into the receiver.

"Whoa, baby, turn down the volume," exclaimed the voice on the other end.

It took a moment through the brain-curdling pain, but I recognized the voice. It was Lonnie Saunders, my editor from Kensington Publishing.

"Ahhhhhhaaaaaaaaaa!" I replied.

"Zack, baby, what's with the screaming?" Lonnie sounded like he was chewing gum.

The best I could manage to reduce the screaming was holding the phone away from my head. People in the grocery store's parking lot were beginning to gather around me. It seemed like they wanted to help, but they were afraid to touch me.

I can sympathize.

"We looked over your book proposals, baby," Lonnie explained. "It's all good stuff, really amazing stuff."

I had just enough sense in my brain to doubt Lonnie's sincerity. When Kensington requested a list of potential book concepts, I had given them two real choices larded with a bunch of ridiculous wizard-themed proposals.

There was no way Lonnie thought the wizard books were "good stuff."

"Wizard erotica. I love it. Potion recipes? Great. You really know your wizards. I love the mercenary wizards book, too, but I think you need to flesh it out a little more. Now this other idea, this darkly humorous apocalyptic horror novel, what can you tell me about that?"

"Aaaaaggghhhhhhhmmmmmmphh." I rolled my face into the puddle of blood as I screamed.

"Right, right, you mentioned an October one date. Do you think you could deliver by September one?"

"Aaarrrgh!" I demurred.

"Whoa, calm down." Lonnie cautioned. "We'll split the difference.

How does September fifteen sound? Good, good. Now there are some things, baby. I love the idea. Love it. But I think we need to change it up a little."

"Aaahmphph." I let my face sink back into the blood as I sobbed my reply.

"You know it, baby. It'll be twice as good. What I'm thinking is, what if, imagine this, instead of end of the world, you do the Internet. And instead of darkly humorous, you just skip the darkly part. Times are too crappy for that sort of thing. People want to be cheered up. Let's make it peppy. Oh, and instead of a novel, it's a guide. Sound good, baby?"

"Do you think he's dead?" asked a woman standing over me.

"No, look." Her husband nudged me with the toe of his shoe. "You can see the bubbles in the blood. He's still breathing."

"Breathing, what's that?" Lonnie seemed to half catch the conversation taking place over my head.

I tried to gasp a response, but all I could manage was a weak gurgle.

"Look, I know you're the best. You can write it all. Write a big hit about the Internet and people or whatever. Sound good?"

The man and the woman helped me sit up. I nearly passed out. The pain had by that point ebbed into a steady throb. I felt cold and nauseous. I was going into shock.

"Aaaaaaaah!" My scream was becoming hoarse.

"Beautiful, baby." Lonnie decided he had waited long enough for my answer. "If you've got any questions let me know. All right? All right? Great, baby. Ciao!"

"Aaaaaah!" I replied, but the line went dead mid-scream.

The scream ebbed and I fell silent. The phone slipped from my fingers. I looked up at the man and the woman trying to help me.

"It'll be all right," the man said.

"Aaaaaah!" I answered.

Not my most articulate series of conversations, but I did the best with what was at (skinless) hand.

Convalescence

My ambulance ride to the hospital is a subject for someone else's book. Perhaps Vince and Janice D'Agostino, the retired couple who found me in the grocery store parking lot and summoned the ambulance. Janice held my good hand while the EMT injected me with some sort of industrial-strength opiate. I don't remember much of anything after that.

The next few hours passed in a similar chemical haze, although I do retain brief flashes of memory. I was visited by several nurses and doctors. I came to know most of these people quite well over the coming days of surgeries and recoveries, but there were two doctors I considered "my doctors."

Doctor Gerber was an elderly man with a lipless ribbon of a mouth. It was the sort of slack and inarticulate aperture that might have seemed at home on a snail or slug. It was adapted perfectly for suctioning up a meal of debris off the side of a gourd.

Doctor Gerber would walk into my hospital room, peer over the rim of his glasses at my chart, glance up and at a point about three feet above my head on the wall, and then walk out. The closest I ever came to having a conversation with Doctor Gerber was a bit of fleeting eye contact and a grunt as he replaced the chart at the foot of the bed.

Doctor Lian was the brusque Chinese doctor who I interacted with the most. He was the one who told me Doctor Gerber was the surgeon who would ultimately repair my hand. Doctor Lian was some sort of weird bone specialist whose job it was to inflict intolerable agony on me daily by drilling a series of screws into my fingers.

"You such a baby," he complained whenever his drill churned through the local anesthetic and I twitched or gasped in pain. "A baby not even wake up if I do this. Just a tickle."

It took two days of drilling and screwing and steel-plating to assemble the bones in my fingers. When Doctor Lian was done, my hand was covered with scaffolding. Painful scaffolding that wept blood and managed to ache through the morphine.

The Erector Set on my hand wasn't even addressing the problem of not having any skin. There was a gelatin-like mitten over my hand. A nurse explained it was "keeping me fresh" and preventing serious infections.

I had completely forgotten about my ill-timed phone conversation with Lonnie, but that small mercy was not going to last. The pleasant opiate haze began to dissipate when Doctor Gerber ordered a reduction in my painkillers. The physical pain was bad, but the boredom was worse. When you're drugged out of your mind you never realize how boring it is to sit in a hospital all day.

My roommate, a literal rodeo clown with a broken pelvis, dominated the room's only TV and loved to yell answers at bad game shows. Buddy Bronc was his clown name; his real name was something boring like John Cooper or James Cobbler.

Buddy said he was "kicked in the taint by an ornery 'spinner' " and was "just glad to have a dick." He always wanted to talk to me about rodeos and having sex, which demonstrated an uncanny ability to identify subjects I never wanted to discuss with a clown.

Just before I arrived, an exceptionally massive nurse had made Buddy intimate with a Foley catheter. He wanted to discuss this inconvenience at length. The pain it caused him was the only thing that could cut through his sex and rodeos talk.

Have you ever read about the candiru fish? It's a tiny silver fish in the Amazon that can follow a wading fisherman's urine up his urethra. Once it's nestled snugly inside the unlucky fisherman's urinary tract, it latches on with barbs surrounding its mouth and drinks his blood.

The candiru drinks blood from the inside of the fisherman's dick. The fish is in his dick. Imagine a version of the candiru you can purchase from a medical supply catalog. That's a Foley catheter.

"Goddamn you piss a lot," Buddy moaned whenever I stepped out of the bathroom. "Keep me up all fuckin' hours."

He was understandably bitter about my urination habits. While I was able to get out of bed and take a leak at night, the severity of Buddy's injuries forced him to turn over that body function to a vampire fish wedged up his urethra.

Sometimes Buddy even managed to combine his urination obsession with one of his favorite subjects.

"Y'all ever peed on a girl?" Buddy asked me late on the third night of my hospital stay.

I confessed that I had not urinated on a woman and voiced no interest in doing so.

"You should try it. You got to drink a whole lot and then save it up. So you pee more and harder."

I was willing to take his word for it.

"Sheila left me last week," Buddy Bronc confided to me during a commercial break. "She took the dogs and all my DVDs."

"Was it the peeing?" I asked.

"That's my wife you are talkin' about there," Buddy snapped.

I apologized and Buddy seemed to accept.

"It's okay. I ain't never peed on her. Sheila left me 'cause I was still married to Rita. So me and Sheila's marriage didn't count. And I said, 'Well, I got the license from Reggie work up at the courthouse.' But I think she just wanted to pick a fight . . ."

Buddy was a terrible clown. While he digressed into a monologue about his girl Sheila, his "fat bitch" sister, and his previous wife,
my mind focused in on the pulsing pain in my hand. It felt as if someone was taking a drag on a very evil cigarette and the burning ember
at the tip was buried inside each of my shattered finger bones. I became hypnotized by the rhythm of the pain and almost drifted off
to sleep when something Buddy was saying snapped me back to consciousness.

". . . give her a call tomorrow. I think I need to have a conversation with that bitch."

*Oh, no. Oh, God, no. Lonnie Saunders called me! He called me
about a book!*

The realization washed over me in a wanna-puke tsunami. Lonnie Saunders wanted me to write a book! Lonnie, the unctuous
chimera of a used-car salesman, sports agent, and pimp, wanted me
to write some sort of godforsaken guide.

Guide to what? What was it? Fuck! Something about wizards?

"Fuck!" I exclaimed aloud.

Buddy looked over at me.

"Which one? Rita? Been at least six weeks. Now Sheila, we
used to . . ."

I hit the nurse's CALL button beside my bed as Buddy began to
describe a sex act he performed on his fake wife that began with
lassoing her in a barn. It ended with dire hillbilly deviance I dare not
recount here without risking the confiscation of this book from libraries.

The door to the room opened and the night nurse stood silhou-
etted in the doorway. Neither busty nor Asian, I would generously
describe Mandy as "structurally sound." She was short and stout,
with legs as thick as rail ties. She filled a Technicolor nurse's smock with
a confused bust that seemed to expand in several directions at once.
No looker, true, but I was glad it was Mandy.

The other nurse, an Ecuadorian girl who was beautiful except for her bad teeth, was a sadist. I once asked for an extra pillow to prop myself up better and she looked me in the eye and pinched my arm. I don't even know if she spoke English. She never even brought me the pillow.

"How are we doing tonight, Mr. Parsons?" Mandy asked.

"When I came in here"—I pushed myself upright—"what happened to my stuff? The stuff that was in my pockets. My phone. Where did it go?"

"Did your wife take it?" Mandy asked. "I saw a bag of your stuff at some point."

I shook my head. Michelle took my car keys, but I had no memory of seeing my wallet or cell phone. I had not thought to ask someone about either until Buddy's rambling reminded me of my phone call from Lonnie.

Mandy helped me out of the bed and together we searched all of the possible nooks and crannies in the room where my phone and wallet could be hiding. Buddy watched our efforts until the morphine pump for his shattered pelvis activated. He grinned and his chin slowly dropped against his chest.

"Found it," said Mandy with a triumphant smile.

She handed me a plastic Ziploc bag containing some coins, a receipt from the grocery store, my wallet, my phone, and two dead flies. The phone was disgusting. The holes on the earpiece were gummed up with blood and the buttons were covered by a thin crust that was almost black. To my amazement, the battery was not dead.

Mandy brought a damp washcloth over and I wiped down the phone until it was reasonably clean and the white cloth was pink. I should add that doing this was not particularly easy when you only have one hand and the nurse seems disgusted by the sight of blood.

I accomplished the task by sitting on the edge of the bed and resting the ankle of one leg on the knee of the other. I then placed the phone upright in the crook of the bent knee, pinched the knee closed on the phone, and proceeded to grunt a great deal as I swiped the wet cloth across the front of my phone.

I had a few voicemail messages from friends and family wishing me well, but nothing from Lonnie. I switched over to e-mail on the hospital's anemic wireless and my phone practically melted down from the number of e-mails it was receiving. Lonnie had unleashed a stream-of-consciousness barrage of ideas and notes for me to "help" in writing the book.

The cryptic and sometimes frightening subject lines for the messages included classics like "tron guy a hit," "what is a 4 cham?", and *"chapter about girl with a dick."* This at least vaguely informed me on the subject matter. I didn't have the heart to actually read any of the e-mails, but that was fine. My conversation with Lonnie was flooding back.

Based on his e-mail subjects, I deduced that Lonnie wanted the guide book to be about the Internet. This was possibly the stupidest idea I had ever read. What sort of moron reads, let alone buys, a guide to the Internet? That is the sort of book a mom in 1994 gets for her kid interested in computers. It was the sort of book that would have a picture of a robot surfing on a river of numbers for its cover.

No, the Internet is far too fleeting and dynamic to ever be adequately tied down. To borrow something from Buddy, you could never lasso the Internet to a fence and convince a horse to have sex with it.

I sighed and fell back on the bed, so dispirited I could almost ignore the screaming pain that exploded as my skinless hand flopped against the mattress. That scoundrel Lonnie Saunders had once again fast-talked me into writing the worst book ever.

Maybe, just maybe, I could weasel my way out of this one. It had to work.

11

I was afraid that if I didn't do something, and quickly, writing a book about the Internet might be the end of my career as an author.

Early Release

In the morning, I made four calls to Lonnie's office in New York before I got through to his personal assistant, Roxy. I had never met her, but we had spoken many times. Roxy sounded the opposite of my admittedly uninformed stereotype of the average personal assistant.

I envisioned the average personal assistant as a young and well-groomed up-and-comer, constantly speaking into a Bluetooth headset to make reservations at upscale restaurants or cancel high-power meetings. Personal assistants were lean and on the edge, wired to please their boss and serve him or her slavishly.

Roxy was nothing like that. She sounded bored and had the rough voice of a woman on the wrong end of decades of chain-smoking.

No, that's being too kind. Roxy sounded like she was half a carton of Pall Malls away from a cancer voice box. A chest X-ray of her would look like a picture from the Hubble telescope. There would be spiral arms and nebulas of malignancy swirling in the twin universes of her lungs.

I imagined her with an unruly head of gray hair, eyeglasses secured around her neck by a chain, wearing a frumpy sweater and lugging canvas tote bags full of crumpled legal pads.

"Yes?" she growled.

"Roxy, this is Zack Parsons. I need to speak with Mr. Saunders."

"Are you the wizard guy?" she asked.

"Uh, yeah, that's me. Look, I had a little bit of an accident a couple days ago and I need to talk to Lonnie."

"He's not in the office right now," she replied.

I sighed with disappointment, but Roxy wasn't finished.

"He's in Chicago," she said, and I heard a loud crinkling of papers. "The Ritz-Carlton. Room eight seventeen. If you want to go over there I'm sure he'd be—"

"I just need to talk to him on the phone," I interjected.

Roxy cleared her throat. It was a wet hack. I could hear marbles of phlegm being shaken inside a brittle paper bag. Her voice dripped with melodramatic annoyance when she continued.

"If you want to go over there, to the Ritz-Carlton, room eight seventeen, I'm sure Mr. Saunders would be glad to see you. He told me not to bother him, though. So you just go on over there and knock on the door unannounced. See how that works out for you."

She hung up the phone before I could reply.

The idea of finally meeting my editor was a bit daunting, but I was in no position to allow my nerves to get the better of me. This critical moment called for courage. Heroic, assertive, type A personality. Getting out of the hospital and to the Ritz-Carlton meant convincing one of my two fairly hostile doctors to let me go.

Doctor Gerber flatly refused when I requested release. By "flatly refused" I mean that he lowered his face a few degrees and pursed his wet noodle lips. It was a deafening rebuke. I tried again with Doctor Lian. Asking his permission made me feel like a kid getting a second opinion from Mommy after Daddy says "no."

"Dumb-Dumb, you go outside you get infection," Doctor Lian explained. "You want to get killer bug, hand fall off? Maybe you get dick poison and dick fall off. Pretty stupid then, uh-huh?"

"I can't skip this, Doc," I pleaded.

"I'm no 'doc,' Dumb-Dumb." Doctor Lian folded his arms across his chest. "Dock where you park a boat. But I not keep you here. You want to go, get deathly disease, go ahead. Go. Be Dumb-Dumb. Spread your wing and fly. Go on, Dumb-Dumb."

"Can't you put something on my hand?" I asked, and waved my skinless, gelatin-encased, steel-haloed hand.

"Oh, sure, I got a good one," Doctor Lian sneered.

He stormed out of the room and came back with a white plastic shopping bag.

"Here you go," he said, and grabbed me by the forearm. He covered my skinless meat hand with the bag and then stretched a fat rubber band down over my hand and wrist. He looked at me and let it snap against my forearm, cinching the bag tight in the process.

"There you go! Weatherproof!"

"Thanks," I mumbled, and grunted as I climbed out of the bed.

"Oh, no, my pleasure. Be my guest. Go on, a whole dumb world await a Dumb-Dumb like you."

I nodded and shuffled past him.

"Come back when you serious," he called after me. "I fix your hand for real then."

The Breakfast Clubbing

Lonnie answered the door. He was much shorter and fatter than I had expected. Pot-bellied and Devitoesque. In fact, Lonnie would have been a perfect doppelganger for the diminutive actor if it weren't for his fraudulent blond pompadour and the bushy, golden caterpillars above his eyes.

His face was flushed and sweaty. He was clad in boxer shorts and an ill-fitting hotel robe that hung open like playhouse curtains on either side of a rolling strip of torso. It was a very theatrical framing for the view of his grotesquely protruding bellybutton.

A girl wearing a similar hotel robe brushed past him and then me and into the hallway. Her black hair hung in her face, but as she passed me I glimpsed eyes puffy and red from crying and streaked mascara. She smelled like stripper perfume and burning rubber. Lonnie hardly seemed to notice her departure.

"Come in, come in," Lonnie invited. "You want some star fruit, baby? A Thai massage?"

"No, no thanks," I replied. "This is an amazing room."

Lonnie's suite was high ceilinged and luxurious. The main room was bathed in the golden light of parchment lampshades and appointed with overstuffed antique furniture that might have passed for Thomas Jefferson's living room set from Monticello. Through the open double doors of the bedroom, I could see that the floor was scattered with cotton balls.

"Yeah," he looked around admiringly. "Not as good as the room I get at the Four Seasons in Manhattan, though. Has a fireman's pole. You just can't get that in Chitown."

Lonnie did a barefoot spin in the middle of the room, his arms spread as if to drink in his surroundings. Articles of clothing were draped haphazardly across the furniture. He scooped up a bra and a white T-shirt.

"Have a seat," he suggested.

I moved aside a silvery sequined dress and relocated a purse from a chaise longue to an elegant teak end table sporting a Tiffany lamp. Round yellow pills spilled out of the purse across the polished wood. I looked to Lonnie and he shrugged.

"Ain't mine, baby," he said. "I am drug-free. Alcohol and Ketamine only. Just kidding. Just kidding, baby. Loosen up. Maybe you should take a couple of those. Kidding, kidding, baby. But seriously, help yourself."

Lonnie was even more manic in person, bouncing from foot to foot like a lizard on hot sand. He seemed to remember he was still holding a bra, and he tossed it into the bedroom.

"Housekeeping," he said incredulously.

I have never hated Lonnie, but I have never trusted him, and his guilty tweaker act was creeping me out.

"Holy shit!" he proclaimed suddenly, bugging his eyes out. "What happened to the mitt there?"

He leaned over to get a better look at my bag-covered hand. I realized that there was a small puddle of blood in the bag, as if it were a cut of meat from the butcher's.

"I didn't know it was bleeding," I said. I lifted it up and looked at the bag, but the rubber band around my arm seemed to be containing the blood.

"What happened, baby?" he asked again.

"That's part of why I'm here, Lonnie. We need to talk about this book deal."

"All right." He bobbed his head affirmatively. "All right, I'm down. That's cool. Let's order up some mimosas and— You like lobster tail?"

"No," I said.

"That's cool; that's fine." He snapped his fingers and paced distractedly.

"Hey, look, I just want to—"

"Here we go!" Lonnie snatched up the pearl-handled receiver of an antique telephone. He stabbed a fat finger into the rotary dialer and winched in the number for the front desk.

"Yeah, this is Saunders in eight seventeen. Yeah. Having a pow-wow up here and I wanted to order some room service. Four mimosas and lobster tails. You want lobster tails?"

"No, thanks," I replied.

"Better make it six mimosas and two lobster tails."

While he listened to the person on the other end he pantomimed shooting himself in the mouth.

"All right," he said. "The door is unlocked, so just come on in."

He hung up the phone and danced his way to the chaise longue and plopped down next to me. Not just next to me, practically on top of me.

"So what's the bug, baby? What's the deal?" He slapped a fat-fingered hand on my knee. "What can Lonnie Saunders do to make you feel good?"

His invasion of my personal space was calculated. He wasn't making a creepy proposition, nor was he being overly friendly. Lonnie had some inkling of why I was there, and the sweaty little goblin wanted to bully me in some small way.

Lonnie was not physically intimidating. I had almost two feet on him. His move worked anyway. It threw me off. I have always been horrible at negotiating or demanding anything, and his hand on my knee creeped me out just enough to ruin my whole pitch.

Lonnie's smile broadened and I realized I must have winced or somehow betrayed my discomfort. Having made his point successfully he gave my leg a squeeze and scooted away from me on the chaise.

I knew I was defeated, but I gave it a try anyway.

"I can't write this book, Lonnie," I began. "A funny guide book is pretty clichéd to begin with and about the Internet? This isn't 1995. People know what the Internet is at this point."

"Come on, Zack, you're *on* the Internet," he said, as if that meant something. "You know all about that stuff. You're an expert."

"You can't write a book about catchphrases and funny websites," I countered. "That's what I know. A bunch of weirdos and their weirdo friends on their weirdo websites. Hell, I'm one of those weirdos."

"So don't write about the websites; write about the weirdos." Lonnie craned his neck as if searching for something. "Hey, do you have any cigarettes?"

"Sorry, I just quit," I said. "Lonnie, look, even if I wanted to write the book, I just . . . I can't."

I waved my bloody bag around. Lonnie snorted with amusement.

17

"So you cut your hand? Don't be a baby, baby. Ernest Hemingway wrote *The Old Man and the Sea* with his ball sack cut open. F. Scott Fitzgerald's house was lousy with raccoons. He almost died from rabies."

"I don't think any of what you just said is actually true," I countered, "but I'm not using this hand thing as an excuse. I'm right-handed and it's going to be many weeks before I can use my right hand again. Maybe many months before I can type or use a pencil."

"Who the fuck writes with a pencil?" Lonnie flicked one of the yellow pills off the end table.

"You know what I mean."

Lonnie fixed me with a serious gaze and flipped one of the pills right at my face.

"Look, this isn't a fun-time party-time negotiation here, baby. We're not talking about your feelings or your poor little hand. Learn to type with your left hand or cut that one off and type with a hook."

"A hook?"

"Or whatever. Maybe they have a robot hand. Look, you cashed the advance check for this book and you don't even have a proposal. We're being nice here. More than fair. You gave us a list of ideas and, frankly, your wizard books sucked. I say that as a publisher looking for wizard books. We are proactively seeking wizard books. They were just appallingly bad. A romance novel called *Wizard Marriage*"?

"The amorous spell caster is an underutilized trope," I replied, feeling a bit outclassed.

"Trope? Slow down there, Proust. You're a joke writer, so write something funny. Write me a funny book about the Internet."

He clapped his hands several times.

"Go find your weirdos. Write about your weirdos. All right?"

It was that sort of moment that I always wish I had spent the time and money on those nunchaku lessons. And that I had brought my nunchakus.

The room service cart arrived before I could roundhouse-kick Lonnie Saunders through one of the exterior windows.

A skinny bald kid wheeled the room service cart up to the elegant table in the suite's dining nook. He carefully arranged the champagne flutes in a semicircle around the centerpiece of a silver-topped dish of lobster tails. Bibs and condiments were provided on a separate tray.

Lonnie tipped the kid well and then motioned me over to the table. He lifted the silver lid from the steaming lobster tails. I hate lobsters. I hate any crustacean. It's the idea of eating what amounts to a giant sea bug that disgusts me. Normal bugs, fine, but I am not going to devour the guts of some oceangoing cockroach just because the government tells me it's safe.

I watched Lonnie lustily forking the fluffy white flesh from one of the lobsters. He would fork two or three butter-dipped bites into his mouth, chew for a few seconds, and then chase it down his throat with half a flute of mimosa.

"Back in colonial days lobster was so cheap they banned feeding lobsters to inmates in coastal prisons," I said, just to make small talk. "At the time it was thought to be similar to eating rats."

Lonnie slammed his fork down on the table and glared at me while he chewed and swallowed his current lump of crustacean meat. At length he warned me, "Don't fucking do that, baby."

"What?"

"Don't bring that David Foster Wallace shit over here and ruin my lobster," he said, and then pushed it away. "Rats? If only rats tasted like this. You're a shitty brunch companion, Parsons."

It wasn't the first time I'd heard that and it wouldn't be the last.

"I'm sorry!" I exclaimed, even though I wasn't.

"It's all right, you're just a clueless little baby. Let's do this then. Let's do some negotiating. What have you got?"

"Well, I—"

"Because I've got a contract that you signed, so keep that in mind when you make your demands. Think about that."

I did and I had. Lonnie's suggestion about writing the book about the weirdos rather than the websites was actually pretty solid. Something along those lines had crossed my mind if, as a last resort, I was trapped into writing this infernal guide to the Internet.

"I need a car," I said.

"No," Lonnie said.

"Just a rental," I amended.

"No," Lonnie replied. "No car. No plane tickets. No gas allowance. If you need to go somewhere for this book you need to get there yourself."

"Recording equipment," I said.

Lonnie got up and walked into the bedroom. He returned with a Ritz-Carlton pen and pad.

"There you go." He slapped it down on the table. "What else?"

"My hand, I—"

"Hook or robot hand," he said, and drained one of the flutes of mimosa. "Next."

"I get the feeling there isn't going to be much give-and-take in this negotiation," I said.

"Yeah, you're probably right," Lonnie agreed. "Why don't we call it a day? You let me finish my lobster and you go on and get started with your book. Sound good?"

What a dick.

"I need to get back to the hospital," I said as I stood up.

Something about the position of my arm and the way I was standing gave Lonnie Saunders a very mistaken impression about my body language. His hand shot out and grabbed mine in a powerful and friendly handshake.

Blood exploded from the ruptured grocery bag and rained down on the mimosas and lobster tails. I let out a whimper and collapsed to my knees in agony.

The flash of white hot pain I experienced in that moment proved to be cathartic. The choice was clarified by the pain. It was crystallized by the gore exploding out of my wounds.

I would write the guide about the weirdos. I would write about the vores, and furries, and creeps who put themselves in fan artwork. I would endeavor to write the comprehensive travelogue and guide to the subcultures that make the Internet simultaneously wonderful and terrible. I would need to carefully observe and interview the people who have made those subcultures fascinating.

It wouldn't be a *good* guide to the Internet's weirdos. It would be an *awesome* guide to the Internet's weirdos.

Before my adventure could begin I had to have a little talk with Doctor Lian about my robot hand.

CHAPTER ONE

The Matrix Retarded

He's intelligent, but an under-achiever; alienated
from his parents; has few friends. Classic case for
recruitment by the Soviets.

—FBI Agent Nigan, *War Games*

The Internet is a slippery creature that defies description and
metaphor.

Sure, the physical Internet can be defined. It can be described
as routers and fiber optic lines, megabytes and gigabytes, bleeps and
also bloops. That sort of description is too literal. By those rules you
could claim a human is a bunch of meat and organs, but then a
bucket filled with meat and organs also qualifies as human.

It is the nature, the elusive essence, of the Internet that cannot
be easily categorized. What the Internet *means*.

Thousands of people with intellects vastly superior to mine have
tried to describe the Internet. These are people with real college degrees, not the sort you buy for $49.99 from a "university" in a former

Soviet state. Their degrees didn't arrive in an envelope that smelled like salted fish and prominently featured a spelling of "master's" that included a "k" and no vowels.

Ted Stevens, the disgraced Republican Senator from Alaska, had a bachelor's degree in political science from UCLA. That is an undergraduate degree and probably around ten IQ points on me. The brutal Darwinism of Alaskan politics ensures no fools ever hold office in that state. Yet, even a man as robustly intellectual as Senator Stevens once infamously warned of the Internet, "It's not a truck. It's a series of tubes."

Thanks?

William Gibson, one of my heroes, described the futuristic Internet of *Neuromancer* as a "consensual hallucination" consisting of "lines of light ranged in the nospace of the mind." Gibson's neon-drenched cyberpunk prose always appealed to me, but that description of the Internet sounds like a bad ride on some spinning playground equipment after huffing glue.

Gibson managed to come up with an extravagant and psychedelic version of dumb. For practical purposes the cyberspace portions of *Neuromancer* might as well have been a technical manual on how to send an e-mail written by Ted Stevens during a peyote-fueled vision quest. They definitely don't get anyone any closer to understanding the reality of the Internet.

The Internet is so slippery in large part because it is vast and ever-changing. Gibson might have come closest on the third try in *Neuromancer* when he referred to cyberspace as something of "unthinkable complexity."

Another nerd hero, racist horror author H. P. Lovecraft, used this technique frequently. When something was "too scary" or "too otherworldly" he would come right out and admit, "This monster is too scary and otherworldly for me to describe." Lovecraft was dealing in impossible angles and colors from outer space.

When a writer attempts to cover the topic of the Internet, he or she is dealing with an imaginary world distributed across millions of computers and created simultaneously by hundreds of millions of people. That sounds like some impossible angles or colors from outer space to me.

Anyone who volunteers themselves as an authority on the subject of the Internet is an asshole. Don't listen to a word they say.

The Internet is too broad; there are too many people filling it up with crap and too many rocks to turn over to ever hope to present a comprehensive picture. Descriptions become obsolescent almost immediately. There are too many tribes, cultures, subcultures, groups, and subgroups to catalog.

Nothing is more cringe-worthy for a frequent Internet user than to see their corner of the Internet described by someone from the outside. Internet subcultures can seem impenetrable to outsiders. They are esoteric, by chance or design, and their denizens communicate using culture-specific jargon and inside references that leave inquisitive outsiders baffled.

When I set out to write this book, I wanted to limit myself to subcultures I had familiarized myself with over nearly a decade of writing for Something Awful. For most of that period our Awful Link of the Day has singled out strange subcultures and weird websites for ridicule. We cruelly mocked everyone from furries yiffing in hotel rooms to miscarriage moms building photo shrines for the bloody corpses of their unborn babies.

It was a rough game we played, maybe even slightly evil, but it was a good sort of evil. Like torturing a terrorist for the location of a bomb or killing a sweet little baby kitten by giving it too many kissy-wissies. That sort of evil.

I hoped that evil experience with the Awful Link of the Day would prepare me for writing this book.

As usual, I was wrong.

Zee Chamber of Horrors

If I were forced at katana-point to offer my best attempt at a metaphor for the Internet I would have to reach for the Bible. I realize that makes me an asshole by my own rules, but trust me on this, Bible metaphors add tons of literary credibility. *The Iliad* was nothing but a big Jesus metaphor.

I just hope Super God doesn't find out I'm using Regular Bible. He's very sensitive about that sort of thing (super apostasy), but he really needs to chill out. Super Bible isn't all that different from Regular Bible. The Psalms are written in Klingon and Super God might have gone a little overboard devoting nine Commandments to booty. Other than those two examples, and David grinding Mecha Goliath on a skateboard, and the part where Moses unleashes a plague of "dudes getting pounded by horse dicks" on Pharaoh, and Super Jesus exploding instead of being crucified, it's all basically the same stuff.

Keeping in mind that all Internet metaphors are stillborn failures, I think that Regular Bible's parable of that damnable apple from Genesis is about as close as you're going to get. Snake Devil tempted Eve by telling her when she took a bite of the forbidden fruit of Knowledge her eyes would be opened and "you will be like God, knowing good and evil." That ruined the good times for Adam and Eve in a hurry, but they knew a lot more than they did before.

Like the apple, the Internet gives each of us access to wondrous and limitless knowledge. But, the revelation of the Internet is that we discovered our vice was also limitless. Our egos and super-egos were joined by our raging ids, unleashed on a seedy world of our creation.

Adam and Eve felt shame and found the need to tie some leaves to their junk. Our forbidden fruit evidently made us shameless and gave us the knowledge to use a camera to show our junk to strangers.

This model didn't seem so bad when the Internet first began and the knowledge was a whole lot less limitless. A bunch of nerds posting to Usenet and bulletin boards about *Star Trek* and boobs and Dungeons & Dragons didn't cause society to collapse into anarchy. It was easy to see how the pros outweighed the cons.

Nerds, the perpetual outsiders and fringe characters, established themselves as the de facto rulers of the Internet. For nearly twenty years their superiority was unchallenged, but as their virtual kingdom spread it attracted new audiences and new enthusiasts. The number of Internet users grew slowly at first, but with the creation of the Web and Internet browsers those numbers began to grow exponentially.

Millions of newcomers were learning that they could establish a new identity on the Internet. Without a body to get in the way, they could literally become whoever they wanted, and as the Internet spread these identities grew in importance. Without geographic constraints like-minded individuals were able to seek out one another around the world. This allowed subcultures to flourish.

These tribes began to form on the Internet almost from the beginning, and many of the subcultures discussed in this book predate the creation of the Web. It was the Web that drove these subcultures to prominence. It made them accessible and appealing to millions. Furries and otherkin were among the first, but stranger subcultures fragmented from the originals or appeared from nothing, and narrower interests found audiences.

If you're going to write a book that deals with questions of identity and tribalism on the Internet, sooner or later you probably need to talk to an expert.

I was three months into the process of writing the book. I had amassed a collection of websites, saved forum posts and IM conversations. I had talked to some old friends in Arizona, erotic puppeteers, conspiracy theorists, End Times believers, and various and sundry other odd individuals.

I was preparing to embark on my journey to meet with and interview as many of these characters I had come in contact with as possible. I could feel the wind at my back and the book project was developing a real sense of momentum, but I still felt a lingering doubt. It was as if there was something missing. I needed a clearer sense of direction.

It took me a few days, but I decided what I needed was the spark of insight that I could not create myself. I needed someone with a professional's perspective. Before I learned who my weirdos were firsthand, I needed to talk to someone who knew how the Internet shapes identity and community.

With a little help from the University of Chicago humanities department, I contacted Anders Zimmerman, a graduate researcher of "cyberspace anthropology" who claimed to be working as "part of the University of Chicago." He referred to his specific field of study as, "Inner Self Manifestation."

Most of Anders Zimmerman's published research involved the use of a sort of sensory immersion technique. In papers he referred to it as "The Chamber," but its exact purpose was confusing to me and his research was light on the specifics. All I knew was that he was searching for the same sort of truth about identity that was at the core of my book.

When I spoke to Anders on the phone he sounded very excitable and very German, an over-caffeinated Freud. The mention of my book project immediately piqued his curiosity.

"Ooh, a buch, ja? I have zee reimagining chamber," he said. "Come to meine shtudio und we can do some experiments."

"What sort of experiments?" I asked.

"Ve re-imagine you," he said, and then added, "In zee chamber."

I was a bit hesitant to subject myself to "zee chamber," a hesitancy that only re-hesitated when my taxi arrived outside a carpet outlet store in Chicago's Hermosa neighborhood.

There are worse neighborhoods than Hermosa in Chicago, neighborhoods with more violent crimes, but this was the sort of area where some really horrible and weird shit might go down. It was the sort of area where a beloved grandma gets decapitated by a scythe or a city bus making its late-night rounds stops to pick up passengers only to find three skeletons sitting at one of the bus stops. Hermosa is the sort of neighborhood where you're walking along and you find a baby laying on the sidewalk and you pick it up and it has your face.

The eerie desolation was nerve-wracking, but it was broad daylight. Anders's "shtudio" was located adjacent to the carpet outlet, behind an unmarked green security door. There was an intercom next to the door with three buttons. A small placard beside the top button read SCIENC, and the other two placards were scratched out. Someone had hastily scrawled a penis and testicles in black marker across the front of the intercom.

I pressed the top button. Nothing. I pressed it again and longer.

"JA! Ja! Okay, vas?" Anders's voice blasted from the over-amped speaker.

I leaned down to the speaker and loudly said, "I'm here to see Anders Zimmerman."

"Ja! Shit, you don't have to shout."

The door buzzed and I hurried inside. It took a moment for my eyes to adjust to the dim lighting. The expansive ground floor was dusty and smelled of machine oils. Large presses or lathes of some sort were covered by plastic tarps. The overhead fluorescent lights and most of the windows were high and painted over. Thin beams of light were breaking through the crackling paint and in their shafts I'm pretty sure I could see asbestos particles.

A heavy door opened and closed somewhere far away inside the building. There was a loud click followed by a buzz as one by one the fluorescent lights switched on.

"Gutentag, Herr Parsons," said Anders from very near to me.

I jumped, realizing the anthropologist had closed to within a few feet of me while I was staring up at the lights like a rube. He was a little shorter than me, a little older, but he had a youthful head of spiked blond hair that was thinning a little bit on top.

His facial features seemed drawn by gravity to his chin, which left a lot of empty real estate above his gray eyes and horn-rimmed glasses. He was dressed like a member of the merchant marine. He was a nightmare vision from a J.Crew catalog in a worn cable-knit turtleneck, ridiculous white canvas pants, and a pair of decaying army boots he had apparently inherited from a combat veteran.

"Hello," I said, and shook his hand. "This is an interesting place you've got."

Anders was given pause by my clicking handshake. He glanced at my gloved hand, a gift from Doctor Lian, before his internal monologue changed the subject. He surveyed the room as if just noticing it.

"Ooh, ja. This is old machine shop, leased very cheaply as long as I keep the machines. This is okay because zee chamber is in zee basement."

Anders directed me toward another security door, this one in better repair and marked with three-dimensional chrome letters that spelled OFFI. I reluctantly followed him to the door, picturing zee basement as a rat's maze of claustrophobic passages choked with rusty, steaming pipes and pressure gauges with needles vibrating in the red.

I calmed my nerves by reminding myself that I had braved the *Twilight Zone* episode that was Hermosa. I didn't see a stray bunch of red balloons floating purposefully down the street. I didn't have my face melted off by a pigeon. Hermosa was a way worse scene than some stupid creepy basement in a factory.

Fortunately, zee chamber in zee basement was nothing like I had imagined. We descended a perfectly normal enclosed staircase and passed through a door into an open and well-lit space. It looked more like an artist's loft than a dank industrial basement.

It was almost the exact opposite of dank. It bordered on pleasant and warm. It was definitely clean. We were standing on cherry parquet flooring. There was a drafting table and stool and two Apple computers sitting atop two black Ikea desks. The desks were so new there were a few assembly stickers visible as we walked past.

The lighting was warm and sufficient, provided by a mixture of overhead lamps in brushed metal fixtures and standing lamps that seemed chosen to go along with a whimsical set of purple couches. I think I even heard soft music playing. Distant strains of Feist.

"Not vat you expected, ja?" Anders laughed, detecting my surprise. "Come, I show you zee chamber."

The chamber was a separate room that resembled a racquetball court. It had three white walls, a white ceiling with starkly bright recessed lighting, and a one-way glass back wall and door. In the center of the room was a chair that looked like an ergonomic dentist's chair. It was black and articulated, with a foot rest and padded armrests. It looked creepy, but also very comfortable. Good lumbar support.

I pressed my palms against the glass to get a better look and I realized that the white walls were not walls at all. They were made from floor-to-ceiling strips of a faintly iridescent white fabric stretched taught over a metal framework.

"What are the walls?" I asked.

"Ooh, you vill see." Anders had taken a seat behind one of the Apple computers. "Come sit down. Vee must talk before you go into zee chamber."

"I'm not going to sit down in there and end up on a beach talking to my space dad, am I?" I asked as I took a seat.

"No, of course not," Anders said with complete seriousness.

He had somehow missed my insanely clever reference to the movie *Contact*. My opinion of him was plummeting.

"Before ve begin I must know vie you have come here to see zee chamber," Anders said. "Vat do you vant to learn from me?"

"I want to learn why people become who they become on the Internet," I replied.

Anders nodded.

"I want to know if the online personality is distinct from the person in the real world," I continued. "Whether they create an idealized self or whether their environment shapes—"

"Ooh, ja, this is the key!" Anders interrupted. "Nature verzez zee nurturing. Do zee lonely become strange from seeking a sense of belonging or is it like-minded individuals they seek? Forget zee uzzer questions. Zee real question is when zee man is given a choice of identity does eet spring from zem or from zee surroundings?"

"Attraction versus actualization?" I asked.

"Ja, something link that. Und why do you think zee chamber can help you answer your questions?"

I wasn't really sure how to answer. I wasn't even sure about zee chamber's intended purpose. I needed a starting point for my journey through the Internet's subcultures and since I wasn't going to be offering any insight I thought I could hijack some from a real expert. My search for an Internet sociologist, psychologist, or anthropologist in my area had eventually brought me to Anders Zimmerman's fairly obscure work.

"I don't know," I finally said. "You claimed to be working on a diagnostic tool and I thought I could subject myself to it."

"Nein," Anders replied. "Not diagnosis. Experimentation. I am not a medical doctor, I am a researcher. I am observer. I do not treat."

"So you tell me. How does the chamber work?"

"Ooh." Anders stood. "You vant to find out, ja? First, some rules for you, Herr Parsons."

He settled himself uncomfortably against the corner of his desk. I winced at the awkward pose. It looked as if it could lead to toilet problems.

"First and most important, zis is not a toy. Zee chamber is a complex scientific instrument and it is not an amusement. Not a joke. You said your book is funny, ja?"

"Oh, don't worry." I held up my hands. "My book won't be funny at all. That's just what the publisher thinks."

"Ja, vell, no jokes. A joke could produce zee false result," he scolded. "Und no getting up. Once vee start you must continue to zee end."

"Why is that?"

"Zis is a complex process und once I start there is no shtopping. I see concern on your face, Herr Parsons. Do not fret, there is no danger to you. If you follow meine instructions nothing vill go wrong."

Being told "there is no danger" and "nothing will go wrong" by a guy who sounds suspiciously like an Igor from a low-budget Frankenstein remake is not really reassuring. However, other than the slightly creepy chair the chamber did not look all that scary.

"Anything else?" I asked.

"Ja, you are not epileptic, richtig?"

"Nope," I said.

"Zen vee are ready, Herr Parsons."

Anders led me to the glass door and held it open. There was a slight pressure change when the opening door broke the seal. I could see the fabric covering the walls sway almost imperceptibly.

"Take off your shoe, but not your sock, und have a seat on zee . . . seat," Anders instructed.

He watched me untie and remove my shoes and then I stepped into the room. Anders followed me in and walked me to the seat. Every movement, everything that should have made a sound, was muffled and deadened by the acoustics of the room.

I sat down in the black reclining chair. It was difficult to settle into properly, but with a little help from Anders I found the right position. At that point it became very comfortable, so comfortable I might have been tempted to nap were the room not so bright. Anders hydraulically adjusted the seat using a foot pedal on the floor and then adjusted the back so that I was facing forward and slightly up.

"Zee chair will turn slowly," he said. "Zis, accompanied wiz everything sometimes make a person sick."

He pressed a tightly folded paper bag into my hand.

"If you feel zee sickness, use zis," he said.

I nodded.

"Remember, do not get up during zee process," he said, and I replied in the affirmative.

Anders gave me one last check, adjusted the chair's height again very slightly, and then stepped back.

"Okay, gut, you are ready," Anders pronounced. "I will give you instructions over zee speakers. If I ask you a question you must answer immediately; do not hesitate. Hesitating can contaminate the response. Inshtinct is zee key."

"I've got it," I said, and gave him two thumbs up.

Anders walked out of zee chamber, sealing the glass door and leaving me alone with the bright whiteness. There was a mechanical thump overhead and the lights within the chamber suddenly switched off.

Faint techno music began to play from three sides. I did not recognize it, but it was driving and repetitive. It was the sort of moronically pounding music that might play over the sound system at a car show as models in bikinis posed next to an ergonomic green Frisbee on wheels. It was hypnotic twenty-first-century Jock Jams.

The music began to increase in volume, and I realized there were also speakers built into the headrest of the chair and a booming subwoofer pressed against the small of my back. The drum and bass was beginning to vibrate my insides. The sensation wasn't entirely unpleasant. Yet.

Digital constellations of colors burst across the walls in synchronization with the music. Red and green showers of pixels exploded with each drum hit. Smaller eruptions of blue and yellow exploded into being with machine gun rapidity and tracked in glowing strips that crisscrossed from one wall to the next.

The room had become a mathematical visualization of the music, hypnotic and a little overwhelming, like the bars on a giant, psychedelic equalizer.

I presumed the effect was achieved by using some sort of projectors concealed behind the fabric and framework of the chamber's three walls. Even knowing this, it was still impressive and a little disorienting.

The chair began to shake. For a moment I thought it was the subwoofer blasting into my spine, but as my view of the procedural fireworks began to shift I realized the chair was rotating. It swiveled on the hydraulic lift until the dark glass of the windows was on my left side, then it rotated back in the opposite direction until the glass wall was on my right.

"You vill listen to my voice," Anders boomed from the speakers as if I had a choice. "You are entering zee Matrix."

On cue the visualizations shifted to the green alphanumeric waterfalls popularized by *Zee Matrix*.

"You leave your body behind und your consciousness flows into zee digital realm. You are not any longer constrained by zee physical body. You can now be whoever it is you choose. Vatever you vant."

The green letters and numbers faded away and were replaced by a dynamic collage of faces. They appeared to be clipped from family photos and class pictures. Most were anonymous, but I recognized Anders among the faces. And there was President George W. Bush. And . . . Shannon Tweed. And was that her again in a red wig?

"Now it is time to discover who you are and who you will be, Mr. Parsons!"

Anders's delivery was overwrought and almost gleeful. He was plainly enjoying his role as the disembodied voice of the Wizard of Oz.

"The new you will begin to take shape from your unconscious and your consciousness. Your instincts will guide you. Are you ready?"

I waited for a moment to be sure he wanted a response and then I answered, "Yes!"

"Good. You are now immersed in zee stream of zee sensory data. You are beginning your journey of discovery. Look at zee images you see before you . . ."

The screens faded to black.

". . . as each appears, speak aloud zee first word zat comes into your head. Do not hesitate. Do not think about your answer."

What might have been simple association was complicated by the audio that began to play along with the images. As the first image appeared—a photograph of a white cat rubbing its face against the corner of a coffee table—words began to bubble out of the speakers on the chair's headrest.

As the cat fully resolved on each of the walls I heard a steady stream of contradictory words and phrases.

"Gold," said a computer-generated woman.

"Pickles," said a computer-generated man.

"Red. Red. Woman. King. Zero. Champion. Guitar," the voices babbled in my ears, switching sides and overlapping.

"Answer quickly!" Anders shouted over the main speakers.

"Cat!" I answered.

"Pumpkin. Pigeon. Book. Crease," the voices continued, my auditory focus shifting through several bands of spoken words emerging from the speakers.

A new photograph faded in on the screens. An image of a gleaming samurai sword held in a clenched fist.

"Finger," said the woman's voice.

"Finger!" I blurted.

The image of the sword dissolved into a photograph of a basket full of apples.

"Crane. Shoe. Hiccup. Porridge," the voices babbled.

"Fruit basket!" I shouted, but I had to think for a moment and resist the urge to simply parrot the words being spoken directly into my ear.

The experience would be alien to most people outside of the former Soviet Union and parts of Cambodia. Maybe a few captured American spies were subjected to something like this by the KGB, but the average person has never been led into an empty room, sat in a dentist's chair, and asked to yell out responses to images while techno music and random words blasted in their ears.

The closest common experience might be attempting to count to a high number and being confused or losing your place when you hear other numbers. That was the sort of maddening mental failure I endured for much of the exercise. It was a constant struggle for my brain to react to the images independently of my ears. I got the hang of it after several pictures, but as it progressed I realized my defense mechanism was simply naming what I was seeing in the photo.

"Very good," Anders announced, even though I was feeling stressed out by the exercise. "Take a moment to regain zee composure. Listen to zee music und relax. Vee vill continue to zee next phase once you tell me you are ready."

The digital fireworks returned and the music grew a bit louder. The chair continued to swivel from side to side. I had to admit, the sensory overload was becoming slightly nauseating.

I fought through the ache in the pit of my stomach and announced my readiness.

"Excellent. You are doing vell, Mr. Parsons."

The music softened a bit as the screens once again faded to black.

"Now vee vill be reversing things a bit," Anders said. "I am going to ask you a series of questions. You vill see images on zee screens, but you are to respond only to my questions. Zer is no right or een-correct answer to zees questions. Answer however you like and re-call your goal is to manifest your inner self."

"Are you ready?" he asked.

"Ja!" I replied.

"Vee begin . . . now!"

Images began to flash rapid-fire across the screens. It was an accelerated version of the earlier collage of faces, but covering a much broader spectrum of subjects. It was an onslaught.

Mundane images, violent images, strange images, and pornographic images exploded in complete disharmony across three walls of the chamber. One moment a black-and-white photograph of a ranch house appeared and a moment later it was covered by a photograph of genital herpes from a medical textbook. A moment later the herpes disappeared behind an image of kids cheering on a roller coaster.

I reeled from the imagery. I was being deluged with disorienting optical static even more intrusive than the words being shouted in my ears during the first exercise.

"Vat is your favorite color?"

The Taj Mahal at sunset. A gauzy glamour photo of three children with Down syndrome standing in front of a Christmas tree.

"Vermilion!" I shouted.

"Name your best quality," Anders instructed.

A stone arrowhead. A fat woman's cleavage. An F-117 Stealth Fighter parked at an air show. The world was spinning. An insane whirling kaleidoscope of colors and pictures.

"My punctuality!" I shouted.

"Vat is your greatest flaw?" Anders asked.

A recreational Jeep stuck in a ditch. A baseball pitching machine. Dolphins leaping out of the water in unison. I could no longer tell what was actually being projected on the screen and what shapes my brain was creating out of the rippling, turning bands of color.

"Ahhh fuck I hate . . . late women," I answered.

A tombstone. A collectible motorcycle. Question after question. Bile crept into my throat. My legs shook involuntarily.

I tried closing my eyes, but an unseen camera in the room betrayed my tactic. Anders warned me to keep my eyes open and chided me about joking with my answers.

A rabbit chewing on a wood chip. A woman nude except for a headband. My friend from childhood?

The questions continued. It felt as if I was drowning in the sensations of the room. Sweat coursed down my temples and over my forehead. I was constricted, almost breathless.

"If you could have two of anything, vat vould you vant?"

A Brazilian football player catching a ball with his face.

"Vaginas," I answered with a gasp. "Vaginas on my . . . hands."

A T-72 tank model kit.

"What is zee name you call yourself?"

The strange way Anders phrased the question had to be intentional.

"Vaginahands?"

"Who is—"

Anders was interrupted by a ringing telephone.

"Excuse me, Herr Parsons," he said.

The images abruptly faded to a deep gray static. A soothing ocean of nothing. The room was dark again. My pupils were so blown out I could barely make out my hands resting on the arms of the chair.

I heard a pop of audio, as if Anders had turned off the intercom. He had only switched channels. When he answered the phone, his words were broadcast through the chair's headrest.

"Hello," Anders answered.

"Becca, I can't talk now," he said in a perfectly normal Midwestern accent. "No, we can talk about this tonight. I'm with somebody."

There was a pause as the person on the other end, presumably "Becca," said something to Anders. I took a moment to absorb this new information. Anders Zimmerman was a fraud on at least one level. He sounded like he was from Des Moines, not Dresden.

I realized that if that asshole was faking a German accent to earn kooky science credibility, well, it had worked. But the proverbial jig was proverbially up.

"It's not Megan," Anders said with evident anger. "She's gone and I haven't—"

Becca shouted something so loud it was audible (though unintelligible) in the headrest speakers.

"No, no! No, sweetheart, it's just some jerkoff who found me through U of C. I don't—"

Ol' Vaginahands had heard enough. It was a struggle to get out of the slowly rotating seat, but with a grunt of effort I flopped out on the side.

It was difficult to navigate by the stroboscopic flash of the digital collage on the wall screens and I tangled myself up on the seat's hydraulics. I spun uncertainly and nearly fell back on my knees. At last, I was able to steady myself by looking at the distorted reflections in the glass back wall. It was much darker than the other three walls.

I shuffled my way to the back wall. With one hand resting on the glass I slowly worked my way to the door I remembered in the middle. My fingers found the latch and I opened the door with a pressurized thump and a rush of air.

Anders was still on the phone when I emerged from zee chamber. He looked up with surprise.

"Herr Parsons, I varned you not to get up!" he exclaimed, setting aside his cordless phone.

I blinked away the stars from the lights. My head was swimming with the aftereffects of the digital torture and I still wasn't steady on my feet, but I was through with the bullshit. I was even content to leave without confronting Anders, but he stepped between me and the door to the stairwell.

"You have not yet manifested your inner self," he said.

Anders was wrong about that. His stupid light show hadn't answered my questions, but he had unwittingly told me exactly what I needed to hear. Thanks to his bizarre attempt to scam me, I could see Zee Retarded Matrix. I didn't cram years of human understanding or journalism school into an hour in a computerized funhouse, but I *did* manifest my inner self.

I was an asshole.

I gave Anders a shove. One-handed. Not enough to knock him over, I'm not a particularly tough or strong person, but it was forceful enough to make him take a step back. He looked at me with surprise.

And let me go.

A Special Delivery

Strange as my visit was to Anders Zimmerman's amazing Technicolor dream chamber, there was an even stranger epilogue.

About a week after I discovered my inner self, I was sitting at my desk working on an article for Something Awful. The doorbell rang and I answered to find a FedEx deliveryman. I signed for a standard FedEx shipping envelope.

I tore open the perforated tab and a single playing card spilled out into my hand. It was the ace of spades—the death card.

On the back was a message written in fine-tipped black marker.

"I see you when you're sleeping."

It was signed with the initial "A" printed in a circle.

I called Anders and received his voice mail. The message I left for him was, well, let's just say it was intemperate. I promised to do things to his face that are a crime just to contemplate. I remember at the end of the call I told him I would jump up and down on him until his guts popped out of the top of his head like a tube of toothpaste.

Anders never returned the call, which was probably for the best. He wasn't the sender of the mysterious message.

By the time I learned the true identity of the sender it was much too late.

CHAPTER TWO

Amateur Physician, Sicken Thyself

The doctor of the future will give no medicine, but will interest her or his patients in the care of the human frame, in a proper diet, and in the cause and prevention of disease.

—Thomas Edison

I had restless leg syndrome. My doctor confirmed it. He said with restless leg syndrome, the symptoms usually get worse at night, or in the evening when it's time to relax. And then he said something else: REQUIP.

—REQUIP® television commercial

One of the downsides of living in the throes of the Information Age is all that damn information. It's right there in the name of the age. Mocking you.

You run into information everywhere, even when you're trying to avoid it. You search Wikipedia for information on bathyspheres and you end up at the wrong end of a series of links two hours later reading about the fat-tailed Dwarf Lemur.

You search for a video of Hillary Clinton crying during the 2008 Democratic primary and you end up getting distracted watching booty claps.

Beware the booty clap videos, my friends. Were there only a map of the Internet there would be a drawing of a clapping booty and a warning to Internet users: Here There Be Booty Claps. Many men have gone searching the Internet for a noble cause and never returned from the booty-clapping Sargasso.

Thong vortices and laudatory asses aside, no subject suffers from a more perilous overabundance of information than health material. A Google search of the word "sex" produces 729 million results. A Google search of the word "health" returns just shy of one and a quarter billion results. That is 100 percent conclusive proof that there is more health information than porn on the Internet.

Yeah, you feel that? That is the earth shattering under your feet.

Fortunately, you can get some help for that as there are about 750 websites for people with earth fragments embedded in their feet.

Hundreds of general purpose health sites cover the full panoply of medical conditions. They contain searchable libraries of medical information and news. Nearly all of these general health sites include a helpful self-diagnosis tool.

These are the tools of the devil. Occasionally, they do manage to correctly diagnose a medical condition. Something with very clear symptoms or very unusual symptoms. You can figure out you're having a heart attack or that all that blood shooting out of your orifices is hemorrhagic fever.

Too bad most medical conditions aren't that clear-cut. Hundreds of diseases can share identical symptoms or a person may only manifest one or two symptoms. Worse still, minor symptoms can often be linked to serious illnesses.

For a hypochondriac, these tools and the wealth of medical information on the Internet can lead people down very dangerous paths into self-treatment and obsession. There is even a portmanteau for hypochondria in the Information Age: cyberchondria.

WebMD, one of the oldest and most comprehensive medical sites, offers a symptom-checker that can produce some truly terrifying results. For example, selecting a knee ache experienced in both legs produces a list of possible causes that includes lupus, Lyme disease, and rheumatic fever. Not listed: jumping off a fence, sleeping with your legs in an uncomfortable position, and "your fucking overactive imagination."

This ability to instantly magnify the most minor ailment into a life-threatening or incurable illness is just one of the dangers of the information overload threatening hypochondriacs. Another dire trap can be found on the fringes of medical science, lurking in the Internet Twilight Zone waiting to be found by the impressionable morons who don't trust doctors. Fake diseases, fake cures, and misdiagnoses are rampant.

I wanted to begin this book without diving in the psychosexual deep end of the Internet. Give readers a little time to ramp up to the strangeness. Internet hypochondria presented me with that opportunity and, by luck of geography, contact with three types of hypochondriac living within driving distance.

Sweet, Deadly Lies

Imagine a world where everything you think you knew to be true was actually a façade created by global corporations working in concert with world governments. Imagine this unholy union bent on poisoning the world's food supply with one of the deadliest toxins man has ever created. The corporations have cleverly concealed the poison as a popular low-calorie sweetener and the government regulators are allowing them to sell it to an unsuspecting population in order to . . .

In order to . . .

"Profit," believes Doctor Bitsy Schwab.

She and her friend Leslie Jefferson are part of Mongoose, one of the many online organizations, forums, and outreach groups dedicated to victims of the artificial sweetener aspartame.

The fear of so-called aspartame disease, and the deadly effects of most artificial sweeteners, is pervasive on the Internet. aspartame disease is also one of the Internet's oldest and most enduring examples of self-diagnosis on a mass scale.

The FDA and regulatory agencies around the world have come to agree that aspartame is a safe food additive. Confirmaton of its safety is backed by research from nonprofit agencies and respected institutions. These findings are dismissed by critics as collusion with aspartame manufacturers, a massive corporate enterprise headed by agricultural and chemical giant Monsanto.

Dr. Schwab and Leslie Jefferson don't trust the FDA. They think aspartame is a deadly chemical and they agreed to meet with me at the conference room of a Holiday Inn Express in suburban Chicago to discuss aspartame's many dangers. Getting in touch with them was the hard part, convincing outspoken advocates of the anti-aspartame movement to talk to me was as easy as asking them once.

Unfortunately, I waited until the last minute to call and book the conference room at the Holiday Inn. I was sorely disappointed when I was told over the phone that the conference room was already booked by a clown ministry for children.

"All three days," explained the apologetic concierge at the Holiday Inn. "I just was in there. They are in clown makeup talking about Corinthians.

"And rapping," he added in a breathless whisper.

According to the same concierge they also had balloons and a man in a donkey suit. The Lord works in mysterious ways.

My next phone call was to Dr. Schwab's office to change the appointment. Dr. Schwab's "office number" rang to a cell phone carried by Ms. Jefferson, who was never officially introduced to me and answered the call as "Dr. Schwab's office."

I could hear a baby crying in the background.

Ms. Jefferson was not pleased when I suggested a change of venue to one of the Holiday Inn's many comfortable rooms not prefaced by "conference."

"What if you're a pervert?" Ms. Jefferson asked.

"I'm not a pervert," I lied.

"I'll call you back," Ms. Jefferson replied, and hung up the phone.

Two hours later I received a return call from Ms. Jefferson. She was eager to lecture me on the value of Dr. Schwab's time, which, she insisted, could be better spent, "Saving real lives." Damn the fictional characters.

"I just need about an hour of your time to talk about the dangers of aspartame," I said.

"Aspartame, yeah?" Ms. Jefferson replied. "She is a leading expert."

"What field does she have her degree in?" I asked, but Ms. Jefferson ignored the question.

"We'll meet you at Ed Debevic's," Ms. Jefferson said. "Same time as before."

Ed Debevic's is the worst place to attempt to conduct a serious interview second to, maybe, a German machine gun bunker on D-day. It's an infamously flamboyant Chicago restaurant where the theme is "annoying 1950s," and everyone who works there looks and acts like someone cosplaying at a *Grease* fan convention. The music is loud and the waiters and waitresses yell and dance on the countertops.

I'm sure it's a hoot for adult children and tourists from Japan who want to be yelled at and humiliated by a giant white lady. For me, it was an expensive distraction and probably punishment for botching the Holiday Inn meeting. I could think of no other reason why a hippy doctor would want to hold a meeting at a restaurant willing to set up a trough of trans-fats and Diet Cokes at your table.

I arrived ten minutes early and requested the most isolated booth in the farthest reaches of the restaurant. The booth really wasn't that isolated, but Vic, the chubby and sexless waiter with the oily bouffant hairdo and rosy red cheeks, insisted it was the best he could do. He accepted my twenty-dollar bribe and tugged nervously at the bottom of his too-tight bowling shirt.

"Won't be too busy for another hour," he suggested.

An hour and two milk shakes later and Ed Debevic's had filled up. It was something short of raucous, but there was the ominous buzz of a countertop dance in the atmosphere. I saw a Japanese man with a cell phone camera out and children yelling. It wouldn't be long now.

I was feeling bloated from the milk shakes and beginning to wonder if Dr. Schwab was going to stand me up. When Vic passed by again I made a critical mistake.

"Can I get a Diet Coke?" I requested.

He glared at me, in the throes of his carefully planned sassy waiter performance for a nearby table, but he gave me a curt nod without breaking character. Just as Vic returned with my Diet Coke, just as the first countertop dance of the evening began, Dr. Schwab and Ms. Jefferson arrived.

"Diet Coke, huh?" Vic shouted over the thumping and cheering for the benefit of Dr. Schwab and Ms. Jefferson. "Why bother, you can never lose enough weight to stop being ugly! Pssssh!"

He set the drink down and whirled away. I glared at his back and then returned my attention to my arriving guests.

Dr. Schwab was a small woman in her late fifties. She had thin features and a face that was deeply lined. Her skin looked fragile and reminded me of flattened origami paper that had been folded and unfolded a hundred times. Her graying brown hair was pulled back in a ponytail that exploded behind her head and disappeared down her back. She was dressed shabbily in layers of old sweaters completely inappropriate for the warm weather. A rainbow-strapped canvas carryall hung from a drooping shoulder. It overflowed with pens, receipts, papers, loose antacids, and all the other debris of an unfashionable woman's purse.

"Hello," Dr. Schwab said. "This is Leslie. I believe you spoke on the phone."

Her companion, Leslie Jefferson, was an immense black woman with bulging eyes and tree trunk arms she kept folded atop two of the largest breasts I have ever seen. Well, I did not directly see her breasts. She was wearing a huge pink Space Jam T-shirt that hid them from view, but I was able to detect the spore of giant breasts distorting her shirt and forcing her to cross her arms at an unusual angle. I sensed them indirectly like deadly radon or the traces of a powerful Jedi.

"Mhmmm, yeah, we spoke," said Leslie.

She grunted and slid her bulk into the booth. Her body shifted and rippled like a bear rubbing its back against a tree. When she had finally settled in she had left barely a third of the bench for Dr. Schwab. The small woman didn't seem to notice she was nearly crowded out of her seat. She deposited her carryall on the table and I could hear the metallic crunch of shifting keys.

"Mister Parsons, this is grotesque." Dr. Schwab pointed to my Diet Coke. "I will not discuss this with this grotesquery as you have it on the table. Was that intentional? To insult me? I'm insulted, but unfazed."

I got up to take the soda over to the counter.

"I wouldn't drink anything out of any of their cups," Dr. Schwab warned.

"Residues and whatnot," Leslie added, and Dr. Schwab nodded gravely.

A scrawny teenager was crooning away from the top of the big counter on the far side of the restaurant. He was singing tunelessly and clad in an ill-fitting prom tuxedo from circa 1958. Through the right eyes it looked like one of the overdressed zombies from *Night of the Living Dead* had shambled into a karaoke bar in hell.

The two ladies drank distilled water they brought in a metal flask ("plastic contains toxic phthalates") from their own wooden cups. They refused to eat Ed Debevic's hamburgers on the grounds that the meat was, according to Leslie, "Hormonally out of whack." They seemed slightly annoyed by the singing and shouting.

I felt no sympathy; it was their fault we weren't enjoying a quiet Holiday Inn where they could have indulged all the flask water and antacid tablets they wanted.

Dr. Schwab and Leslie settled on a pair of Cobb salads that they meticulously dissected onto napkins before eating. They seemed to relax a little once they were actually cramming lettuce into their mouths, but the incident with the Diet Coke had set the tone.

I was of the enemy. I was in league with the world governments and the aspartame manufacturers.

"Let me just ask you directly," I said, not knowing how else to begin. "What are the side effects of aspartame? The risks?"

Dr. Schwab wiped her mouth precisely with a napkin before answering.

"There aren't risks associated with NutraSweet and all aspartame sweeteners. There aren't side effects. It's poison, not a food additive."

"But they put it in food, so it is a food additive," I countered.

"Exactly," Dr. Schwab said.

She exhumed a musty accordion folder from her carryall and pulled out a thick stack of papers held together by an industrial-strength paperclip. She passed the papers across the table to me.

"You need to familiarize yourself with the works of the experts," she said.

I only had time to skim the rambling fifty-page document assembled by Dr. Schwab. While she and Leslie crunched away on their salad, I learned about a neurosurgeon named Dr. Russell Blaylock and the books of a diabetes specialist named Dr. H. J. Roberts.

Dr. Blaylock is a crusader against aspartame in food and fluoride in drinking water. He maintains a monthly health and wellness column on the rightwing News Max website and has appeared repeatedly on *The 700 Club*. His book, *Excitotoxins: The Taste That Kills*, takes aim at aspartame and monosodium glutamate or MSG.

His colleague Dr. Roberts penned a supposedly authoritative book on the dangers of aspartame titled *Aspartame Disease: An Ignored Epidemic*. Aspartame disease is the name given to a multi-symptom illness that experts like Dr. Roberts believe is caused by aspartame toxicity. His book on the subject is over a thousand pages in length and joins other books by Roberts on artificial sweeteners as well as books on the dangers of vitamin E supplements and vasectomies.

I was initially suspicious of someone who seemed to be making a career out of finding deadly toxins in everyday items. I decided to trust Dr. Roberts as a source of information once I learned he also wrote a book about a 1985 visit by Princess Diana to Palm Beach, California. *Princess Diana: The House of Windsor and Palm Beach* includes "inside information" garnered by Dr. Roberts because "his wife, Carol, was the mayor of Palm Beach at the time."

I was curious why a crusader against aspartame would be so concerned with a brief visit by Princess Diana to the United States that he would write a book about it.

My questions were answered by Dr. Schwab's summary, "Dr. Roberts includes information relating to Diana's problems (mood, bolemia[sic] and more) that may have been caused (or made worse) by the substance called aspartame."

I looked up and re-clipped the stack of papers.

"You couldn't have read all that," Leslie said.

"You believe aspartame killed Princess Diana?" I asked.

"She died in a car accident, don't be ridiculous," Dr. Schwab scolded.

"She could have died from aspartame eventually," Leslie added.

It took prodding to get Dr. Schwab to answer my original question about the dangerous effects of aspartame. She finally caved when Vic stopped by the table and asked if I needed another Diet Coke. I waved away the question, but Dr. Schwab was incensed.

"You know," she began with an imperious tone, "that Diet Coke you love so much is more toxic than paint."

"Acrylic or oil?"

"Wall paint, stupid," Leslie interjected. "Don't be stupid."

I doubted I could survive drinking a can of paint, but I was pretty sure I could endure the same volume of Diet Coke. I said as much and Dr. Schwab shook her head.

"You would vomit from drinking that much paint; your body knows it's poison and gets rid of it. Your body thinks Diet Coke is something good. It processes it as something good. But it isn't."

"It isn't good?"

"No!" She slapped her palms on the table. "Aspartame is a poison. They use it to kill ants just like they're using it to kill you."

"So what does it do? How is it killing me? What are the ill effects of aspartame?"

"Death," Dr. Schwab said. "Death if you're lucky. Death eventually. Before you die though it rots your whole body. Diabetes, obesity, high blood pressure; it turns to formaldehyde in the eyeballs and causes blindness, headaches, cancer—they have found tumors of aspartame in people's brains. Phenylalanine causes tumors. Multiple sclerosis, lupus—"

"Lupus?" I interrupted.

"Yes," Dr. Schwab said. "Memory loss, seizures, chronic joint pain, birth defects, Gulf War disease."

"I thought depleted uranium caused Gulf War disease," I said, indicating the popular rumor about the mysterious illness.

"Those soldiers drank Diet Cokes and Diet Pepsis all day long in Iraq and it gets very hot. All of the symptoms they describe fit in perfectly. Thousands of them. Monsanto knew about this; they know it will break down into methanol in the heat and that it's a poison and they continued to ship it overseas."

"They made Agent Orange," Leslie interjected. "Look at how that worked."

"Why isn't there a Gulf War syndrome for the current Iraq war?" I asked. "They've got to be drinking tons of Diet Coke over in Iraq now, and it's been going on for years."

"There will be," Leslie interjected. "There will be a Gulf War syndrome. We already see it. I got an e-mail from a woman whose son is in Iraq and she said he gets these painful headaches and can't sleep every night."

"He's in a war zone," I said.

"Exactly," Leslie said. "Exactly. He is in a war zone with Diet Coke."

"There is no enemy more deadly than artificial sweetener," Dr. Schwab agreed.

"What about the Nazis?"

"There has been more than one Holocaust," Dr. Schwab said. "One Holocaust is going on right now from aspartame."

She had just doubled down and upgraded aspartame's crimes from mass murder to genocide.

"How many people have actually died from aspartame?"

"Countless," replied Dr. Schwab.

I pressed her for an estimate.

"Ten million," she said. "Maybe more or less by a million. It's incredible. There are thousands dying all over the world from it and doctors won't even acknowledge it. They assume it's natural causes or other things."

"Like depleted uranium," I suggested.

"Other things. Whatever. Environmental factors. The symptoms resemble a variety of serious illnesses. Or they're covering it up for payouts."

"So we need to stop using it?"

"Stop, but be careful," Dr. Schwab said. "You have to wean yourself off, because your body stops producing natural enzymes. You can have seizures or even go into a coma like a diabetic if you just quit cold turkey."

I was a little surprised by this aspect. I had read about many of the supposed health risks relating to aspartame, but I had no idea that quitting it could be like quitting a serious drug.

"How is that possible?" I asked. "If not drinking Diet Cokes could cause you to have seizures and lapse into a coma, wouldn't there be an epidemic of these sorts of problems? There are millions of Americans who drink diet sodas. What if they switched to water?"

"Aspartame is in water," Leslie said.

"Trace amounts," Dr. Schwab amended. "Enough to prevent withdrawal. Enough to be toxic."

"Don't they have to list that on the label?"

"You pee it out and then they bottle it," Leslie pronounced with no further explanation.

"Aspartame is in over seven thousand products," Dr. Schwab said. "Often it's so far down on the list of ingredients you wouldn't even notice it. It's in medicines and foods. You have to be very careful to avoid aspartame."

"So how do you avoid it if it's in water and all this other stuff?"

"You educate yourself and . . ."

Dr. Schwab held up her thermos.

"Make your own water."

I left Ed Debevic's with two things certain in my mind: I was going to drink the first cold diet cola I could get my hands on and I was never going back to Ed Debevic's. My thirst for diet cola wasn't some outrageous need to show up Dr. Schwab. I needed something with aspartame because I believe that old cowboy wisdom that when your horse throws you in the dirt you better get right back on before it decides you don't belong in the saddle.

If I didn't act quickly my natural paranoia would take over and I'd fall into the horrible spiral of aspartame fears. If that happened my nightmares were sure to become a twisted, *Grease*-themed, aspartame apocalypse. Rizzos dead in the street from Gulf War syndrome. The Scorpions thrashing like epileptics in pools of Diet Dr Pepper.

I stopped at a gas station a few blocks away and made haste for the cooler in the back. I grabbed a Diet Coke, paid for it, and popped it open the moment I was back outside. It tasted crisp and jagged. It was refreshingly unlike something that should prominently feature skull and crossbones on the label and be kept out of reach of small children.

As I savored the deadly beverage, my mind snapped back to the parting comments from Dr. Schwab. We were standing just outside the door at Ed Debevic's. I was eyeing my car, the thick stack of papers tucked under my arm. She was clinging to my bicep with a small hand, urgently telling me about Donald Rumsfeld.

"It may be a joke to you, but this is a deadly game to him. He was on Reagan's transition team when he took office. He helped pick the FDA commissioner who approved aspartame. His former company, Searle, makes aspartame. They created it!"

I nodded, wanting to get away from Dr. Schwab and her huge doom-saying friend.

"Listen," she said. "Listen. You know, 'Beware the military-industrial complex.' No, no, it's, 'Beware the pharmacological-food industrial complex.' If you hear only one thing from me, if you only put one thing in your book, put that in there. These guys are putting their drugs in everything you eat and drink."

Something in the sad desperation of that moment overwhelmed my cynicism. It wasn't that I believed all the books claiming every food and drug and new sweetener causes every imaginable ailment, it was that I believed that she believed them.

There are those in the anti-aspartame groups cynically trying to make a profit from junk science and fearmongering. Even Princess Diana knew that. But many are honestly attracted to the topic by a need to believe that an evil force is manipulating the world, that a malign intellect is responsible for their woes.

I recognized the same desperation in dozens of other anti-aspartame devotees on the Internet. Some of them were conspiracy theory kooks, but many of them were people suffering from real problems who turned to the aspartame groups to explain the unexplainable. The case against aspartame was sold on peer pressure combined with a bewildering amount of allegedly scientific information.

Even I found it difficult to sort through which doctors were credible and which were just claiming credibility to line their pockets or empower themselves. It was easy to sympathize with people struggling with mystery illnesses, easy to understand how they could be made into believers.

It is the case with many of the subcultures born or nurtured on the Internet that devotion to the subculture can spread like a disease into the real world. There are hundreds of accounts of well-meaning anti-aspartame activists evangelizing to relatives and even strangers with serious illnesses. It's one of the favorite subjects on forums devoted to the dangers of aspartame.

The results of this evangelizing can be mixed.

"I recognized the signs right away," wrote one Internet poster. "Her daughter looked very sickly and was complaining of joint pain and weakness. Her mom said she had lymphoma and I saw she was drinking a Diet Sprite. Believe me I tried to warn her, but she wouldn't listen. No matter what I said about the phenyl she wouldn't listen. The stewardess asked me to calm down and I told her what was happening, and she gave me a look like she knew but there was nothing she could do. I had to sit there and watch them poison their child on the plane. It was an unpleasant flight."

When confronted with contradictory findings from reputable sources, the anti-aspartame activist hardens his or her position and decries the sources as tainted by connections to "Big Aspartame." On the Internet they retreat to their topic-specific forums, where the rare opposing viewpoints are offered by easily dismissed newcomers or those curious about aspartame who dare to question the one-sided research.

The attitudes set up a members-only mind-set. Those who understand that aspartame is a real danger are the insiders, and those who don't understand are either ignorant or part of the aspartame conspiracy.

"We live in a world of sweet lies," Dr. Schwab said as she followed me to my car. "Deadly lies. But if you see the lie, you can beat the lie."

I didn't know how to answer, so I just waved good-bye.

Congratulations, You Are Special and Horrible

Dr. Schwab, Leslie, and the Internet's anti-aspartame movement convinced me they are suffering from Internet hypochondria, but they have as much in common with conspiracy theorists. I wanted real hypochondriacs and all these ladies were giving me were some convoluted stories involving Donald Rumsfeld and creepy medical testing.

The stack of papers Dr. Schwab gave me didn't convince me any better than the anti-aspartame websites. There were no believable links between aspartame and the hundreds of physical ailments reported by supposed victims. The multilayered aspartame conspiracy became more improbable and convoluted the more I read.

I was waiting for a poisoned spy dart straight out of a Robert Ludlum book to shoot through a window and hit me in the neck. No doubt some shadowy aspartame agency taking me out for knowing too much.

Only, I didn't know too much. I felt like I knew less than when I started. Figures, dubious data points about brain cancer, maybe, but I wasn't any closer to the Internet hypochondriac.

I needed classic hypochondriacs, not people talking about the Trilateral Commission and the New World Order. I needed people with no ailments who believed they had a real medical condition. I needed to talk to people drowning in the fathomless ocean of medical information available at the deep end of a Google search.

Among hypochondriacs on the Internet there is a singular ailment that seems to be self-diagnosed more frequently than any other. It afflicts millions who had lived their lives knowing they were different, knowing they were special, but not fully understanding why. It is a self-diagnosis so insufferably egotistical that you might feel yourself hating someone for claiming the illness.

And yet, when you read the symptoms, you might just realize you too are suffering from . . . *Self-Diagnosed Asperger's Syndrome!*

To date, Asperger's syndrome is the only illness confirmed to be contagious through the transmission of HTML.

According to the Nemours Foundation's primer on autism for parents, "Asperger's syndrome (AS) is a neurobiological disorder that is part of a group of conditions called *autism spectrum disorders.*" It is a form of high-functioning autism that in many cases allows the sufferer to operate in and interact with the world around them on a fairly normal level. It is a real illness that can be crushing for individuals and parents.

It is also fast becoming the antisocial nerd's number one scape-goat.

For many Internet users Asperger's syndrome (pronounced "ass-burgers") has become almost synonymous with "asshole." It could be that the telltale symptom of the autism-like disorder is a lack of empathy, which would make someone with Asperger's syndrome seem an awful lot like an asshole. Then again, it could be that approximately 500,000 assholes have self-diagnosed with Asperger's syndrome on the Internet.

These "Internet Aspies" wear the unofficial diagnosis like a badge that absolves them of any responsibility for bad behavior. This diagnosis excuses their strange obsessions and hostile outbursts. It is validation of their lives as unique and beautiful dorks and it pre-exonerates them for any stupid or disgusting behavior they might exhibit.

Tell your mom to fuck off? Asperger's caused it! Refuse to do anything other than play video games, eat pizzas, and go to the bathroom for a solid month? Asperger's! Spend more than 25 percent of your income on Legos when you live in a trailer? Asperger's!

A careful look at the list of symptoms related to Asperger's can demonstrate why antisocial nerds turn to the syndrome as their favorite "get out of responsibility free" card.

The *Diagnostic and Statistical Manual of Mental Disorders*, or DSM–IV, lists the following six criteria for diagnosing Asperger's:

1. Qualitative impairment in social interaction
2. Restricted, repetitive, and stereotyped behaviors and interests
3. Significant impairment in important areas of functioning
4. No significant delay in language development
5. No significant delay in cognitive development, self-help skills, or adaptive behaviors (other than social interaction)

6. Criteria are not met for a specific pervasive developmental disorder or schizophrenia

It might seem like the diagnosis of a normal mental disorder at first glance, but let's pause to consider how each of those criteria might manifest outside the austere pages of the DSM–IV. Let's throw out all that technical terminology and boil each down to its essence. Allow me to rewrite them as, say, an adult child really into Legos and Linux might see the list.

1. I'm not going to prom because I want to level my gnome.
2. I draw Sonic the Hedgehog with breasts and dicks for nipples.
3. I don't know how to do my own laundry.
4. I type at sixty-five words per minute.
5. I took an online IQ test and I am 5 points below Einstein and also Charmander is my PokePersonality.
6. I only threaten suicide when I want something worth over $100.

"Ah!" you might exclaim as you read the revised list. "Why, I have trouble getting along with people and have never had a girlfriend! It must certainly be Asperger's syndrome. I have unusual hobbies that might be considered 'nerdy' or 'obsessive' or 'creepy' and that must be a case of the Asperger's! I am way smarter than these other people! Must be Asperger's!"

Just like that, you have convinced yourself that you are an Internet Aspie. That you are "spergin'." You are a special dude, with special problems, and special explanations for your total dickhead behavior. Blaming Mom and Dad is old hat; these days you've got a new and magical invisible friend to blame for all of your bad behavior and questionable life choices.

It's easy to sit in judgment based on my Internet observations, but I had to meet an Internet Aspie. It turned out to be a lot easier than hooking up with the aspartame ladies.

I've been friends with one for the past eight years.

Andy Ferris is nearly seven feet tall, with a big potato-shaped head and apple cheeks faintly scarred by acne. The corners of his red-lipped mouth are perpetually twisted downward into a frown. Even when he smiles he looks to be sneering uneasily, like the director's cousin cast to play the villain in an exploitation movie.

Andy was twenty-two when I met him. His hair was already thinning. By twenty-six he looked like he asked his barber for "the windswept Hitler." He is an unfortunate victim of bad genetics compounded by aggressively bad hygiene.

Andy is pudgy and doesn't really have a firm grasp on how to dress, resulting in T-shirts that fail to cover his stomach. His facial hair is so unpredictable that I have always assumed he times himself while he's shaving. Irregular patches of dark hairs sprout randomly from his cheek or his chin depending on the day.

I once invited Andy to a party and he literally stood in the corner. At that event he was a gentle giant cowed by the crowds and intimidated by strangers, but he mingled easily with friends and was capable of conversing at length about any number of his hobbies. Once Andy decided you were his friend, he was generous, loyal, and gregarious.

Near the beginning of the process of writing this book, I had an instant messaging conversation with Andy during which I let slip that I was devoting part of a chapter to self-diagnosed Asperger's syndrome. He seemed irritated by the notion.

"WTF wrong with that?" Andy asked.

"It seems like a pretty marginal disease to self-diagnose," I replied. "It takes a doctor to really diagnose something like that."

"Doctors don't know shit," Andy argued. "I know I got it."

The antisocial *World of Warcraft*–obsessed cat was out of the

Lego bag. Although Andy remained hostile to my premise that there was something possibly wrong with self-diagnosing Asperger's syndrome, he agreed to meet in person and discuss the issue.

Andy lived alone, finally, in a small one-bedroom apartment in Fort Wayne, Indiana. He had spent the preceding twenty-eight years living with his mother. As I pulled up in the parking lot outside his apartment building, I have to admit I was a little nervous. It was two years since I had seen Andy and I was not sure what to expect.

Andy answered the door to his apartment wearing an ill-fitting *Animaniacs* T-shirt and a pair of gray sweatpants with a couple of really suspicious holes in the knees. His usually patchy facial hair was replaced with a thin mustache that drooped over his upper lip and a scraggly goatee.

He was holding a paper plate with a steaming microwave burrito in one hand and in the other he was holding a half-empty two-liter bottle of Dr Pepper. It was a wonder how he managed to turn the doorknob with his hands full. Then my gaze drifted behind his shoulder to the apartment.

The apartment was a plain white-walled series of boxy rooms with stained off-white carpets. These rooms were chaotically filled with junk. Toys, computer equipment, DVDs, books, empty pop bottles and cans, socks, bags from fast-food restaurants, and basically every other sort of debris you could imagine a jobless homebound nerd amassing.

I only saw the mess in the living room at first look, but it continued throughout the apartment, worsening near the bathroom and Andy's filthy bedroom. He didn't give me a tour, but the door to his bedroom seemed unable to close. This permitted me a glimpse of heaped clothing, a bare mattress, and a poster for an anime called *Bleach* that appeared to center on a man with red clown hair, a very sharp face, and a giant sword. I noticed several fist-size holes in the bedroom's drywall.

"Thanks for cleaning up," I joked.

"No problem," he replied humorlessly.

He explained that he emptied half of the dishes out of the kitchen sink and the garbage out of both industrial-size trash cans.

"There was some stuff in the bottom of one I couldn't get out, but I got these scented garbage bags so you can't smell it," he said.

I did not plan to test his claim.

I sat down with Andy after the whirlwind tour of what he referred to as "Andy HQ." He hunched over his paper plate and noisily gulped down his burrito, pausing whenever he got an especially hot bite. When that happened, he would sit up straight and breathe loudly through his mouth in an attempt to cool off the steaming meat and cheese. When he had finished his last bite, he gulped Dr Pepper straight from the bottle, emptying most of the remaining liquid.

He punctuated the Caligulan display with a wet-lipped belch that reeked of reconstituted beef paste and "hot" flavored ketchup. He wiped the orangish-brown residue from the corners of his mouth with the paper plate.

"You eat like a monster," I observed.

Andy thought that was funny, although I stand by the comment. We had known each other long enough that he was not shy or inhibited around me. We fell easily into conversation and I enjoyed catching up on his life.

He wanted to talk about my new hand that I kept hidden beneath a black leather glove.

"Can you crush things with it?" He wanted to know.

I offered to break a pencil, but he insisted I smash an egg over the sink. When I pointed out that anyone could smash an egg in their hand, he shrugged and insisted again.

There was a mechanical pop as the mechanism in my hand overcame the shell of the egg. My leather glove was covered in the oily egg white. I held the yolk and pieces of shell in my cupped hand before letting it slip into the sink.

"That is fucking awesome as shit, dude," Andy observed.

I rinsed off the glove and towel-dried it before we returned to Andy's couch to discuss his living situation.

I learned that Andy was still jobless, relying on his mother for his rent and frozen burritos. He was unashamed of this arrangement, but said he wasn't sitting idle.

"I put my résumé out there," he said. "Got some good hits, too. And my mom knows a temp agency that's hiring. I could do some data entry."

In the meantime, Andy was inspired by the news of my book and had started on his own Great American Epic.

"It's based on *GoldenEye*," Andy said.

"The movie?" I asked.

"No, it's based on the Nintendo Sixty-Four game," Andy said. "The plot is what if double-oh-six had the *Moonraker* laser from multiplayer and instead of faking his death in the Arkengelsk chemical facility level he kills James Bond and then escapes. But James Bond is really alive only he is burned by the laser and James Bond works with the Russians to get revenge on double-oh-six who has been promoted to double-oh-seven—"

"I don't think that's how it works," I interjected.

"Whatever," Andy said with irritation. "He could still be a double-oh-six. The point is it's like *GoldenEye* from the Nintendo Sixty-Four, but played through in reverse by double-oh-six with James Bond as the bad guy. And you know what the coolest part is?"

"That isn't the coolest part!?" I laughed.

"No, no," he said. "Check this out. The James Bond dude who wrote the books never even wrote a *GoldenEye* book. They just made it up for the movie! So now I can be the guy who wrote *GoldenEye*."

"That's borderline retarded, Andy," I said.

"You can think that, but you won't be the one making that face when I am in your face after selling a million copies of my book. How many copies do you think your book will sell?"

"I do—"

"Five hundred if you're lucky." Andy cut me off. "Five fifty tops, maximum. Mine will sell fifty-eight times that number."

Andy was becoming breathlessly agitated at the one-sided argument he was having. I changed the subject to games. He was looking forward to the then-upcoming Conan MMORPG and he mentioned several times that it would "incorporate nudity and extreme violence." These two qualities were what Andy sought most in all forms of entertainment.

I can only imagine the bared "hooters" and decapitating *Moonraker* laser headshots that featured prominently in his alternate reality *GoldenEye* novelization.

Once Andy calmed down, I steered him carefully away from any more flashpoints for his temper. Being friends with him for most of a decade, I had learned what topics sent him over the edge. His libertarian politics were a particularly sore point between us.

Libertarianism is a subject I have observational reasons to suspect is shared among many self-diagnosed Internet Aspies.

I could never prove one is the cause of the other, because there are a number of demographic issues to consider. Both groups are populated by predominantly young, white, affluent males. These same people seem to enjoy nerd rap songs and retro gaming.

An obsession with video game tits and bloodshed fit the profile. Writing a dorky novel about *GoldenEye* seemed right in the wheelhouse of an Internet Aspie, although I suspect a person suffering from real Asperger's syndrome would have written something in private code that was completely incoherent to the average person.

I decided I had collected enough observational material and it was time to risk Andy's wrath by asking directly about his self-diagnosis. That was a fatal mistake.

"Can we talk about your Asperger's syndrome?" I asked tactlessly.

"What?" Andy looked at me and ran fingers through his thinning, greasy hair.

"Your self-diagnosed As—"

"I heard ya the first time," he groused. "I thought we agreed no talking about that."

"No. No, Andy. That's the whole reason I came here."

"Oh, the whole reason?" Andy was getting pissed. "You came here just to talk to me for your book? No other reason? You didn't want to hang out with—"

"Yes! Of course, Andy! We've been friends for—"

"Fuck off," he said, and waved a hand at me dismissively. "Friends don't drive hours and then the first words out of their mouths are 'What about you being a crazy douchebag?'"

In my opinion, Andy did a very poor impersonation of me.

I sighed and said, "Andy, I've been here for over an hour."

"So?"

"Forget about it," I said.

I began the arduous process of calming Andy down. He still wanted to argue about it, but I managed to direct him back to calmer subject matter. Eventually he sat down on his lumpy couch and played some ridiculous fighting game on the Xbox. He beat me almost every time with the girl with the visible underboobs, although I got him once or twice with the guy wielding a sword bigger than his leg.

When I tried to gently nudge him back toward the Asperger's syndrome conversation, Andy glared at me and flared his nostrils. After the third or fourth attempt he tossed the controller down on the carpet and threw the classic closed-fisted double birds at me.

He let them sink in for a few seconds and then got up from the couch and stormed out of the room.

I heard a loud grunt and a thump as if Andy had moved something very heavy. The door to his bedroom slammed closed.

Sitting in the apartment by myself, I began to smell a sweet rotted stench. I realized it was emanating from one of the two trash cans.

"Andy, come on," I pleaded through his closed door.

"Fuck off!" he shouted back.

In his own hostile, nonverbal way, this was Andy's attempt to convince me that his Asperger's was real. He never pulled anything quite like that before, and although his anger seemed real, I could not help but believe his behavior was a stunt.

It became clear Andy was not going to emerge from his bedroom while I was still there. I gathered my things and prepared to leave.

I shouted, "All right, I'm going."

"Later, bro," Andy called back through the closed door without a hint of anger.

Morgellons? I Barely Knew 'Em!

When it comes to fake illnesses caused by the Internet, nothing can hold a candle (or a mysterious blue fiber) to Morgellons. This fake disease is the perfect alternative for a hypochondriac who wants to have a unique and horrible illness experience without selling out to "the man" and choosing a real illness.

How many other diseases have an official website specifically to promote their existence?

As is the case with all good epidemiological research, Morgellons was discovered and named by an amateur who refused to accept the advice of a series of medical professionals. Mary Leitao's two-year-old son began to suffer from sores around his mouth and he complained of "bugs."

Like any concerned mother, Mary took her son to a variety of doctors and dermatologists in an attempt to diagnose the problem. None of the doctors could definitively determine the source of the sores and rashes afflicting Mary's son. Some of the doctors even believed that the problem was with Mary and psychological in nature.

Mary refused to accept this diagnosis. Using her bachelor's degree in biology and her expertise as a concerned mom, Leitao examined her son using microscopes.

What she found started a revolution in Internet medicine. She discovered strange red, white, and blue fibers supposedly sprouting out of her son's sores.

Leitao could have been glad to learn her son was slowly growing an American flag. She could have viewed it as an opportunity and turned him into a patriotic icon celebrated by America. Instead, she was horrified by the strange discovery.

With nowhere else to turn, Mary Leitao founded the Morgellons Research Foundation to "study" the "flag disease."

Experts from the CDC and elsewhere have studied Morgellons and found that the fibers are a bunch of malarkey and most of the cases are something they call "delusional parasitosis." In layman's terms, "crazy made-up bug disease." Other individuals suffer from real dermatological ailments, but refuse to accept that they have a contact allergy or a skin infection instead of some kooky fibers sprouting out of their body.

Mary and her friends continue to accumulate evidence from sympathetic medical officials in much the same way questionable doctors provide testimony against aspartame or real doctors say just enough to leave the possibility open.

Could Morgellons be real despite all evidence to the contrary? Could Mary Leitao be right? Yes, anything is possible.

Could the Bible code unlock the secret of time travel? Yes, in exactly the same way.

At the fringe of the Morgellons community is another group who believes the fibers and the sores and the strange sensations associated with Morgellons are part of a larger government or alien conspiracy. Microscopic photographs on these sites picture fibers under magnification and include meaningless captions like, "Fluorescent Nano Arrays and Crystalloid Matter" for an image of some white dots on a slide or "Closeup of Gel Mass with Embryonic Features" accompanying an image of a thread with some gray gunk adhering to it.

If you remove the mention of aliens or CIA brain implants from the fringe sites, they are functionally identical to the regular Morgellons sites. They're all about collecting threads and pieces of gunk and picking at scabs and then taking pictures. Many sites feature arrows added to point out particularly suspicious grains of sand or flakes of dandruff.

One alien Morgellons site quoted a U.S. Air Force colonel certifying the authenticity of a bunch of scabs as extraterrestrial. The Morgellons Research Foundation site quoted a 2006 ABC *Primetime* interview with a guy named Ron Pogue from the Tulsa Crime Lab in Oklahoma. According to ABC, Pogue said the fibers were "some strange stuff" and "not lint." Mark Boese, also from the Tulsa Crime Lab, believed the fibers were "consistent with something the body may be producing."

Alien implants, strange not-lint, and possibly human hairs are just a few among dozens of theories about Morgellons and each theory had its expert source. Which expert was I to believe in that sort of situation!?

Before I talked with a real live Morgellons sufferer, I wanted to talk to an informed non-idiot about the illness. I spoke on the phone to a Chicago dermatologist who asked that her name not be used in the book.

"If you say anything about this stuff you get swamped with letters and phone calls," she complained to me.

Since she chose the coward's option of remaining anonymous, it fell to me, your beloved author, to create a name for my dermatological expert. After a session of super prayer that rejuvenated my super faith in Super God, I decided to add weight to her words by bestowing on her the name and title of Doctor Elspeth Morgellons, Doctor of Morgellonic Science.

"Is Morgellons real?" I asked Doctor Morgellons.

She laughed.

"One word answer, 'no.' "

"You can use more than one word," I said, hoping to familiarize her with the process of talking.

"A lot of the symptoms are real," Doctor Morgellons said. "Even if there is not a physical cause these people have real problems. That is why I think it's so important to exhaust all avenues of treatment for the underlying causes, be they psychological or physical. Particularly when there are children involved.

"But is there a disease called Morgellons? The answer is 'no' to that. Absolutely not."

"Have you dealt with any Morgellons patients firsthand?" I asked.

"A few," she said. "They come in all wound up from things they read on the Internet. These message boards they get on . . . they're convinced they have Morgellons. Some of them bring in these boxes."

"Boxes?"

"Yes. Tupperware or Ziploc bags. They put their scabs and fibers in them and then bring them to show me to prove they have Morgellons."

"And they don't prove it?"

"No." She laughed again. "No, usually it's just scabs, stray hairs. Sometimes there are other fibers, maybe manufactured, but these wounds they have are either caused by an underlying disease or they are self-inflicted. They feel an itching sensation and then they cause the sores to form by scratching until they open themselves up. Their bodies do the rest."

"What do you tell them when they come in?" I asked. "How do you break the news?"

"There you have it," Doctor Morgellons said. "That's the crux of the problem right there. Some of them simply will not accept a diagnosis of anything other than Morgellons, but most will. Particularly if there is a clear cause. I made the mistake once of telling one of my patients she had Ekbom's syndrome."

"What's that?" I asked.

"Another way of telling her she was imagining things. I should have known she would look it up on her Internet group, but I tried to tell her that and give her a placebo. She had sores all over her shoulders and on both cheeks. She called me that night and left a very nasty message on my voice mail. I haven't heard from her since then."

"But sometimes telling them the truth works?" I asked.

"Yes," Doctor Morgellons replied. "Fortunately, many of them will listen to reason. It can just require a lot of convincing. It's an exhausting illness to have to treat in these patients."

"Caught!" I exclaimed. "You just admitted it was a real illness requiring treatment!"

"What? No, I . . . what do you mean?" She stammered, totally busted as hell.

"I'm sorry, doctor, I have to update my website with this information. Thank you for your time," I said, and hung up the phone.

At long last, definitive proof from a real medical expert that Morgellons was a real illness requiring medical treatment. When the Morgellons people caught wind of this, there would be shockwaves throughout the community.

But, wait, which community? Which faction would I honor with this news?

There were the original Morgellons people, who considered themselves the real Morgellons people, and then there were the crypto Morgellons people working on the fringe of Morgellons science.

The decision was clear. When in doubt, the crazier the better, and I had just the man to be my contact. Dr. Don Fuller. I knew him from a cryptozoological and etheric healing mailing list. He never specified in his posting to the list what field he held his doctorate in, but he claimed to specialize in "magnets and protective orgonite technology."

During the three months or so I had subscribed to the list, Dr. Fuller seemed very interested in "combating artificial alien infestions[sic] including nanofiber Morgellons and reptoid mind control implants." When I e-mailed him, I let him know I was working on a book covering Morgellons and that I had turned up some interesting insight into Morgellons plague.

Dr. Fuller was glad to chat with me via instant messenger. We set up an appointment to speak, but it took four separate scheduling attempts before Dr. Fuller managed to show up.

"My computer is a goof," Dr. Fuller offered as his explanation. "Every time I want to do something on it the goofy thing goes haywire."

I assured him it was no trouble.

"So whatcha got for me?" Dr. Fuller asked.

"I have interviewed a dermatologist for my book. The real deal. She slipped up while we were discussing Morgellons and she admitted that it is a real illness requiring medical treatment."

I felt pleased to be able to share my incredible breakthrough on the subject, but Dr. Fuller was less than impressed.

"So?" He messaged back. "Have known Morgellons was real for years. Since original tests on nanofibers."

I was crestfallen. This was my big addition to the field of Morgellons research and it was being scoffed at by one of the champions of the field.

"I thought it was still being disputed," I contended.

"Maybe by the people who are still part of the problem," Dr. Fuller countered. "Everyone who knows anything knows Morgellons is real. Just open your eyes. Look at the evidence. Look at Clifford Carnicom's work. This is well-known factual stuff."

"Yeah, but you claimed on the mailing list that it was an alien implant," I shot back, feeling a bit irritated at being rebuffed.

"An artificial self-replicating illness created by aliens and implanted in the water supply and in certain foods."

"Which foods?" I asked, wanting to avoid any self-replicating nanofibers.

"GM foods," he said. "Monsanto and Dow are all over the place with them."

"I thought you said it was an alien creation!"

"LOL!"

Oh, the indignity! Dr. Don Fuller was laughing out loud at me!

"Kid, you got bad info. Monsanto, Dow, and the military contractors are all working together. They're a front for the reptoids."

"So how do we fight back?" I asked, still stinging from Dr. Fuller's rebuke.

"Neodymium magnets and orgonite technology," Dr. Fuller replied. "You neo your sores and implants for a few hours, disable their energy fields so they stop replicating, and then you surgically remove them. You use the orgonite etheric collectors to consolidate your energy and disrupt the reptoid attempts to control your conscious brain."

"I thought you said the reptoid implants and Morgellons were two different things." I was becoming confused.

"They are!" He messaged back. "The reptoid implants are larger and inserted during abductions. The Morgellons nanofibers are produced when your body responds to certain triggers."

"So your body makes them?" I asked.

"Yes," he replied. "Your body is slaved to the reptoid energy wavelength and is forced to produce Morgellons buds that will grow into colonies."

"How do you disable them to prevent them from replicating if they can just send out an energy signal that makes you make more?"

"Ah, but that's what the orgonite is for. You use the orgone energy to jam the reptoid signal."

"Which is in food produced by Monsanto?"

"Right," Dr. Fuller replied.

"And they make aspartame, too?"

"Right," Dr. Fuller answered.

"Thank you for your time," I said, and bid Dr. Fuller good-bye.

My world was becoming stranger by the moment. It was a little hard for me to believe that Morgellons and aspartame were related, but if I had two unimpeachable medical experts like Dr. Bitsy Schwab and Dr. Don Fuller telling me the two were connected, that was information I could not ignore.

I was beginning to feel as though I might be getting in over my head. If I had known then what I know now I might have backed off; I might have stayed away. I could have called Lonnie and told him to shove his book up his ass.

Like a fool, I continued to chase the truth, blissfully unaware of the terrible price I would pay.

CHAPTER THREE

Ron Paul Has a Posse

> I would like to leave people alone and I think young
> people are that way and I think anybody who uses
> the Internet would like to be left alone.
>
> —Dr. Ron Paul on MSNBC's *Morning Joe*

The 2008 U.S. presidential contest was a historic clash of titanic figures. Old legends were broken, like the venerable John McCain and the once-inevitable Hillary Clinton. New legends were shaped in the crucible, like the mighty Barack Obama and the moose-slayer Sarah Palin. These were historic times!

Yet, to the denizens of the Internet, no man cast a greater shadow over the election than a slight, white-haired congressman and pussy doctor from Texas by the name of Ron Paul. This long-shot Republican primary contender injected a contrarian libertarian voice into the Republican debates and rankled many in the GOP establishment.

Libertarianism is uniquely popular on the Internet, appealing to the self-interest, the intelligence, the relative wealth, and the youth of the Internet population. The core principles of libertarianism can be summarized in two words: FUCK OFF.

Libertarians don't always mean it in a bad way, but they mean it.

Socially liberal and fiscally conservative in general, libertarians don't want smaller government, they want a minimalist government. The purists believe tax is synonymous with theft and the only useful purpose of a federal government is to provide for the defense of the nation and practice an isolationist foreign policy.

To the surprise of many, Dr. Ron Paul almost inadvertently became a fund-raising dynamo. Internet contributions poured in from libertarians and disaffected Republicans. Many of them opened their wallets of their own volition, eager to give to a conservative who represented a clean break from the sins of the Bush administration. Even some Democrats, impressed by Ron Paul's consistent rejection of the Iraq war, became Paulites.

Relying entirely on grassroots support, Dr. Paul raised more money than any Republican candidate in the fourth quarter of 2007. On November 5, 2007, Internet supporters raised $4.2 million for Ron Paul as a "moneybomb" of timed donations. This set records for one-day fund-raising. The moneybomb stunt was repeated in December, raising over $6 million for Dr. Paul and shattering their own record.

Things were not always perfect in the Paulosphere. Ron Paul's Internet supporters were forced to reconcile their own libertarian views with Dr. Paul's socially conservative views, like his opposition to abortion and his semi-evil stance on gay rights.

Then there was Ron Paul's old newsletter, *Dr. Ron Paul's Freedom Report*. For many years the paper was run by blatant racists. According to some, this included libertarian and Ron Paul associate Lew Rockwell writing under a pseudonym. While these articles were appearing in the newsletter, Dr. Paul's name remained on the masthead.

Dr. Paul and his supporters cried foul when the newsletters, dating back to the early 1990s and before, became an issue in the media. Dr. Paul claimed, "Libertarians are incapable of being racist, because racism is a collectivist idea." Nobody knew what the fuck he was talking about except for libertarians, who already loved him, so it was a pretty terrible defense.

Fair or unfair, the taint of racism clung to the campaign in the media, and his legion of Internet fans failed to translate into victory in the Republican primaries. He garnered fewer than two dozen Republican delegates. As Republican challengers to John McCain dropped out of the running, Paul stayed on into June thanks to his huge Internet bankroll.

Dr. Paul finally acceded to John McCain's lead in the primary. He noted McCain had the number of delegates needed to become the Republican nominee, "but if you're in a campaign for only gaining power, that is one thing; if you're in a campaign to influence ideas and the future of the country, it's never over."

The huge sums of money banked by Dr. Paul's 2008 presidential bid were transferred to his political action committee, Ron Paul's Campaign for Liberty. His legions of Internet soldiers, though demoralized and reduced in number, soldiered on.

Not Obtained by Sudden, Slow-Moving Flight

"We just thought, 'Blimps are cool. Ron Paul is cool.' What could be more American than a blimp? When ya think of a blimp ya think of America."

I nodded and left my own mental associations between airships and political movements unspoken.

I was driving to Elizabeth City, North Carolina, with Ron Paul supporter Tucker Mayhew in my passenger seat. His younger sister, Taylor, was sleeping stretched out on the backseat. She did not want to come along. She was not a Ron Paul supporter. She preferred *High School Musical*.

Tucker's mother had insisted we bring Taylor to "see Tucker's blee-ump."

The blee-ump didn't belong to Tucker, he was just one of the hundreds of donors that had contributed to the more than $350,000 raised on the Internet for the Ron Paul Blimp. Rabid fans of Ron Paul were almost giddy with excitement over the idea of the blimp.

I had to admit, the idea was as simple as it was ingenious. People love blimps, yet they did not know much yet about Ron Paul. A grassroots group of Ron Paul supporters believed the best way to introduce Ron Paul to the American people was by piggybacking on America's overwhelming affection for things written on the sides of blimps.

Do you remember what it says on the Goodyear blimp? It says "Goodyear," but I bet you remembered that. Because it works!

It was like the old adage, "The way to a man's heart is through his stomach." Just like that, only they replaced "stomach" with "blimps" and "man's" with American's.

"The way to an American's heart is through his blimps."

Close enough.

Tucker was an early supporter of the idea. He was kicking around the Ron Paul corners of the Internet that helped to spawn the concept. He remembered people talking about it before there was even a website. He showed me a screenshot he had saved on his computer of a post on a Ron Paul forum that he believed proved he was "in on the ground floor."

"This sounds *fucking* awesome!" Tucker declared in the post, although he chose to use nine exclamation points. "Imagine if we put this bad boy over every football stadium in a primary state. Everyone knows about Goodyear and everyone would know about Ron Paul."

I spent the last few days kicking around North Carolina and waiting for the blimp launch to go ahead. It had been scheduled for almost a week earlier and had been subsequently delayed every time until today. With each cancellation, I would return to my hotel and work my contacts trying to get closer to the Ron Paul Luftwaffe.

I can only guess my associations with Something Awful and a few mocking articles about Ron Paul slammed some doors in my face. No one in the upper echelons of the blimp project wanted to talk to me.

So I turned to the lower echelons and Tucker Mayhew, a second-year law student with a bad part in his hair and a pair of Transitions lenses in golden frames. He favored long coats and bow ties, the perfect image of a somber conservative law student. The exact sort of attorney you would want in your corner if you were suing a school district so your kid could learn creationism instead of geometry.

That image was ruined whenever he opened his mouth and spoke in a whiny drawl. It wasn't even a North Carolinian accent. It was as if Professor Frink from *The Simpsons* had been raised in the backwoods of Appalachia.

In contrast to his douchebag name and his douchebag way of dressing, Tucker was a pretty nice guy. He was nice enough to invite me over to his parents' house for macaroni and cheese with hotdog buttons, nice enough to offer to introduce me to some of the big brains behind the Ron Paul blimp, and nice enough to invite me to drive him to Elizabeth City. His mom was the one nice enough to invite me to bring his nine-year-old sister along.

"I don't have a lot of friends at college," Tucker confessed to me during our two-hour drive to the blimp launch. "It's hard to meet people. The Internet makes it easier. There has been a bunch of Ron Paul meets on campus. I even met my girlfriend at one."

Tucker showed me a wallet photo of a girl who looked like she should be rolled in bread crumbs and deep fried. But she had a pretty face.

"She's got a pretty face," I said, my eyes darting back to the road.

"Not a bad bottom either," Tucker said.

Forgotten wells and corpse piles had better bottoms, but no sense debating the finer points (or blunt ends) of Tucker's girlfriend. I reached over to fiddle with the radio. I had to do something to prevent the awkward silence that followed from killing us all.

"So why Ron Paul?" I asked as I fiddled with the radio. "What makes him so special?"

Tucker took a moment to respond. He was licking pudding from the foil top of a pudding cup.

"Waddya mean?" he asked, his words murky with pudding.

"I mean, what is it about Ron Paul that makes you guys so crazy about him? Why is he different than Mitt Romney?"

Tucker snorted with derision.

"Romney? Mister Double Guantanamo? No. The Iraq war was a lie. The whole War on Terror is a lie."

"So vote for a Democrat," I suggested. "Obama or Clinton or one of the others."

"Oh, that's even better," Tucker said. "The Clintons back in the White House or the most liberal senator who will raise taxes like crazy? Yeah, no thanks. And Democrats are only barely better than Republicans on foreign policy. They started Vietnam after all."

"Okay, those are a bunch of reasons why not to like the other guys," I said. "Why Ron Paul?"

Tucker had a dreamy faraway look in his eyes and a tiny dollop of chocolate pudding in the corner of his mouth.

"You gotta believe in something," he said, his voice thick with emotion or possibly more pudding. "I believe government is the problem not the solution and I believe we gotta stay out of foreign countries. I believe . . . in minding our own business and let . . . let the free market take care of things."

Dawn was breaking over North Carolina. It was about to be a misty, cold, miserable morning. My map printed from the Internet took us through the middle of the sleepy college town of Elizabeth City and then sent us south along the Pasquotank River. Taylor woke up like a dog sleeping during a long car trip, sensing the shift in speed and the dramatic tension as the humans approached their destination.

"Ron Paul is gay," she said, rubbing sleep from her eyes.

It took us another twenty minutes to find the airship's launching point, delayed by a wrong turn into Elizabeth City's modest airport.

The launching sight was a dreary field owned by Airship Management Services, the company renting their blimp to an LLC started by Ron Paul supporters. Liberty Political Advertising was a completely grassroots effort with no involvement and barely a mention from the Ron Paul campaign. This sort of polite disavowal from Paul became a standard practice. His overzealous supporters and their deep pockets, when combined with strict campaign finance and spending laws, meant Paul could barely give these oddball groups a wink of approval.

The unofficial nature of the event showed in the disappointing attendance and the lack of media attention. A few dozen people were milling about next to a large wooden Ron Paul REVOLUTION sign. Some sat in lawn chairs, huddled beneath camping blankets and sipping travel mugs full of coffee. The more hale and hearty youth were in sweatshirts and even T-shirts, laughing and enjoying the spectacle of the blimp being topped off in preparation for its launch.

CSPAN, of all things, was blasting loudly from speakers.

It didn't strike me as an atmosphere befitting something as conceptually awesome as a blimp launch. Not exactly a crowd getting pumped up and *rocked like a hurricane.*

Tucker tried to introduce me to Trevor Lyman, but he was talking to someone from a real media outlet and I did not feel like standing and watching him get interviewed. Lyman was half of the brain trust behind the Ron Paul blimp, the other being Elijah Lynn, the Alan Colmes to Lyman's stocky, square-jawed Sean Hannity.

Lyman was too busy with the camera, but I shook hands with Lynn briefly. He seemed friendly but preoccupied with preparations for the launch and not interested in answering questions. Alan

Colmes probably isn't a fair comparison for Lyman. He was more like a really pale and shifty-eyed Willem Dafoe.

Looming behind us at a respectable distance was the blimp. They were already preparing to launch and the 190-foot-long white blimp was hovering about a foot above the ground. It was impressive. It was a giant, white bomb of buoyant truth swaying gently from side to side on its mooring cables.

I understood from Tucker that there had been a great deal of effort and money sunk into the printed graphics displayed on the side of the blimp. It was emblazoned with the Randian question, "WHO IS RON PAUL?" in twelve-foot-high text. Beneath that, in smaller lettering, was the suggestion to, "GOOGLE RON PAUL."

Investors, supporters, well-wishers, and people who planned to attempt to shoot the blimp down with rocket launchers could track its progress on the blimp's website. A map displayed its current location and regular updates were made to its schedule of appearances depending on the funds raised by the LLC.

"It'll fly right over the interstate on the way to rallies and cities," Tucker said, marveling at the huge flank of the blimp. "People will see that."

"And then they'll Google Ron Paul?" I suggested.

"Right," Tucker agreed.

"From their car?"

"Well, they've got phones you can Google on," he said.

"While they're driving?"

"People do it," he said, growing a bit irritated. "Or they could be stuck in traffic. Or what if they're a passenger?"

"Then they could Google Ron Paul on their phone," I suggested.

"Right," Tucker agreed. "Or write it down and Google it when they get home. Or . . ."

He trailed off and never finished the thought.

"Can I ride in it?" Taylor asked, and started to run toward the blimp.

I watched as Tucker chased her around the field, reaching after her and always stumbling a few steps behind her like a Keystone Kop. People were posing for photographs behind the big Ron Paul REVOLUTION sign with the blimp in the background. I'm pretty sure I saw a woman with a monkey on her shoulder.

A bearded man with wild black hair was sitting in the grass playing a bongo and chanting, "This is what democracy looks like! This is what democracy looks like! This is what democracy looks like!"

I wondered why democracy did not have any black people or hot babes.

"Your blimp is hella gay!" Taylor squealed.

Tucker still lagged behind her. His shoes were beginning to clot with mud.

"I could run her down," someone suggested behind me.

I turned and was looking a chestnut quarter horse right in its brown eyes. The man who made the offer was sitting atop the horse, dressed in cowboy hat and patriot regalia, an American flag in one hand and the reins of the horse in the other.

"I think he'll catch her," I replied.

"I was just kidding." The man chuckled.

He sighed and surveyed the sparse crowd. He seemed satisfied, maybe even impressed.

"We're gonna kick some ass this year," he assured me.

When the Ron Paul blimp finally launched that morning an uneven cheer went up from the crowd. The white blimp looked like a suppository as it rose slowly into the unwelcoming gray sky. The man on the horse rode back and forth with the American flag. People took pictures and laughed.

"You can't stop something like that," I heard someone say.

The Iowa caucuses were less than three weeks away.

The Salad Days

It was cold early January in New Hampshire, a scant three days after the 2008 Iowa caucuses and two days before New Hampshire's first-in-the-nation primary. The whole state was lousy with journalists and politicians.

Early polling favored Barack Obama to take the state on the Democratic side following his upset in Iowa. John McCain, who famously beat George W. Bush in the 2000 Republican primary, was polling ahead of Mitt Romney on the Republican side.

The other story in New Hampshire was Ron Paul, riding high on the news of his fourth-quarter fund-raising and his surprising 10 percent performance in the Iowa caucuses. No one outside his rabid supporters seriously expected Dr. Paul to win the state. It had a long history of libertarian leanings and the overwhelming (some would say overbearing) presence of his volunteers in New Hampshire suggested strength, but he was just too far behind in the polls.

None of that mattered to true believers, including my friend Todd Glenn. Todd was a diehard Ron Paul supporter, a Paulite, as he proudly referred to himself and his friends volunteering for the campaign. He was in New Hampshire supporting Ron Paul and had convinced me to join him, purely as an observer, to "see what was happening."

I was an unapologetic Obama supporter, which was fortunate because the Obama volunteers had an unofficial neutrality agreement with the Paulites. Both groups loathed Hillary Clinton's mobs of thuggish middle-aged supporters and most of the Republicans, so it was an unspoken bond that extended to politeness between the two groups.

It was a quiet détente in the frozen north, small favors that weren't orchestrated by either campaign. I heard of charitable Obama canvassers passing hot coffee and doughnuts to Ron Paul supporters shivering on a street corner. In return or just by chance, Ron Paul supporters were reluctant to tear the signs from the hands of Obama supporters during the inevitable visibility scrum behind live TV broadcasts, but woe betide the Clinton supporters.

Things were just peaceful enough between the two groups that I was able to hang around with Todd without drawing any unwanted confrontations from his new friends. A few asked me about Obama or confessed hope that he would win the Democratic nomination. Most of them just shrugged when they heard I supported Obama or said something like, "At least he isn't Clinton."

Todd and seemingly five hundred Ron Paul supporters were staying at the house of a widowed farmer. The bowlegged old farmer asked to be called Wicket. He smiled constantly, wore overalls and flannel shirts, and had the scraggly chinned look of an extra from the Robert Altman version of *Popeye*.

On the evening I arrived, Todd showed me to a patch of floor and gave me a blanket and a cloth sack of clean laundry to use as a pillow. Wicket trundled around his packed living room, dispensing steaming black coffee from a silver pot. He offered warm creamer packets and sugar from the kangaroo pouch of the apron around his waist.

The Paulites were pale, overgrown men. There was a roughly even distribution of chubby twentysomethings with terrible facial hair and skinny twentysomethings dressed like they were from the dorkiest chapter of the Nation of Islam. The room was packed with loose hormones directed at the handful of younger women staying at the farmhouse. You could see the polite fear in their faces as they were separated from each other and surrounded by little groups of awkward suitors.

Older, longtime libertarians, many of them locals not planning to spend the night at Wicket's farm, made up for their lack of youthful enthusiasm with a crystallized burning hatred of both Bush and the Democrats. They stood off to one side, gathered around a battered sofa, and discussed gun rights and secession. The older libertarians watched the kids with a mixture of bemusement and, oddly, low-key hostility toward the latecomers to libertarianism.

The buzz at the farm that night was that Dr. Paul was being "silenced by the media" and particularly Fox News. There was a Fox News Republican debate scheduled for the following night and Ron Paul had been excluded from the proceedings with little explanation. The Ron Paul supporters justifiably pointed out that both Fred Thompson and New York mayor Rudolph Giuliani were polling worse than Dr. Paul, yet both were invited to the debate.

The bad news of the debate was tempered by a bit of good news. A few of the volunteers staying at the house had word that Ron Paul was going to be hosting a live town hall in Manchester, New Hampshire, to counterprogram the Fox News debate.

"It's gonna be tomorrow," said a bearded man in his mid-twenties I knew only as Junior.

"Tomorrow night?" I asked.

"Same time as the Fox debate," he replied. "And they're gonna put it on the internet, too. Ron Paul 2008 dot com."

"Who needs Fox!?" Todd exclaimed.

Junior grinned. His eyes glistened like black buttons in the poorly lit farmhouse. His face was still reddened from visibility walks in the cold.

"Y'all gonna go?" Junior wondered.

"Hell yeah," Todd replied, and then looked to me. "Right? Right?"

It was weird seeing Todd, a perpetually sick manic-depressive, acting so enthusiastic about anything, let alone an elfin old man from Texas. How could I deny him the one light in his benighted existence?

"Of course," I replied.

"Awesome," Junior said. "Hutch is gonna be there. It's gonna be awesome."

It was not awesome, I will go ahead and lay that out there right now. Hopefully that doesn't spoil the end for you too much.

I woke up the next morning sore to the bone from lying on the hardwood floor. The room was hot and smelled liked B.O. and farts. My hair was plastered to my face with sweat and my arms had red marks from the rough wool blanket Todd gave me.

Most of the Paulites were still sleeping, but Wicket was up and bustling around the farmhouse's large kitchen. Most of the appliances looked to be from the 1950s, but he had a large stainless steel-fronted refrigerator.

"My younger brother makes venison sausage," Wicket said, and opened the freezer to show me piles of frozen sausages. "Want some eggs?"

I took a plate of eggs and sat at the table, shoveling the under-cooked yellow clumps into my mouth while two pale and stricken-looking girls sent text messages.

"Do you have a car?" one of them asked me.

Todd didn't even have a car. I shook my head. The girl returned to desperately texting, no doubt trying to find some sort of escape from the rural colony of gassy hornballs with bad facial hair. I wished them luck.

I finished my sloppy eggs and took my plate over to the sink to wash it off. Wicket was still scrambling eggs in a huge nonstick skillet almost big enough to serve as a wok.

"Don't worry about it," Wicket said as I reached for the faucet. "I'll wash 'em all once they're done."

"Oh, thanks," I replied.

He leaned over to me a bit and said, "If ya hurry upstairs you can get a shower before the hot water is all used up. Only enough for a couple more of ya."

I heeded his advice, showering quickly in the claw-foot iron tub located upstairs. It was relaxing to wash off all the sweat and I knew I probably smelled terrible. Unfortunately, I was soon sharing cramped quarters with seven other folks from the farmhouse who had not bothered or been able to catch a hot shower.

Transportation into town was an issue and several of the more rugged Paulites set off on foot down the country road in the direction of Manchester, where the town hall was to be held in the evening. It was over three miles of brutal cold slogging through plowed snow banks that had a hard crust of overnight freeze. The alternative was walking on roads with no lane markers.

I'm not even sure they made it. If you're ever in Manchester and you see a Sasquatch with a Ron Paul toque, well, you know who he ate.

Thankfully, Junior provided us with a ride into town in a cargo van owned by a Ron Paul supporter with a roofing business. Eight of us piled into the back, sitting on stacks of roofing tiles and over-turned buckets stained with frozen tar. Most everyone smelled like day-old corpses washed up on the banks of a tropical river.

Without a well-organized volunteer corps like the Obama campaign, the Ron Paul campaign operated as an activated militia. This worked fairly well in New Hampshire, where the grassroots support for Dr. Paul was well established.

The van dropped us outside a Quiznos on Elm Street and we hooked up with other volunteers already milling around chanting the clever Ron Paul slogan, "Ron Paul! Ron Paul! Ron Paul!" There were maybe two dozen of them being led by a Jewish kid named Eli who never got off his cell phone the whole time I was there.

The plan, from one of the other chanters, was to gather as many supporters as possible and then begin marches back and forth in the more heavily trafficked areas. A few cars honked their horns at us, whether in support or in derision it was usually hard to tell. People seemed to be chanting and waving their signs to stay warm.

This was the pattern for most of the day, with occasional breaks to eat or warm up in one of the restaurants in downtown Manchester. The real excitement came whenever our group ran afoul of another group of supporters.

There seemed to be a particular hatred for followers of Mitt Romney. Many of them were imports from Massachusetts or Mormon paratroopers from Utah, dressed in new ski coats and neckties. The Ron Paul supporters, many of them locals, detested this sort of carpetbagging. They shouted "War monger!" or chanted "Mitt should quit!" when Romney's supporters wandered into earshot.

The "brought in" rumor also circulated about Clinton's supporters and to a lesser extent Obama's. Only Ron Paul supporters were considered genuine. I opted not to mention the fact that most of the people staying at the farmhouse were from out of state.

The closest things came to getting ugly was an incident around two in the afternoon. Five Giuliani supporters drove up in an SUV and decided to follow behind us holding Giuliani placards. There were two college-aged kids and three adult men that looked to be of Italian ancestry. I doubt they were Mafiosos, but the word spread that they were for obvious reasons.

Ron Paul supporters, Todd included, began to heckle them for losing the Iowa caucuses and being so far behind in the New Hampshire polling. This heckling continued for several minutes with the Ron Paul supporters drowning out any chant the Giuliani supporters tried to start.

Finally, a young woman with stringy brown hair began to yell at the Giuliani supporters about 9-11. Earlier in the day the ringleader of our group asked her to knock off some 9-11 conspiracy theory evangelizing. In close proximity to Giuliani's "minions" the urge became irresistible.

"Giuliani and Bush caused nine-eleven!" she shouted. "Three thousand people died so we could fight Bush's war! Giuliani is a terrorist!"

"War criminal!" someone added from the back.

This was too much for one of the Giuliani supporters. He hurled his placard Frisbee-style at the woman and charged the nearest man. That happened to be Todd, someone who has been in several fights and won none. Todd had just enough time to yelp before the Giuliani supporter leveled him with an open-handed slap to the side of the head.

"What now, motherfucker!?" The man shouted. "You all are the fucking terrorists! Who's a fucking terrorist now?"

A few of the Ron Paul supporters jockeyed to fight the guy, but were held back. I pushed past them and dragged Todd out of the line of fire. The Giuliani supporter gradually backed away and the group of them retreated back toward their SUV, perhaps realizing they had crossed a line.

Todd was uninjured, but stunned by the incident. He developed a red handprint on his face for the next few minutes. The 9-11 truther with the stringy hair thanked Todd and flirted with him for the rest of the visibility march.

In the late afternoon we retired to an Irish pub called Murphy's Taproom for beers and hot food. Murphy's served as the unofficial HQ of Ron Paul supporters in Manchester. We warmed up and had beers and swapped war stories with other groups of Paulites.

While Todd and the truther paired off to talk about having crazy 9-11 is a hoax babies I mingled with some of the other patrons. It was just a stroke of luck that one of the main topics of discussion was Internet organizing. Several supporters had laptops out and were updating blogs or using ronpaul2008.com, a campaign and social networking site that has since been taken over by Dr. Paul's Campaign for Liberty PAC.

The common denominators among the Paulites seemed to be youth, an interest in the Internet, and general disgust with conservative belligerence and liberal "political correctness." Taxes were also a big topic and some vague idea that liberals wanted to "tax us to death."

Among the younger Paulites there seemed to be an inordinate number of lawyers and people who could at least believably pretend to be "constitutional law" experts. The younger Paulites also seemed fairly affluent, whereas many of the homegrown New Hampshire Paulites seemed to be salt-of-the-earth types.

The hostility between the young and old was still evident in the way people grouped together in the bar. Here the tension seemed lessened after a tiring day of walking together and holding signs. Spirits were further buoyed by beer and the excitement of the upcoming town hall. When one of Ron Paul's painfully awkward ads came on the TV, the bar fell silent and then cheered wildly at the sight of the Ron Paul supporters featured in the ad.

"Live free or die. New Hampshire," said one of the men in the ad.

The rest of the ad was drowned out by the deafening cheer in Murphy's. After it had died down I walked over to the bar to get another beer.

"I think that chick from the commercial is on my Facebook," said the man standing next to me at the bar. "The hot one."

I wasn't sure who he meant.

I was on my fourth or fifth Boddingtons, living free and not dying, when word began to spread that we were mustering to move out to the Ron Paul town hall. A woman I believe was campaign staff arrived with a huge printed banner for us to carry. Many of the Paulites were drunker than me. A few had brown smudges around their mouths from peeling and eating chocolate coins stamped RON PAUL LIBERTY DOLLARS.

The building where the town hall was being held was a large multistoried red brick compound that resembled a cross between a schoolhouse and a mental asylum. The choice of venue was purely utilitarian: one of several companies leasing space in the building was Manchester's public access station MCAM-TV 23. This was the station that carried a simulcast of Dr. Paul's town hall discussion across much of New Hampshire and on the Internet.

Dozens of us marched through the snow, chanting and hollering and attracting honks and shouts from passing cars. The groups of Ron Paul supporters were converging on the public access studio. Their ranks had thinned out some as many left to travel the short distance to Milford and protest the Republican debate. The anger at Ron Paul's exclusion from the debate was bubbling.

"I'd rather die on my feet than live on my knees," remarked one particularly heavyset Paulite.

"They won't forget us," agreed his friend. "They will remember the name Ron Paul."

Another one of the Paulites was concerned that we might be killed by Republican agents.

"Should have brought my guns," he joked. "We could set up some sandbags and make sure they don't try to stop us."

"I'd die for that," someone pitched in, and the conversation temporarily shifted to fantasies about a bloody battle to protect Ron Paul while he bravely transmitted his town hall.

Most of the remainder of the march was given over to a discussion of fiat currencies and the monstrous injustice of the Federal Reserve. This was a favorite topic of Paulites, but I was unable to feign interest in "worthless paper money." If Amazon.com wanted to start accepting sacks of gold nuggets then I was fine with the currency switch, but it was hard to care.

The legendary Hutch was waiting for us at the station. He was a tall, chinless white guy in his thirties. He had thinning brown hair pulled back into a ponytail and he wore big wire-frame glasses and a jean jacket with REVOLUTION embroidered on the back. He referred to his Blackberry and murmured into his Bluetooth earpiece frequently as he directed the arriving groups of Paulites to set up along Commercial Street.

I wondered aloud what all the hype was over Hutch.

"He's one of the guys who came up with the fund-raising stuff," Junior told me.

Not the moneybombs or the campaign's branding. That was Lyman, the genius behind the blimp. Hutch was somehow involved with the way Paul was handling his campaign donations. He seemed to be a dull process figure within the campaign, but the supporters claimed he had official ties to Paul and spoke with authority.

Though disappointed, the Paulites deferred to him when they learned they would not be allowed into the town hall. Word had already gotten out about that, but many had hoped to find a way inside.

Hutch produced a laptop and directed Paulites to an exterior wall of the building where an open wireless network would provide Internet access. Tech-savvy Paulites practically orgasmed over Hutch's attention to detail as they crowded around the window hijacking bandwidth from a router named "LAB2."

I held the fort atop one of the snow drifts lining Commercial Street, waiving a Ron Paul sign and motioning for passing cars to honk. The supporters near me took turns stealing over to the laptop and trying to get the TV station's website to load the streaming video. There was a lot of griping about crashed sites and dead video streams, but the feeling by the end of the town hall was that Ron Paul had knocked one out of the park.

The mood was jubilant. People were hypothesizing about "hidden support" in New Hampshire not being detected by the polls.

Some theorized that America might have watched Fox News, but the locals watched Ron Paul and that was all that mattered.

Supporters hugged one another. I saw Todd making out with that 9-11 truther girl near the wireless hotspot.

I saw Hutch smoking a cigarette by himself and I sidled up to ask him about the town hall.

"It was amazing," he said with a grin. "We are going to kick some ass in New Hampshire. Giuliani is going down."

He smiled and tossed his cigarette into the snow. At that moment former New York mayor Rudolph Giuliani was polling third in New Hampshire.

The Post-Ron Paulcalypse

Rudy Giuliani went down. He was a complete failure of a candidate, a humorous footnote in the margins of the campaign history book.

And Giuliani beat Ron Paul in New Hampshire.

Giuliani ended the night in fourth place with 9 percent and Paul had only 8 percent. The two of them were fighting for the scraps near the bottom of the Republican roster.

New Hampshire was Ron Paul's best hope, the place selected as the home to libertarianism's utopian Free State Project. A New York neocon beat Ron Paul there. It was a crushing blow to the movement.

"I can't believe this." Todd called me from New Hampshire as the results poured in.

I was in my hotel room in Boston on the day of the primary, enjoying some sort of lung infection and trying to eat my way through the room service menu.

"What's wrong?" I asked.

"They're stealing it from him!" Todd shouted, his voice quivering with emotion. "Those motherfuckers are stealing the election from him. There are counties with zero votes for him and Carol knows people who voted there."

"Who is Carol?" I asked.

"My girlfriend," he said, as if I should have known. "We met on the campaign."

I recalled the stringy-haired truther from a couple days earlier. I took a burning swig of overpriced room service Scotch and hit RE-FRESH on the ABC News results page. Obama was losing.

"Obama is losing," I said.

"What? Who cares? They're stealing the election!"

We were two sinking ships passing in the night. Cut off by the fog. Semaphore flashing uselessly.

"I've gotta go," I said, and hung up the phone.

It was selfish to dismiss his angst, but I was almost as invested in my man as Todd was in Ron Paul.

I can only imagine how the poor Bill Richardson supporters felt that night, huddled in their adobe houses, pondering the crushing defeat of their bumbling Latino hero.

Who didn't love Bill Richardson and all those stories he told? There was that time he showed Saddam his shoe and almost started another war with Iraq and there was that time he accidentally dropped nuclear secrets and spilled them all over the Chinese. Who didn't want to pinch that fat little face and those freckles drawn on his cheeks?

But, vote for Bill Richardson? Really? No way. I loved *Life Goes On* but I didn't write in Chris Burke for president.

Barack Obama went on to recover from his defeat and engage in a historic and brutal primary campaign against Hillary Clinton. Ron Paul carried on as well, but for all intents and purposes, the cold stony earth of New Hampshire was the final resting place of his 2008 election bid. He was always a long shot, but to be dealt such a crushing defeat in the state most ideologically in line with libertarianism dispelled any illusion of victory.

Ron Paul's Internet supporters were among the last to give up on their candidate. Many refused even after Dr. Paul had conceded in June 2008. Seeming to sense that he could end his campaign, but did not even have the power to disband the community that had formed around his movement, Ron Paul for President transitioned to Ron Paul's Campaign for Liberty.

This lively PAC supports libertarian candidates with absolutely no chance at winning and libertarian causes that most Americans find crazy. Presumably, they have been active in the fight to legalize colloidal silver and blood root salves, have worked to inform Americans about the dangers of aspartame, and are getting to the bottom of why the Pentagon was shot with a stealth cruise missile on 9-11.

Nah, that's a cruel straw man of the beliefs of Internet libertarians. I am sure Ron Paul's Campaign for Liberty supports real libertarian ideals like charging people money to drive on your personal road and eliminating superfluous government agencies like fire departments, police, the Center for Disease Control, and whatever that agency is where Hellboy works. If you want the faerie king and a bunch of Nazis to unleash the golden army, then Ron Paul is your man.

While Ron Paul's PAC continues to trudge along, the most interesting developments in the Paulosphere are the result of independent ventures from supporters. That delightfully enterprising spirit that brought America the Ron Paul blimp is alive and well.

One such idea is Paulville. Located on the salt flats in Hudspeth County, Texas, the goal of Paulville according to its website is, "to establish gated communities containing 100 percent Ron Paul supporters and or people that live by the ideals of freedom and liberty."

It's a "privately held co-op" or, to put it another and more amusing way, a libertarian commune. When your philosophy decries collectivism at any level, how successful can you expect your collectivist community to turn out?

As of the writing of this book Paulville has attracted dozens of libertarians . . . to post on their forums. Most of the more recent posts on the forums either come from foreigners and people with better ideas for Paulville than "buying up a tract of remote salt flats and selling them back to people." It's hard to come up with a worse idea than that, but the Ron Paul supporters on the Paulville forums have certainly tried.

Begun in March 2008, Paulville is a resounding success on par with the Free State Project in New Hampshire. According to the Paulville website, to date "a couple members" have stopped by the fifty-acre plot of land to "check out the area."

No utilities, no paved roads, no shopping or commercial development. Who wouldn't want to pick up their life and move to Paulville to eke out an existence on a salt flat? Maybe you could become a subsistence farmer there.

I wonder what sorts of crops grow in salt. Turnips? How many gold Pauloons could you get for a salt turnip?

I called Todd Glenn to get his opinion of Paulville and find out when he planned to move to Texas.

"Fuck off," he replied, and hung up the phone.

It seemed like the right answer.

CHAPTER FOUR

Otherkin—Dragonkin

Pretty much anything with caffeine is related to dragons.

In my experience, when you are living in the countryside, you notice every excruciating detail of your environment. You notice the stone goose in a pink frock someone has placed next to their driveway and wonder what terrible chain of mistakes and miscalculations led to its arrival in their yard.

You notice the misspelling of "electronics" as "eletriconics" on a hand-painted window display and contemplate the belligerent inattention to detail something like that would require. You even notice the secondhand baby clothes store that looks so depressing you can almost hear the sobs of multi-miscarriage moms shuffling in with bags full of unworn onesies.

The city isn't like that. The city is so full of sensory information that you can't process all the details or your brain would overheat. After about a week of living in a city the kaleidoscope of nail salons and shoe stores and weird Greek pizza places might as well be the dark outlines and simple colors of a cartoon background. It gets so bad you expect muggers to leave clouds of dust in their wake as they flee or your brain reduces an entire neighborhood to a repeating row of condos and dog parks.

To notice country-level details in the city you need to be trapped on foot with nothing to do and nowhere to go. Aimlessness and listlessness are prerequisites to processing more than just the contours of the overflowing urban environment.

Being locked out of your apartment or car is a good start. When you're in that situation everything you desire is trapped just out of reach. You have to stand around and let the normally blurry details of the city come into focus while you wait on someone to come to your rescue.

Someone like a locksmith. The same one who made you wait for two hours in a Best Buy parking lot when your car's steering column locked up inexplicably. What an asshole.

"Locked out," I told the locksmith.

"Where?" he asked.

I told him.

"Half hour," he said, and hung up the phone.

"Half hour" is locksmithese for, "Two hours, if you're lucky, and you'll thank us for showing up at all."

I walked from the pay phone to a nearby gas station, bought a soda and something with a cream filling, and tried to drown my sorrows in carbohydrates. It worked for a while, but I had unwittingly sat down on a curb frequented by a homeless guy I like to call WBE or Worst Beggar Ever.

WBE, as you may have inferred from his name, was the worst beggar I have ever seen. He was white, which is already a huge homeless demerit. Business guys in suits downtown, regardless of their race, don't want to hand money to a white panhandler. It's too close. It messes with too many preconceptions.

It's like seeing your dad crying or your mom kissing another man on the lips. White bums are very upsetting for a lot of guys in the prime begging demographic.

WBE was appropriately bearded and smelly, but he looked young. All too often youth is wasted on the homeless. Young and white suggested a slacker who had just slacked a little too aggressively. Maybe he was the sort of guy who passed up a rent check for an ultimate fighting pay-per-view and ended up on the streets and stoned out of his gourd. There are plenty of homeless people like that, but alas, WBE had even greater demerits against him.

WBE had a dog. Not completely uncommon, although I think it's inappropriate for someone without a home to take on a dependent. It was a little, white fluffy dog with a brown kerchief tied around its neck. The sort of dog a very fat woman might own.

"It's a bison frise," I imagined him telling a gorgeous woman. "His name is Meatball."

Then she would pat the dog on its head and slip WBE her hotel key. Later that night they would all orgasm dozens of times. Even Meatball.

Yes, I was jealous of a homeless man. You never saw how happy he looked when he was sleeping.

The dog was just as annoying as the owner. It was so well behaved. No yapping or chasing other people walking their dogs. I have taken dogs to obedience training and could not get them to stop barking at geese flying at a thousand feet overhead. I wanted Meatball to be startled by honking horns or run wild at the sight of a pigeon.

WBE and his Lassie-like puffball dog had a final trait that eclipsed all others as an irritant. It was a trait I witnessed firsthand many times while getting gas or something to drink. It was a trait I ran afoul of that day I was locked out of my apartment.

"That's where I sleep," WBE groused at me. "Got a cigarette?"

He asked for a cigarette before I even processed his initial comment. I stood up with a grunt.

"You're smoking one," I observed.

"Yeah."—he took a drag from the cigarette in his mouth—"this one's almost out though."

I gave him three cigarettes. He nodded and put them into the plastic bag wrapped around his wrist.

Then he stretched out on his back in the shadow of the gas station. He set a tin can next to his head and closed his eyes. There were a few pennies in the can. This was how WBE went to work. He fell asleep on the concrete curb next to the air machine for tires and assumed people would leave him change.

No sign. No security measure. No effort.

Maybe Meatball would finally show some emotion if someone messed with the tin can. I abandoned the thought of kicking his can across the gas station lot and I walked back in the direction of my apartment.

I realized I still had a good deal of time to kill, so I settled on a bench across from a barbershop. It had a generic name, something involving a pun and the word "shear" or one of those other words reserved for usage in hair-related puns. Beneath the name on the wooden sign was the phrase, "Come in nappy, leave out happy."

The barbershop seemed empty and dark even though the sign on the door declared it to be open, but it was difficult to see inside. Too many posters cluttering the front window. During my interminable wait for the locksmith, I studied the details of each of them.

The one that sticks in my memory depicted a black woman in her twenties contemplating the dire state of her frizzy afro.

"This thing is out of control," she seemed to say with her rolled eyes and six-inch-wide purple collar.

There was more to this woman and her lawless tresses. She had the time to fantasize about what her life would be like with a different hairdo. In this fantasy, depicted in a second photograph inside a thought bubble, the woman's hair had a chiseled, Grace Jones look.

This haircut was evidently pleasing to a man wearing an 8-ball leather jacket. He was dancing next to the woman and her new haircut and this seemed to be making the woman very happy in the smaller photo.

I questioned the scientific validity of the woman's thought experiment. In addition to her hair, she changed out of her purple jacket and was wearing a gold lamé top and a leather skirt belted with what looked to be parts from an aircraft engine.

The new haircut I understood, but that outfit too? She should have known better than to introduce two variables.

Large white text on the poster advised the use of a spray-on hair product so that you could "become the person you've always wanted to be." It was a curious affirmation to employ on a poster advertising a sculpting spray for women's hair.

Was it a call to nostalgia? To a childhood dream of gold lamé shirts and hot nights with an Arsenio lookalike? Or was it a suggestion that this spray would burn away the person who was standing there reading the poster? Maybe a new you, the ideal you, would arise like a phoenix from the damp hair clippings surrounding the barber's chair.

I spent more than an hour on that bench across from the barbershop, watching customers enter nappy and leave out with a smile on their face. The clientele was uniformly Puerto Rican, young, and tended to favor close buzz cuts and fades with Spanish words carved into the back. The customers were nothing like the woman in the poster. Their hair didn't sparkle.

My mind wandered back to that poster and that phrase. I began to imagine myself in the gauzy purple world of the woman in the poster. Arsenio Halls and gold lamé receded into the misty distance.

I had plenty of time to kill with a single question: who was the person I've always wanted to be?

Robocop seemed like a good start. He can shoot through a woman's dress and hit a rapist in the crotch without injuring the woman. I figured that could be adapted into a pretty solid stage act. He can also see through walls, which would come in handy a lot more often than you think. Just off the top of my head, Robocop would never be served with court papers. Good luck with that subpoena, Dick Jones.

Being Robocop wasn't too realistic. I don't live in Old Detroit and I'm not a cop, but I was still able to fantasize about possessing the qualities of Robocop. He's stoic, he upholds the public trust, and he always does what's right even if it means he can't defenestrate the bad guy.

I also recognized that emulating Robocop would have its disadvantages. Robocop is not particularly communicative. He spends his free time asleep with a titanium spike in his brain dreaming about being murdered and losing his family. He can't take off his pants or make love to a woman since only the front half of his face is still human.

I reasoned that there wasn't much use to punching through a cinder-block wall if there was never going to be a gorgeous woman on the other side. What I ultimately came up with as I sat there on that bench was a fantastic chimera.

The me I always wanted to be was a cross-pollination of Robocop and Zorro maybe with a little bit of the pickup artist Mystery thrown in. I would be the sort of cyborg who would burst through the wall of a drug den, shoot a "Z" into the rapist's crotch, and then stand framed in the hole in the wall and ask Senora Isabella what she would do if she could never see me again.

It would be amazing as long as she wasn't an OCP employee. My programming prevents me from neggin them.

Somewhere during the imagined process of being profusely thanked by Isabella on piles of gold lamé pillows I spotted the locksmith's van driving past my bench. After paying him way too much to pick the door of my apartment I returned to my fantasy.

It was ridiculous. I could never be a cyborg Casanova. Omni Consumer Products would never manufacture a Zorro line of cops. It was pure fantasy. Hardly worth entertaining. I blamed the damned poster for sending my mind off on a tangent of disappointment.

I realized, to my great chagrin, that Worst Bum Ever was probably the closest I could ever come to my fantasy. I would slide out of society, abandon my responsibilities. Then I would make a fortune while I slept in the shadow of a gas station, a bag of cigarettes around my wrist, my loyal dog at my side, and a gorgeous woman slipping her hotel key into my change can.

That stupid phrase from the poster has stuck with me ever since that day. "Become the person you've always wanted to be." I wrote it down on a scrap of paper and taped it to the mirror in my bathroom.

It's a de-affirmation. It reminds me to set my sights lower. To stay realistic with what I can accomplish.

It's that poster reaching out and telling me that I just can't be anything I want. There are reasonable limitations. I believe I can't fly. I believe I can't touch the sky.

I think that wisdom applies to everyone. You can't just decide to be what you've always wanted to be.

There is a thriving subculture on the Internet of those who disagree. They believe you don't just have the potential to be whatever you want; you *are* whatever you want.

Other Than Human

According to version 4.0.1 of the Otherkin FAQ, Otherkin are, "Those people who believe themselves to be spiritually and/or physically other than human."

So that rules out humans, leaving us with . . . well . . . basically everything else.

The majority of Otherkin draw their identities from mythology. Dragons and elves, Tolkien and ancient mythology, anime, and video games. Other creatures of folklore like vampires, werewolves, and space aliens are also very common identities. The FAQ even mentions previously unknown types of Otherkin "that have not shown up in known legends or fiction" and lists as examples "star-dragons" and "Elenari."

If you're interested in keeping track, Elenari are elves, but they are from a different planet or dimension. Their sub-races include the Tulari, Draestari, Listari, Dai'ari, and Kalthilas. I gleaned this information from the Elenari FAQ, which was in turn compiled from the writings of TalLeonan. Is he an ancient druid from space? Perhaps, but he did all his writing on Usenet and a mid-1990s Otherkin mailing list called Tir Na n0c Digest.

It's easy to look at five hundred pages about space elves and dismiss it out of hand. I admit that was my first instinct.

But, looking past the seeming implausibility, many Otherkin genuinely believe in the mythology they have adopted. They can be openly hostile to newcomers and those they view as "faking" becoming an Otherkin. Indeed, the efforts of pranksters from sites like Portal of Evil, 4chan, and even Something Awful have created an inherent distrust of outsiders.

I recognized this could make finding volunteers willing to participate in my book a difficult process. I had already resigned myself to trickery with some of the subcultures covered in the book, but I wanted to stay honest when dealing with the Otherkin.

I contacted six Otherkin who frequented related forums or ran their own websites. I explained the purpose of my book, to explore without prejudging them, and I convinced two of these initial six to meet with me in person. One was a young man named Christian who was new to the subculture, and the other was a more experienced veteran by the name of Roger.

I wanted to find out how committed these two were to the lifestyle, their own personal takes on the mythologies, and how being other than human affected their relationships with normal humans.

The Dragon

"I love dragons, man," said Christian Joseph Heathcliff Ross.

He paused and then leaned back dramatically in his chair.

I was sitting in his St. Louis apartment drinking a glass of grape-flavored Kool-Aid. Christian liked to loudly chew the freezer-burned ice cubes. We had just met about ten minutes before.

Christian insisted I refer to him in the book by his full middle name of Christian and not his first name of Joseph.

Shortening his name to "Chris," something I did several times during our conversation, caused him to purse his lips and take a deep breath through his nostrils. Before he finished his irritated, whistling exhalation I corrected myself each time.

"Christian."

"The funny thing is," he said, "I am totally an atheist. I have been since, like, age ten."

Christian was a young-looking nineteen. He lived alone in a shabby studio apartment in St. Louis. He made the rent each month by working part-time in a community college's computer lab.

"I don't go to school there, so it's sort of an unusual arrangement," Christian said. "I basically watch college kids browse the Internet and help them print stuff."

He appreciated his job for the "unlimited free printing," which allowed him to cover his living area in multipanel color images of dragons and anime characters in roughly equal measure. The dragons tended toward realistic depictions of "western" dragons, with a lot of artwork that seemed related to the film *Dragonheart*. The anime characters were almost uniformly buxom and underdressed.

"There have never been any serious incidents at work," he said without prompting.

I asked him about nonserious incidents and his expression soured.

Christian's teenage awkwardness manifested during our conversation as a restless anxiety. His unkempt hair hung in his face and his Adam's apple poked out of his neck like the fist of a swallowed doll. He plucked self-consciously at his T-shirt and rarely met my gaze.

He had poor volume control and would become very excited when discussing his interests. As he spoke, the volume and pitch of his voice would fluctuate wildly from one sentence to the next. This was not a young man going through delayed puberty; this was a young man getting his ass kicked by delayed puberty.

I arranged to speak to Christian after trading several e-mails with him. It was an easy process. He seemed eager and excited to discuss his lifestyle at length.

I identified Christian as a potential interview subject by reading his posts on a relatively popular Internet forum for Otherkin. Christian counts himself among an enduring and growing subculture on the Internet for men and women who believe they are directly connected to the supernatural. They believe, in varying ways, that they are something *other* than human.

"It means I'm me," Christian said, "but I'm also this other soul inside my body. An ancient soul."

The ancient soul trapped in Christian's body had a name. Christian pronounced it "Lower Barth" but he spelled it "Lauere Baartet" in the e-mails he sent me prior to my visit. I wondered if it was possible to mispronounce the name of the extra soul trapped inside his body. Christian took offense to the suggestion and pointed out that Lower Barth had a voice and communicated with him in English.

"He's a dragon," Christian asserted. "From Germany."

Lauere Baartet, Christian's eighteen-hundred-year-old alter-ego, possessed a sixty-foot wingspan and a neck Christian claimed was "as long as a whale." His reptilian body was rusty-red with a yellow segmented underbelly and was covered in armored scales.

"They can withstand a spear or sword," Christian explained.

Gunfire was also nothing to Lauere Baartet.

"The bullets would just bounce off," said Christian. "He's never been shot, but it would be harmless. Like rain."

Lauere Baartet's powers were nearly limitless. Christian ticked them off on his long fingers, but gave up counting after the first ten.

Lauere Baartet could fly into space or travel into an unseen magical reality. He could breathe fire, cold, acid, and conceal himself in black smoke. Lauere Baartet could control minds and communicate with people while they were sleeping.

"His intelligence is off the charts," Christian effused. "Like Einstein only . . . think about . . . really, really old."

Lauere Baartet was a draconic guardian angel to Christian, both protector and avenger. I hoped my interview went well. I didn't want to be set on fire, frozen, and covered in acid just for asking the wrong question.

For Christian, being an Otherkin meant being in direct contact with Lauere Baartet, the German dragon from AD 200, but there are few limits to what manner of supernatural entity might inhabit someone's body. In the realm of Otherkin, elves, angels, demons, vampires, and more obscure creatures have all found their way into the bodies of various Internet users.

"It's different for everybody," Christian said. "Just because it's one way for me doesn't mean it has to be that way for everybody else. Together me and Lower Barth are a dragon. Some people just are dragons. Elves especially are bloodlines."

I asked him what he meant by "bloodlines."

"Like you're just . . . ," he paused. "You're an elf. You inherit it. There's nothing else to it."

Christian explained that it could be this way for dragons as well. Some Otherkin exist physically as the creatures they associate with. They pass as human or otherwise conceal their lineage by changing shapes. Others, like Christian, are in intimate contact with a powerful supernatural spirit.

"I've always known I'm special," Christian proclaimed early in our conversation. "So don't think this is just made up. This is real."

Christian repeatedly stressed the authenticity of his claims throughout our conversation. He was very earnest, but also unapologetic about the strangeness of what he was telling me. I asked him when he first knew he was an Otherkin.

"Like I said, I always knew I was special. I always felt different. I think the first time when I started to know what I was, was when I was about eight. My dad brought home a video of the movie *Dragon-heart*."

Christian gestured to one of the images of the dragon from that movie taped to his wall.

"That was when I knew what I was, man. I just didn't know what to call it. I knew I had a dragon inside me. I could feel that energy and the power of the dragon. The voices started around the same time. At first he sounded like Draco, from the movie, but I think that was just Lower Barth's way of communicating with me without scaring me."

"What did he say to you?" I asked.

"He told me everything would be cool," Christian said. "He talked a lot about my destiny. There are like ten prophecies about me."

When pressed on the content of the prophecies, Christian claimed they were written in an "ancient German dialect" that a friend of his was translating. The manuscripts were in a "monk order" and had not been completely "scanned in" by the monks.

"They're powerful," he said. "That's all I know right now. My friend found them and they're powerful. Dragon prophecies are always powerful."

Christian learned the term for his unusual circumstance years after first learning of Lauere Baartet. He was searching the Internet at the age of thirteen and came across a group of people who referred to themselves as Dragonkin.

"It is amazing to realize that you're not alone," Christian said. "You spend all these years thinking you're the only dragon left and then one day you just find out there are hundreds of them . . . I don't know. It's like finding out about the Matrix or something."

Playing Games

I was entering my fifth hour at Christian's apartment and he was showing me a collection of Gundam Wing robot models he assembled and painted over the years. There was something garish and unwholesome about his little robots. The pinks and purples and yellows of their color schemes twisted the right angles of robots into a doughy abstract.

Each model he showed me was more poorly painted than the previous model. They were Christian's version of Louis Wain's degenerating cat artwork. I mentally slapped myself when I realized how much I was looking down on the kid for his Gundam robots. I may not watch Gundam, but I could probably name every single Transformers or GI Joe toy.

"I never really watched Gundam," I confessed.

He snort-sighed his disappointment, but continued on.

Christian handed me a robot painted bright green. It had a yellow head and a big purple shield on one arm. My fingers wrapped around its fragile waist and Super Glue crackled. Its left arm and fist, holding a broadsword painted lumpy silver, dropped to the carpet.

"Oh, shit," I said. "I'm sorry."

"You might as well throw the whole thing on the carpet," he said, and then sighed. "It's ruined."

I could not tell if he was joking. I looked him in the eye and tossed the model onto the carpet. Its other arm came free from its torso, a white ring of Super Glue visible on the bright green paint of its armpit.

Christian snort-sighed again and crouched down to pick up his fractured Gundam.

"I didn't mean it," he said. "God."

Christian seemed to calm down after eating some sort of Pizza

Hut concoction with a cheeselike paste adhering to the bottom of the pizza. I paid, unaware that the next day I would be dumping money into Roger's hot wing habit.

It was as Christian was telling a joke about Senator John Mc-Cain that I realized he was like an infant. He was crabby with me over the Gundam because he was hungry. Once he shoveled some greasy triangles of Pizza Hut's Frankenstein creation into his maw he became friendly again.

We resumed the interview, but with many interruptions and digressions. One tidbit gleaned from these sidetracks was that Christian loved White Wolf role-playing games. I knew from reading Otherkin forums that many Otherkin gravitate to White Wolf's games, but I had not known that prior to our meeting Christian enjoyed these games.

White Wolf games are similar to games like Dungeons & Dragons, but with a greater emphasis on story, character, and uncomfortable romantic interludes in a room full of ostensibly heterosexual dudes. White Wolf games include Vampire, Werewolf, Mage, and a game entitled Changeling about postmodern fairies that is particularly popular among Otherkin.

One shared trait of almost all White Wolf games is the idea that the players and their characters are part of a secret magical world. The vampires or werewolves or changelings are the only creatures aware of this magical dual reality to which the rest of humanity is ignorant.

"I like Changeling the best," Christian enthused. "I have a vampire campaign I've been playing for a while too . . ."

He delved into excruciating detail on the subject, relating events in his role-playing sessions in much the same way the most boring person you have ever met might describe a recent dream. As he babbled on about vampire gypsies using some magical power called "chur-mer-stry," I wondered about the cause and effect of White

Wolf games. Was it just a coincidence that so many Otherkin play White Wolf games? Were some of them using the role-playing system as a guidebook for their own "awakenings"?

I asked Christian directly.

"No way," he said. "None of the people in my group even know I'm Dragonkin. I knew about myself way before I played any of those games. Even D&D."

"You said your awakening was six years ago. You didn't play any of those games before the age of thirteen?"

"I played Vampire maybe, but it's totally different," Christian said. "Maybe some people, some sheep, follow along with what those books say. Some people might follow along with *Lord of the Rings* or other people following along with the Bible say they're an angel. But those are fakers. Those are the people who want to be Otherkin but they're not really. They're just posers."

Christian's lips were purple from drinking grape Kool Aid.

"You can make up whatever story you want on the Internet," he said. "You can't make up a story to yourself."

The Power in Everything

It's probably not a good sign for a professional journalist to become bored with the person they're interviewing. Fortunately, I am not a professional journalist. I have no ethical or moral responsibility to the truth or to good conduct or to integrity. None of that nonsense.

Christian was boring me senseless and it was my prerogative to behave like a child. I wanted to forsake my nerd ancestors and shove this tool into a locker.

My head lolled over the back of the chair and I stared up at the ceiling as he talked. I was one story about White Wolf games away from starting to whistle while he explained vicissitude. He pronounced it "viska-tood" and in the context of his stories about *Vampire: The*

Masquerade it seemed to be the ability to make your character turn into a giant meat monster.

My attention drifted to more personal and immediate fantasies while Christian detailed his meat monster rampage. I was fantasizing about creative ways to kill myself by heading to the drugstore I saw on the way over and offing myself with something in there.

I considered chugging acne medication and climbing inside a jumbo trash bag to asphyxiate myself. I finally settled on a fantasy in which I bought diabetic syringes and took them back to my hotel room so that I could inject air directly into my carotid artery.

Yeah, I thought. That should do the trick.

"A dragon is elemental."

"Huh?" I lifted my head and felt the blood rush back into my face.

"I said"—Christian snorted with irritation—"that a dragon is elemental. It is like fire, but it's in everything."

It sounded like the Force. More pop-culture nonsense. I told Christian that it resembled the Force and he scowled, too angry for one of his snorts.

"Yeah, if you don't know your butt from your elbow, maybe," he said. "The Force is in everything. Like an aura or something. Only certain things are draconic."

"Reptiles," I suggested.

"Some, but it's not just animals, man. Inanimate objects have a nature. They either are draconic or they aren't. If you know what you're looking for you can see the associations. Some different Otherkin have associations, too. Everything in the universe is like that."

"How did you learn about this?"

I had read nothing about a system like this on any of the Otherkin websites I researched. There was plenty of New Age mysticism blended in with the Otherkin spirituality and philosophy, but nothing that explicitly tied all matter in the universe to dragons.

"Experiments, man," Christian replied. "I had to just watch stuff. Observe a shitload. It's like, you know, if some girl has a pretty face. If you think her face is pretty that's something you know, right? You've learned how to see prettiness. But you can't, like, put it down as an equation."

"So you've learned how to see which objects are dragons," I suggested.

"Yeah, yeah," Christian agreed as he became animated on the subject. "It's not like they're a dragon, though. It's just the nature of the dragon. They're draconic. Some of them come from dragons. Like if a dragon blacksmith makes a sword it could be draconic. Or sometimes it's just because, like, the object is something a dragon would like."

"It appeals to dragons."

"Exactly!"

Christian was on his feet. He seemed excited that I understood his theory.

"I tried to explain it on the forums and nobody understood," he said. "Some of them tried to, but I don't think they really got it."

Christian was referring to a popular Otherkin Web-based community forum. It was his current haunt, and one I thought I had thoroughly sifted through before coming to meet him.

"So I could hold up any object and you would be able to tell me whether or not it is draconic?" I asked, and used his term.

"Right, unless it's a psychic blank or a powerful dragon is shielding its nature," he said with extreme seriousness. "I can't penetrate their obfuscations."

I walked over to the shelf holding Christian's dusty Gundam robots and I picked up one of the fragile models. Christian's eyes bugged out a little at the thought of me handling his precious droids.

"What about this one?" I asked.

"Draconic, but that's easy. All of my stuff will be draconic. It's been around me too much."

"That sort of ruins the demonstration," I said.

I was already thinking of a possibility. My suicidal fantasies earlier had reminded me of the nearby drugstore. It was within easy walking distance and Christian seemed excited about the prospect of demonstrating his ability.

I suggested we take a stroll to the store to do some field experiments.

"Let's rock and roll!" Christian declared, and jammed his bare feet into a pair of well-worn running shoes.

A short walk through the muggy St. Louis evening and we arrived beneath the fluorescent lights of Walgreens. It was the beginning of the summer and the aisles were overflowing with the sort of cheap beach equipment and foam coolers that you buy at a drugstore on the way to the beach because you forgot to buy them at a regular store.

"What about that?" I pointed to one of the end cap displays of Pepsi.

"Dragons," he answered immediately.

"And those?" I pointed to the adjacent shelves of Coke.

"Dragons," he replied. "There was no cola war as far as dragons are concerned. Pretty much anything with caffeine is related to dragons."

"Mountain Dew?"

"Yeah," he said. "Dr Pepper, Jolt, energy drinks, coffee, and even chocolate. All dragons."

"Okay, well what isn't related to dragons?"

Christian scratched at the peach fuzz on his chin and looked down the food aisle.

"Ah." He grabbed a bag of puffed rice cereal. "Bagged cereal is elves. I know that from an elf who told me about cereals. If it's in a bag it's elf, if it's in a box it's dwarven."

I reached over and slid a disposable camera off the rack.

"What about one of these?" I asked.

"Not dragon," Christian replied. "Hard to say for sure. I've heard vampire for digital cameras and fairy for the sorts of cameras with film."

"Fairies make cameras?"

"No." He scoffed at the thought. "Of course not. I mean, you can't be a hundred percent sure, but there's no reason to think that. Just because an object is attuned or infused with the essence of a certain kind of Otherkin doesn't mean that Otherkin made whatever it is."

I was a little confused by the answer, but I was at least beginning to grasp the concept.

"All right," I said. "What about these?"

I held up two Mexican-style glass candles covered in religious artwork.

"Angelkin, no doubt, bro," Christian said, barely giving the candles a second look.

Angel Otherkin were among the most common Otherkin on the Internet, and among the least popular. Questions about the authenticity of their awakenings were much harsher and more persistent. Christian seemed to extend that disdain to objects he decided were related to angelkin.

I walked down the aisle full of paper products and picked up a stack of paper plates.

"These!" I called.

"Dryads," Christian replied. "And the plastic ones are dinokin, dinosaurs and prehistoric sauroids, which are cousins of Dragonkin but they lack our royal heritage."

I was definitely beginning to understand his methodology. He was using an advanced technique of aura reading similar to Karelian photography known as "total bullshit."

"This is total bullshit," I pronounced, and tossed the paper plates back onto the shelf.

"How dare you?" Christian spluttered. "I let you into my home and you repay my hospitality with this sort of insolence?"

I'm no expert on ancient dragon spirit debate techniques, but referring to someone's "insolence" is probably not a winning approach.

"My insolence?" I recalled Anders and zee chamber. "My apologies, my liege."

I shoved past Christian on my way out of the Walgreens.

I had another Otherkin to interview in Missouri. Maybe he wouldn't be such a massive chode.

CHAPTER FIVE

Otherkin—Elfkin

> Go not to the elves for counsel, for they will say
> both yes and no.
>
> —J. R. R. Tolkien

Roger Wayne Malthus was sweating profusely from his encounter with a video game at Dave & Buster's in St. Louis. His balding hair was plastered to his forehead and his cheeks were flushed red. He stood next to me at the bar, his bulky upper body leaning forward and his pudgy fingers clasping a hot wing with surprising daintiness.

Roger was a big man, the sort of big man who preferred heavy metal T-shirts and black jean shorts worn with unlaced combat boots. The Roger sort of man.

Like Christian, Roger was reluctant to come out of his shell. He was forthcoming in our e-mails, but setting up a meeting ended up requiring a bribe. My book budget was quickly being drained by the trip to Dave & Buster's for hot wings, beers, and video games.

Despite using me like a cash machine, Roger was growing on me. The thirty-something big man was gregarious compared to Christian.

His Cannibal Corpse T-shirt was an amusing choice for a place over-run with kids on a Saturday afternoon.

"It's called 'awakening,' " Roger said. "It's the process where you remember your past life or learn about the truth. Your past, your power, et cetera."

Roger waved a half-eaten hot wing in the air. Red sauce matted his unruly beard. He wiped his mouth clean and took a long pull from his beer before continuing.

"The awakening is as different as your Otherkin identity. It's unique. Some people are awakening their whole lives. I knew a mummy—"

"A mummy?"

"Yeah," his eyebrows lifted. "Real son of a bitch. Liked to shit all over the new guys. He said he was thousands of years old and he would just lord that over everybody. The dragons are like that, too. I posted on the same forums as him. I was going to make a T. rex Otherkin account to totally one-up him, but he went into one of his 'century-long slumbers' right after that. Caught him posting on a car forum for Hondas like a week later."

Roger laughed at his own story and took another swig of beer.

"Anyway, that guy was a true believer in the idea that real Otherkin could spend centuries unlocking all of their knowledge and power. And he hardly believed anyone was a real Otherkin."

"What about you?" I asked.

It was the one subject Roger was reluctant to expound on.

"What's there to tell?" he asked. "It was all in the e-mails."

Roger rolled up the sleeve of his Eaten Back to Life T-shirt and showed me a tattoo on his bicep of a seven-pointed star. I recognized the symbol from my research into Otherkin.

"The Elven Star," I said.

"Bingo," Roger replied, and let his sleeve fall back into place. "My name is Glade Shadow. I am an elf."

Unlike Christian, Roger did not view himself as possessed or shar-ing his body with a supernatural spirit.

"I'm just an elf," he said, holding out his hand as though I might see elf particles clinging to his fingers. "I figured out my mother was an elf and both of her parents are elves."

"Wouldn't that make you a half-elf?" I asked.

"Ah." Roger grinned. "A half-elf is possible, but the elf trait is dominant."

I never stopped to consider the Punnett square for elves.

"You mentioned the awakening," I noted. "Tell me about yours. How did you know?"

"I think I always knew in some sense," Roger replied, echoing Christian's sentiment. "For a lot of us it's about personality. The werewolves and vampires have these predatory urges or they get a little crazy during a full moon. For me it was a mix, because I'm physically an elf."

He held up his hand again.

"See," he said. "Almost no hair."

It was true, there were just tiny golden hairs on his fingers.

"I don't have a ton of hair on my fingers, either," I said, and held up my hand.

He took my hand and lifted it up to the light.

"Yeah, see, you have more," he said. "Way more, and they're darker."

I didn't argue and Roger continued to enumerate his elven characteristics. Good eyesight, quick reflexes, and pointed ears.

"Wait," I interjected. "You have pointed ears?"

"As a baby," he said. "You should see my baby pictures. It's like Spock. But being around people you have to fit in, so my ears rounded out."

I was skeptical, but I kept it to myself. Roger continued on to his personality traits. He had a good sense of humor, he was very logic oriented, he was introverted, and he enjoyed nature.

"I'm also very nocturnal. I'm on the computer all night."

"Is that something elves are known for?" I asked.

"Some elves are nocturnal, some aren't. It all depends on the type of elf."

When I asked him how many different types of elves there were he just shrugged. The hot wings were running out and I could sense that he was eager to test his elven reflexes on some fighting games.

"Don't take this the wrong way," I said, knowing before I continued that he would take it the wrong way. "My concept of an elf does not really match up with you. What you just listed to me sounded like pretty normal personality traits, and not the sort of thing that would convince me I was an elf. How did you know for certain?"

Roger laughed it off. I felt guilty for taking the issue seriously.

"It's okay," he said. "You picture Santa's elves or Legolas. Elves are as widely varied as humans. You just know inside what you are. Like that internal gyroscope."

"So you can't actually prove to somebody that you're an elf?" I pressed him.

"Most Otherkin usually can't," he said. "Who cares? This isn't about other people, this is about my own identity."

Roger gave me a sly grin.

"But I can prove it. I have powers."

I was intrigued, but Roger wadded up a napkin with his orange fingertips and disappeared back into the din of the arcade. My proof would have to wait.

Power Revealed

Roger's ride was a rust-speckled 1989 Chevy Cavalier with a crumpled driver's side door. He climbed in on the passenger side and awkwardly crawled across to the driver's seat. The shocks creaked ominously beneath his bulk.

"You can ride with me," he invited.

I took one look at the swamp of Burger King and Taco Bell wrappers in the passenger side foot well and I declined. The trash was just the topper. The vague and slightly creepy nature of Roger's offer put me off riding in the same car as him.

He had offered to take me out to his house and prove his "elven heritage" to me. I had a suspicion Roger's proof was something that if he exposed in public would force him to register on a special list with the Missouri Department of Corrections.

I was beginning to regret not buying that rape whistle.

Roger seemed to accept that I wasn't going to be riding with him. He turned the key in the ignition and the Cavalier protested for several seconds before sputtering to life. Danzig suddenly blared out of the cassette deck.

"Irty black summer!" The diminutive muscleman cried before Roger turned the stereo down to a reasonable level.

"You can follow behind me," he said. "It ain't far."

Every part of my animal brain told me to flee as far away from Roger and his Danzig tapes as mechanical science would allow. My rational brain told me that I couldn't leave this story without witnessing whatever terrible "proof" Roger was willing to reveal.

My damned smarty-pantsed elitist rational brain won out and successfully suppressed my flight instinct.

Following behind Roger in my car was easy enough. His Cavalier had a tendency to pull left and seemed to top out at around fifty miles per hour. He was constantly wrestling with his car's alignment just to stay in the right lane and the elven gods of Tir na nog alone know why Roger insisted on taking the interstate.

Cars blazed past us with their horns blaring. Roger calmly extended his left arm out the window and maintained a constant middle finger from St. Louis to our exit forty-five minutes later.

The suburb of St. Louis Roger called home was a mostly white blue-collar suburb. Autozones and Applebees. Taco Bells and trailers. It was the sort of featureless corrosion of a city that turns the infill of America into a depressing nationwide franchise of hogslop and car parts for the working class. The Pizza Hut proletariat.

While I was waxing Marxist about the wasteland of capitalism, I nearly missed Roger turning off down a side street. My tires squealed to take the turn and a baby in a car's backseat gave me a very hateful look. Almost immediately, Roger turned again, down a dusty asphalt road with an unofficial fifteen mph speed limit posted. The shipping container–like structures on either side of my car could mean only one thing: trailer park.

A trailer seemed the perfect fit for Roger. To my surprise, he navigated through the entire length of the trailer park and pulled up outside the park's lone permanent structure. It was a gray-green condo with neatly manicured flowers outside. One half of the structure was the trailer park's front office. The other was Roger's family residence.

"Take your shoes off," he advised, holding the screen door open as we both kicked our shoes off onto a long porch covered with Astroturf.

We were greeted almost immediately by Roger's mother, a short and stout woman with a bad bleach job and a missing front tooth that whistled when she spoke. Each "s" added a whistling "p" and each "w" joined to a resonant hoot that sounded like blowing across the top of a bottle.

"Who-*sp* this-*sp*?" she asked with apparent irritation.

"A friend," Roger explained. "He's doing a book."

I introduced myself and explained that I was writing a chapter in my book about Roger. She shook her head.

"I don't know why you'd write about him," she tooted. "He ain't done nothing this year."

She glared at him and then back at me.

"All year," she added.

"I'll be back," Roger announced, and disappeared into the bowels of the house.

"Uh"—I struggled for a topic—"what do you do?"

"I run the front office," Roger's mother said, and then settled onto a kitchen chair with a groan. "Ankles all swole up."

I asked her about her ankles, but Roger's mother wasn't interested. She wanted to talk about being in my book.

"Can you put my picture in it? Like in the paper?"

"Not really," I lied.

"I had mine on the front for Fireman's Festival and they messed it all up." She sighed. "There was me and then a yellow me, only the other me was green."

"They printed it wrong," I suggested.

"Then I called them and they said it was on the Internet. I told Roger and he went on there and it looked fine. He printed it out for me. Don't know why they couldn't do nothin' right."

She reached across the table and rested her hand on mine.

"Roger is real good with computers," she said. "He could do anything he wants with that. But he just plays his games and his music. And Lord knows what else. Pornos I bet."

Roger's mom was the sort of woman who likes to talk "at" people. Like a storyteller, only without much of a story. She rambled on about getting a bridesmaid's dress "taken up" for "Syl's thing at the Legion." She blew smoke in my face as she described how she had a wart frozen off her foot.

"Then they scraped it out," she said. "I tried putting a button up in there when I got another one. You know, the pin on the back of the button. You know what I mean. That hurt too bad, so I had to get it taken off again."

After about fifteen minutes of this, I felt certain Roger had abandoned me with his mother as some sort of punishment. I was contemplating my exit strategy when he emerged from the darkened hallway at the back of the house. A smell not too different from an open sewer followed in his wake.

"Christ Our Lord," his mother exclaimed. "Did you leave the fan on!?"

Roger reddened and shouted, "Yes!"

Roger's mother heaved herself up from her chair and swept into the bathroom at the rear of the house to strike matches and deploy air-freshening sprays. Roger's embarrassment was palpable. He wouldn't even look me in the eye.

"Did you see it? See my mom?" Roger said, craning his neck to look over his shoulder. "She's an elf. My dad was part Indian, too. Cherokee. Indians are more magical than most humans."

"Do you think I could see your power?" I asked.

Roger fidgeted. It seemed strange for him to proudly bring me out to his house and then shrink from the idea of doing what he had promised. What Roger did not know, but might have suspected, was that I had extensively researched his claims of supernatural powers prior to our meeting. These claims included, but were by no means limited to, the powers of healing, darkness manipulation, nocturnal vision, and limited mind reading.

Those were just the powers I saw repeated more than once. In his conversations across various forums and websites, he made numerous other casual claims of powers, including shape changing, mind domination, and something he called "dream sending."

"I'm trying to think what would be best," he explained, staring down at the table and fidgeting.

Roger stalled for time and tried to change the subject. He tried to get me drunk, but I refused his repeated offers of beer and whiskey. As tempting as getting fall-down drunk in a stranger's house might seem, I was committed to erring on the side of caution. I wanted to be able to exit at a moment's notice.

Roger's next tactic was to perform poorly executed stunts. I think he hoped I would be so impressed by one I would declare it to be his power and the demonstration would be considered a success. He prefaced each stunt with, "Watch this." He never implied they were related in any way to his elven heritage.

His first stunt involved covertly adjusting the gas feed on a disposable lighter to make it shoot long tongues of hissing fire. It ended poorly when the flame refused to extinguish and spread down the length of the lighter. Roger yelped and dropped it on the floor and stomped on it, luckily extinguishing the flame. He was relieved that the carpet was undamaged.

"Too much gas," he explained. "But watch this."

His next stunt was a variation on the old "magnetic pen" magic trick using his empty beer bottle. In this trick you hold a pencil in one hand and then grab your wrist with your other hand. You let go of the pencil, yet it stays magically attached to your hand thanks to an extended index finger. When you let go of your wrist the pencil drops.

The beer bottle turned out to be a poor substitute for the pen. Part of the way through his first attempt, he dropped the bottle loudly on the tabletop, summoning his mom from the back.

She stomped around and flared her nostrils, detecting the lingering singed-plastic aroma from the lighter accident.

"You two burning stuff?" she asked suspiciously. "You better not be smoking weed in my house."

She returned to the back with a bottle of Yoo-hoo from the refrigerator.

"Look," I said, "I need to get going. If you've got some proof you need to show it to me."

"Okay, okay," Roger said. "You don't have to be a dick about it. Come on."

He was irritated. I was irritated. To him I was pressuring him needlessly to perform a magical act like some sort of trained monkey. The magical sort of trained monkey. To me, Roger was just killing time and hoping I would go away, but he couldn't acknowledge defeat.

He stomped out of the house onto the Astroturfed porch. Large gnats were swarming by the thousands, concentrating in buzzing clouds around the outdoor lights of the house and the trailers. They didn't seem to bite, but they landed on our faces and flew into our mouths, so we quickly stepped into the darkness where the cars were parked.

"I can see in the dark," he said. "Infravision."

I was familiar with the term from Dungeons & Dragons. It was similar to infrared sight in D&D, but for Roger it meant something a bit different.

"I can sense the energy of things. The radiations of them."

Night vision was a pretty good power, even if he played with the definitions. It was something I could test.

"Here, write something on this," Roger said as he handed me a warm square of paper from his pocket.

He also handed over a pen, making me wonder why he used the beer bottle in his earlier magnetic pen trick. I kept the paper hidden from his view and wrote *"I love Danzig"* on it.

"Now walk over there." He directed me down the trailer park's asphalt road. "Far enough so I can't see you."

That seemed to make the experiment impossible, but he quickly added, "I have to concentrate and focus to use my infravision."

I nodded and backpedaled down the road. An elderly man on his trailer's latticed porch stared at me from the comfort of a ragged recliner.

"Are you boys playing football?" he asked in a quivering, sing-songy voice.

"No, we're doing an experiment," I replied.

"That's good!" Roger called.

"What?" The elderly man leaned forward on his chair.

"It's an experiment," I repeated.

"Hold it up better!" Roger shouted.

"You should play football," the old man declared, and settled back into his chair.

I held up the piece of paper. Roger squinted his eyes as if he was staring into bright sunlight. He lifted his fingers to his temples and made a grunting sound.

"IIII . . . LLLLLOOOOOVVVVVE . . . ," he elongated each word, "DDDDDAAAAAANNNNN . . . DANZIG! I love Danzig!"

135

His celebration was short-lived. I was standing almost directly next to the old man's porch light.

"There's too much light around here," I said.

"He can read!" the old man interjected. "God almighty, what a day! The boy can read!"

"Fine," Roger sulked. "We can go out in the field."

As luck would have it, the trailer park bordered an undeveloped field of tall grass and a few scraggly trees. Roger's house actually spilled over into the grassy lot and there was a roughly mowed semicircle that I presumed was his backyard. We waded into the knee-high grass and repeated the experiment, but things weren't working out so well. Roger was unable to discern *"fuck ducks"* on the sheet of paper I was holding up.

"There's too much ambient energy," Roger explained. "It's overpowering the fine details."

I didn't understand.

"Like, the grass is glowing, and so are you and that sheet of paper. But the glow is so bright I can't see the writing on the paper. It's like a shadow."

I tried to picture the world as Roger was seeing it, but the best my mind would conjure was the green code seen by Neo in the Matrix. I suppose it was similar to that, only a little more flamboyant.

"It's the details I have trouble with," Roger asserted. "I can navigate just fine."

Minutes later, I stood in the waist-high grass, my legs already stinging from the scratchy fronds and biting insects. I watched from my vantage point about fifty feet into the field as Roger drove his rusty Cavalier into the tall grass. He drove up next to me and rolled his window down. Bugs leaped from the grass and swarmed his headlights.

"We're gonna go through the trees once and come back," Roger explained.

"How fast are you going to go?" I asked, wary of riding with him in pitch black.

"Fast enough, but if we hit something it won't kill us," Roger smiled. "But we ain't going to hit nothing."

It was a bad time for double negatives. I should have known that, but I foolishly agreed to this new version of the infravision experiment.

I climbed into the passenger seat, my feet disappearing into the pool of fast food wrappers in the foot well. There was something wet against my ankle. I think it was a slug. The other possibility was a loose human eyeball.

"Ready?" Roger asked.

"Ready," I lied.

It was wide open for as far as the headlights could reach. With a click, Roger shut them off and we were plunged into the velvet black. The night was impenetrable to human eyes, but clear as daylight to those of the drow, duergar, dwarves, gnomes, and Rogers.

The engine rumbled and the car's tires shredded the prickly grass and spun for purchase in the pulpy remains. The car lurched forward and then we were moving at great speed into the unseen black. Roger held the fingers of one hand to his temple to focus his infravision. Even if he could not see, we had at least a few hundred feet to cover before we would risk hitting a tree.

Bang!

The car stopped in an instant and as it did I could hear the distinct screech of metal bending with terrific violence. The sudden din of impact echoed in our ears. The engine died. The only sound was the distant buzz of insects and something dripping from under the hood of the car.

Roger appeared to be dazed, but unharmed.

For a moment I thought I had lost the use of my right arm, but I gradually realized I was holding the door so firmly that I had locked up my elbow. I let go and shook my hand free. My neck hurt where the seat belt had cinched tight.

"What happened?" I asked.

Roger heaved himself out of the driver's side without answering and looked at the crumpled hood of his car. I joined him. The bugs had fallen silent around us as though they were as startled as we were by the crash. To my surprise it appeared Roger had hit nothing. The front end just seemed to be bent and crumpled. Steam wafted from beneath the hood.

"Fuck," Roger said quietly.

He was standing at his crumpled car's front bumper and looking down at something.

"Fuck, fuck, fuck," he repeated.

I climbed out of the car and joined him to inspect the damage. I was expecting to find that we had run down a kobold or goblin. Instead, it was a gray gas meter or pump of some sort, about the size of a dog. It had a solid-metal body like a flattened grape and it was topped with a gauge and pipe arrangement.

Thankfully, there was neither the sound of escaping gas nor the aroma of a gas leak. The stout plug was fused to the ground and apparently undamaged by the impact.

A door banged open at the rear of Roger's house.

"What the fucking Christ is going on out there?" Roger's mom screamed.

He looked up and I could see his pale face growing whiter. The horror set in for Roger as his flashlight-wielding mother began to cross the backyard. She was coming straight for us and with each step she unleashed another string of weapons-grade obscenities.

CHAPTER SIX

Fanfic

> Gimli only nodded. For four months now, they had
> been trying to have a child, without success. They
> had tried everything anyone suggested: positions,
> tests, examinations, and most recently, herbal teas.
> But for some reason, no matter how hard they tried,
> Legolas had yet to conceive.
>
> —From *Fertility* by Cheysuli

It took five weeks of following leads and rumors and an undercover
stint as an author of *Kim Possible* stories to get me close to Janus.
He was the mysterious mastermind behind some of the world's most
popular erotic fan fiction.

As I drove to meet him I actually felt nervous. He was one of
the kings of the Internet and there I was only minutes away from
our arranged meeting at a Home Depot.

Denizens of the Internet called the postmodern mash-up of pop
culture and uncensored sexuality "fanfic" for short. The writers were

peddling fantasies to an insatiable audience, wantonly infringing on copyrights and damaging trademarks.

Janus was at the top of the game. His stories were highly anticipated must-reads, spanning genres and incorporating some of the most popular characters. Those characters often included Janus himself.

Janus didn't limit himself to the characters of a given movie, TV show, book, comic, or video game. He wasn't limited to "slash" and wasn't just crossing over characters from one movie to another. He practiced literary self-insertion. Proudly.

"After all," one of his followers argued, "Dante traveled to his own Inferno. Chaucer wrote himself into *The Canterbury Tales*. Why shouldn't the author include himself as the protagonist when exploring his sexuality within the framework of a *Teen Titans* episode?"

"He's the best," that same Janus follower e-mailed me. "You've got to talk to Janus for your book."

I familiarized myself with some of his masterworks. My introduction, on the advice of that fan, was *Henrietta Potter*, a reimagining of Harry Potter in which Harry drinks a potion that turns him into a girl and he must be saved by Janus.

"Why are my tits hurting?" Harry wondered as his tits grew.

Harry looked in the mirror at his growing tits. And then he felt a pop and his dick flipped inside out and started to grow a clit out of a ball. He was so sensitive.

"It hurts!" Harry cried and stumbled back.

Janus leapt forward over a desk as Malfoy laughed and ran out of the room and he caught Harry Potter as he . . . or was it SHE?! . . . was falling.

"Janus?" Harry yelled, his voice changing and his face getting girlier. "I am . . . a girl."

"It's okay," Janus replied "Your safe now."

Janus's hand touched Harry's boob on the side as he set him (HER!?) down on the floor and Janus could see Harry's nipples getting hard.

"You're a girl!" Janus said. "Completely."

"Yes I have a pussy now" harry agreed.

Janus captured the pathos as well as the eros of that Kafkaesque metamorphosis. His 35,000-word *Henrietta Potter* catapulted sex-changing Harry Potter to another literary level, easily eclipsing the dozens of pedestrian *Harriet Potter* imitators.

Janus was also responsible for the seminal James Bond self-insertion epic. It was entitled *Married Christmas*, a Christmas-themed James Bond epic spanning eleven chapters that featured Janus taking over as 007 and screwing his way through most of the Bond girls.

James Bond's death in the first twenty pages was one of the most riveting scenes in fanfic history, but Janus took it to another level with his self-insertion.

"007 is dead!" Shouted Miss Moneypenny as she stood up from the lifesign meter.

"Oh no!" Said M. "Tell Q to activate 001."

"001?" Miss Moneypenny said with fear. "Are you certain?"

"Yes." M said and pressed the button to activate the activation sequence.

Slowly Janus Bond, the clone of all the James Bonds DNA and sexual power, began to thaw in the cloning vat. He was more handsome than any other James Bonds by a factor of five and no woman could resist his hypnotic commands.

"Miss Moneypenny." Janus said looking at the hot blond and her big boobs. "Take off your clothes."

Miss Moneypenny did and looked down at Janus's weiner which was 14 inches long.

"Its too big she said," she said.

"Shaken not stirred," Janus replied with a smile as he thrust into her howling hooch with a primal force.

"AAAAH!" Monepenny yelled as Janus Bond put his 14-inch dick into her and her boobs vibrated with an orgasm.

In the novella-length work the fictional Janus eventually tires of his bachelor lifestyle and marries Christmas Jones, as played by Denise Richards in *The World Is Not Enough*. The wedding takes place on Christmas Eve.

Those two highly regarded pieces were only a tiny fraction of Janus's body of work. In the realm of fanfic, he represented quality over quantity, but as an outsider the volume of work he had produced was staggering. His portfolio included nearly fifty short stories, seventeen novella-length works or multipart serial stories, and three full-length novels. And those were just the works published on the Internet.

One of my best sources on the subject was a woman named Pivo. She was eager to talk, especially on the phone, and her long career as an author of He-Man and She-Ra homosexual erotica had brought her into contact with Janus.

Pivo was a self-described "huge fan" of Janus. She joked that she used the term literally; a glandular disorder contributed to morbid obesity. She was nearly bedridden and she acted out her fantasies by describing Man-At-Arms tickling He-Man's "purplish boi nipples" with his mustache.

Pivo believed the rumors about a secret "hard copy" cache of Janus's writing dating back several years. Some thought this lost folio numbered in the thousands of pages and included rare or forgotten TV shows and movies.

"I'm talking VR 5/Alf crossover slash," said Pivo. "Supposedly he's got one where he inherits Airwolf and somehow uses it to blackmail the Nanny into a hardcore bondage session. This is dark stuff from his formative years."

I was interested in the archival Janus, but I was more interested in Pivo's claims that she met Janus once.

"He's not who you think." She laughed. "Pretty much the opposite of that. You're going to be really surprised. But yeah, I met him at a regional role-playing con several years ago. When I could still make it to them."

She sniffled before continuing.

"I can give you his info. At least his personal e-mail. One he'll answer."

Janus did not reply to my first three requests for contact, but something in my fourth must have thawed his icy heart. I received a cryptic e-mail with the subject line, "okay." The body of the message mysteriously read, "godofgates."

All of my years on the Internet and it still took a night's sleep before I had my "eureka!" moment and realized what the message meant. I fired up every possible instant messaging client and plugged "godofgates" into as many of them as possible. After several tries, it worked, and I was chatting live with Janus.

"Why do you write?" I asked.

"To tell my story," Janus replied.

"Can we meet?" I asked.

"No," Janus replied, and logged off.

This sort of feeble interview process continued for several days. Each time I was able to get off one or two questions, but whenever I veered toward any sort of real life contact Janus logged off.

"Which of the characters you write about do you identify with the most?" I asked on the sixth day.

"All right," Janus replied.

"All right?"

"I'll meet," Janus announced.

He gave me the address of a Home Depot in Columbia, Missouri.

"Not far from my house," Janus messaged. "I'll meet you in the parking lot. Park as close to the front of the store as you can and stand outside your car by the trunk."

It was a creepy suggestion, but I felt like there was no other way I was going to meet the real Janus. I suggested a slight scheduling change, but otherwise I agreed to the meeting. In a little over a week I would finally meet the real Janus.

When the day arrived for the meeting, I was still in St. Louis doing research for the chapter on Otherkin. I checked out of my hotel around noon, killed some time seeing sights in St. Louis, and then drove the two and a half hours to Columbia. There isn't a whole lot to recommend about Columbia, at least from my admittedly cursory look at the city. Kudos, I suppose, for the very easy to find Home Depot.

It was early evening. I parked the car three rows back from the handicapped space up front, stepped out, and waited by my car's trunk. I grew nervous and paced. As each car drove up in the parking lot, I wondered if the driver was Janus.

A teenager with a shaved head. A fat old man. A wild-eyed black woman talking on a cell phone.

As the cars passed and the minutes ticked by, I wondered what my meeting with this mysterious figure might produce.

Zack Parsons Meets Janus at the Home Depot
by Janus

Zack Parsons was supposed to meet Janus at the Home Depot. He looked at his watch and it said five minutes till. Zack looked up and he didn't see anyone coming to the Home Depot.

Suddenly a Porsche's tires peeled out in a cloud of smoke and a Porsche pulled into the Home Depot. It did a ninety-degree turn and slid right at Zack but he was too shocked to move. The car kept sliding closer and closer making a loud shrieking sound and then it stopped and it was an inch away.

Suddenly a man leaped out of the driver's side of the Porsche and then Halle Berry got out of the passenger side. She was wearing tight khaki hot pants and a white belt and a crop top that was pink and Zack looked at her boobs about to fall out.

"Eyes over here!" shouted Janus, and Zack realized it was Janus.

Janus was as handsome as possible. Halle Berry kissed Janus and felt his ginormous rod like a coiled cobra in his jeans ready to strike.

"Let's go inside!" Janus declared. "You like my woman?"

"Uh I guess, Mr. Janus," Zack muttered nervously as he looked around like a punk bitch.

"Call me Janus," Janus said, and threw his Porsche keys to Halle Berry so she could park the Porsche.

They walked inside Home Depot and they realized suddenly that it was cheerleader night. There was a cheerleader bus parked in the lot and all of the cheerleaders were inside.

"Look at all these cheerleaders," Zack slobbered, and his mouth fell open because there was all kinds of fine-ass women that he had never seen before.

"Don't even think about it, scrote!" Janus laughed, and all the women were looking at him anyway.

The cheerleaders were building a new shower with new tiles so they could soap each other up and lez out. They were looking at tiles and getting hot thinking about lezzing out in the shower.

Zack and Janus walked over to the cheerleaders and two of the fine-ass cheerleaders turned around to look at Janus. One of them was tall and had huge titties falling out of her sweater and it was a half-sweater so you could see the bottoms of her boobs and the cleavage at the top. She was a blonde and was also wearing a skirt and her other friend had black hair and looked like Jessica Simpson with black hair and bigger, rounder ass cheeks.

"I'm Trixy," she said, and held out her hand.

Zack reached for her hand but Janus slapped it away. He took her hand and he kissed it. "And who is your friend here?" he asked.

"That's Kelly," said Trixy, and Kelly held her hand out and also Janus kissed that hand.

"Hey what's goin on here??" shouted the coach, and everybody looked over and saw it was a fine ass older woman with big titties and a track suit.

"Mom!?!?!" Zack shouted.

"Yep, I'm your mom," agreed the coach. "Bet you didn't know I ran a cheerleader school . . . hey, whose your friend?"

Zack tried to answer but he was too stupefied to answer. Zack looked away when Janus kissed his mom's hand. What a disgrace! This was too embarrassing to endure.

"Oh I am enchanted to be sure," Mrs. Parsons, Zack's mom, said. "I see you met Trixy and Kelly. Sometimes we lez out together in the tour bus."

"Mom, I can't believe your sayin' this shit!" Zack yelled.

"Deal with it; I am my own person," Zack's mom said, and hugged Janus. "Hahahaha!" Janus laughed loudly. "Maybe I'll go back on the tour bus and check out the show."

He gave Zack's mom a suggested wink. Zack had tears in his eyes and he felt like a bitch. Zack couldn't say shit because he was an important man; all he could do was look through tears in his eyes when Janus pulled down his mom's shirt and started kissing all over her giant titties—the same titties Zack used to kiss on when he was a baby.

Well, at least I can have Trixy and Kelly, thought Zack, but he had to think again as those two girls started kissing each other and grabbing on Janus's unit. They pulled his jeans down and the cobra sprang out like it was one of those draculas on a haunted house ride and you come around the corner and it goes *blah,* only it was a dick.

"That's the biggest dick I have ever seen!" yelled Zack's mom with joy, and bent over some carpet samples so Janus could see her butt.

"Damn, look at that filthy butthole, Mrs. Parsons! I am gonna fuck that all up!" Janus hooped.

"Mom, stop!" Zack shouted as Janus's thick anaconda plowed turds up Mrs. Parsons's butthole.

"No!" Zack cried, but Janus pushed him down and watched as Trixy put her big juicy pussy on Kelly's head.

Zack was utterly humiliated. He could do nothing but watch as the cheerleader orgy started with his mom and Janus at the center like the eye of a hurricane of stinky-ass sex.

Zack Parsons Meets Janus at the Home Depot
by Zack Parsons

There were a few slight discrepancies between my account of the meeting and the accounting I asked Janus to provide, but the real story was no less shocking. All right, the meeting was slightly less shocking. And at least 25 percent less erotic.

Janus didn't arrive in a Porsche with Halle Berry. My mother was not waiting in the Home Depot with a host of nubile DIY cheerleaders. The meeting did not devolve into an orgy and I did not cry.

Incredibly, the biggest lie in Janus's account was the size of his penis. I abridged most of the pornographic detail out of his version of things, but it was described alternately as a "16-inch monster" and a "20-inch horse cock."

The real Janus's penis was exactly zero inches in length.

"Eileen," Janus said, reaching out through the window and shaking my hand.

"He" was a middle-aged "she." Eileen aka Janus looked to be in her thirties with prematurely graying hair pinned back in a prim bun. She was petite, perhaps just breaking the five foot mark, and mod-estly dressed (as I later observed) in a calf-length floral dress and white sneakers. A small golden crucifix hung from her neck.

She looked at me uncertainly over a pair of thick, open-framed glasses.

"You're a woman," I observed.

"That's right," Eileen agreed with my assessment. "I have been most of my life."

I briefly wondered if she had undergone some sort of sex change, but her snorting snicker suggested she was making a joke.

"Are you a lesbian?" I pondered aloud.

"Come on," she replied. "If I were a lesbian do you think I would write all those stories about giant penises?"

I wasn't too sure what sort of stories lesbians preferred to write. Maybe in their erotica women had enormous vaginas capable of hold-ing huge objects and extra articulation in their foot-long fingers and tongues.

"Let me park my car," Eileen said.

She parked her Honda Pilot SUV next to my car. On the back of it I noticed a bumper sticker that read, IN CASE OF RAPTURE, THIS CAR WILL BE UNMANNED. On the opposite side, just above the bumper, was a Christian fish sticker with a little silver cross in the fish.

The bumper stickers struck me as strange in light of her chosen hobby in a way her gold crucifix did not. Wearing the cross on a neck-lace seemed more like a vague symbol of allegiance and maybe a last-ditch defense against vampirism. The bumper stickers were more aggressive. *I love the Lord* sort of stuff.

I made a note of the bumper stickers and planned to bring them up if the interview went well.

"There we go," Eileen said, turning off her SUV and climbing out.

A large denim purse hung over her shoulder. Through the opened zipper, I could see napkins, receipts, makeup, and a few tampons. Eileen seemed to have trouble making eye contact, but she was smiling and assured enough to walk alongside me into the Home Depot.

There was definitely an edge to her. She flitted from one side of the aisle to the other, evidently interested in every bit of building material, back splash tile, and light fixture for sale at Home Depot. I kept quiet, giving her time to unpack naturally rather than forcing the issue.

"You won't use my real name?" she finally asked.

"I won't even use your real fake name if that is what you want," I replied.

"Good," she said. "I have a position to maintain in the community. You understand?"

I nodded.

"I don't think my husband would like to, I mean to say, he knows what I do, but he isn't aware of the, ahm, the . . ."

"The extent?" I offered.

"That," she said. "And the specifics."

"He's never read your work?"

"Some of the early stuff," she said as she picked up a clay patio tile. "He read a little when I was writing *Sharpe's Rifles* and *Horatio Hornblower*."

She looked away and half-mumbled the names she used for the popular British characters, "Sharpe's Rapers and Whoreatio Jizz-blower."

"I had heard you were into some dark stuff," I said, recalling the rumored archives.

"What have you heard?" she asked. "No, nothing that bad. It wasn't that bad. I mean, it was really poorly written. Not like my new stuff. Which is much better written."

"I heard it was S&M stuff. Violence and rape," I said.

She winced at my words and then glanced around, as if to see if anyone was in earshot.

"Well, yes, I suppose. But it was all moral. The rapists were punished or raped bad people."

"I'm interested in your morality," I said. "You have written some pretty graphic stuff. How do you reconcile that with your religion?"

Eileen looked at me and scowled.

"There is nothing there. One doesn't have a thing to do with the other. Believe it or not, it is perfectly possible to be a good Christian, a faithful Christian, and still write about . . ."

She lowered her voice.

". . . intercourse."

"I thought it might qualify as impure thoughts," I said. "Don't get—"

"Well maybe it does, maybe it does," she hissed. "What if it does? So if I am a sinner, does that mean I can't ask for forgiveness?"

"No, I—"

"One thing I have learned, Mr. Parsons, is that we all sin all of the time. All of us. Think about that. You are sinning right now. You are sinning thinking about my naked body and the terrible things you want to do to it. But you are holding in all that anger and that need."

The idea that I was thinking about raping Eileen was preposterous. I was just as likely going to rape some PVC pipe in the plumbing department. More likely, even.

"That's uncalled for," I said.

"It's the truth," Eileen replied. "I will pray to the Lord for you every day."

Her eyes flashed with anger, as if she was on the verge of completely losing her temper. Then that flash was gone. Eileen dipped her head and turned away. I continued to follow her down the aisles but I kept mostly quiet. I asked her a few other, very basic questions. Things I thought would not upset her further.

"What series have you put the most thought into?"

"My *Due South* and *Facts of Life* crossover slash," she said, examining a caulking gun. "It's a love triangle between Natalie, Fraser, and Vecchio. Janus appears briefly to . . . well . . . you know . . ."

Eileen made the "finger in the doughnut" hand signal. "He does it with Blair and Tootie."

"At the same time?"

"No, of course not," she scoffed. "Blair would never share her man."

We moved a little more briskly through the power tools. Eileen did not seem interested in lingering by the drills.

"Your stories have won a lot of acclaim within the fanfic community," I observed.

"Oh, I don't know, maybe. There are a lot of awards I haven't won," Eileen said.

"What's the one you would most like to win?" I asked.

"Well, one site I'm on a lot gives out an award for best scene in a shower or bathtub. I've been working on some *Silkwood* self-insertion. Janus does some really hot decontamination. Good use of hoses and brushes. I think I've really got a chance this year."

"What's a story you regret writing?" I asked.

"Any of the kids cartoons," she answered quickly. "Most of all SpongeBob. My sister's daughters were watching it over at our house and I thought it was a hoot. I wrote some stories about it. Some Patrick and SpongeBob slash stuff."

"Why do you regret that one in particular?" I asked, drawing up short of a woman with a screaming baby in her cart.

Eileen watched the mother go, waiting until she was completely out of earshot before answering my question.

"I don't think starfish 'cum,'" she said.

"What?" I laughed.

"They ejaculate, but they release it as a cloud. I described it all in terms of big messy splatters and wads of splooge."

"But in the aquatic environment it would have been a cloud drifting around?"

"Right. On Wikipedia it said both species sexually reproduce externally, so at least it is sort of right."

"I don't think real sponges or starfish can talk. That seems like a slightly bigger discrepancy."

Eileen looked at me sternly and said, "How do you know? Can you speak their language? Maybe they talk. Maybe they do."

Janus and the Killer Angels

My sometimes contentious and always uncomfortable interview with Janus/Eileen concluded with me offering her fifty dollars to write an erotic fanfic version of our meeting. At first she was excited by the idea. She confessed, "I almost never get paid to write things."

By the time I got back to my motel and fired up the laptop she was wavering. Her e-mails included repeated usage of the phrase "I'm not going to prostitute myself." I was eventually able to calm her down and coax a contribution from her, but it took a lot more time and finessing than I had in me in that beaten up Missouri motel room.

I had two weeks of downtime to look forward to between my interview with Eileen and my next interviews, so I loaded up my car and prepared for the long drive back to home base in Chicago. I had picked up the audio book download of Michael Shaara's civil war epic *The Killer Angels* for the drive home.

I pulled onto the interstate, enthralled by *The Killer Angels*, wondering what Eileen might do with General Longstreet and whether Janus would fight for the Union or for the Confederacy. I was picturing Janus, now a creature entirely of my mind's eye, defiling a southern belle. The image distracted me from the audio book and the traffic and I snapped back to reality just in time to realize a large, black SUV was bearing down on me.

I swerved over a lane to avoid it, but the passing SUV kept on me, chasing me toward the shoulder. I realized in a terrified instant that I would either have to allow it to hit the side of my car or drive off the road. I had no idea how much of a drop there was off the shoulder of the interstate. I could see there was a drop, but not how much of one.

I laid on the horn as I swerved off the road. The instant the wheel left pavement and plowed into the grass the car seemed to be sliding on ice. I slammed on the brakes as my car dipped and began to spin in the grass.

As I lost all control I caught a fleeting glimpse of the SUV as it passed me. Two faces in ski masks peered out at me from the back windows, like *Jacob's Ladder* had just robbed a liquor store. One of them made a throat-slitting motion. I tried to read the license plate, but I was already spinning away.

My car came to rest a scant few feet from the tree line of a thickly wooded marsh area. My heart was pounding like a bongo at a Ron Paul blimp launch. It was a miracle neither me nor my car seemed to have suffered much damage. When I climbed out and surveyed the side of my car, I saw a few scratches, and there were a few burst blood vessels in my head but I would live.

While I waited for the tow truck to arrive I went over and over what had happened in my head. After a few minutes and many re-plays I came to the only logical conclusion. Someone was trying to kill me.

CHAPTER SEVEN

Ill-Suited for the Pursuit of Fursuiters

> Outside of a dog, a book is a man's best friend.
> Inside of a dog, it is too dark to read.
>
> —Groucho Marx

I was standing at the baggage claim in Pittsburgh International Airport wondering why my pair of small black Samsonites had yet to appear on the conveyor. Most of the other passengers on my flight had already picked up their bags and departed. No doubt headed for their hotels to prepare for the coming days of Anthrocon 2008.

It was down to me and a guy bulging out of a Simpsons T-shirt one size too small. He was also wearing red suspenders, cargo shorts, socks with sandals, and a pair of prescription glasses with flip-up sun shades. This was a man who desperately wanted to never have sex. Or so the uninformed might have thought.

The baseball cap with pointed ears glued on and the fluffy ringed tail emerging from the back of his shorts were two dead give-aways that he very much wanted to have sex. Just maybe not in the way you or I think of sex.

"These things take forever," he complained.

A battered red clamshell suitcase emerged and he began to prance up and down with excitement. He edged around the side to where his luggage was slowly trundling down the conveyor. His tail swished from side to side thanks to his practiced hip swaying.

"Good luck with yours," he said as he hefted his bag up. "Are you going to the con?"

"No," I lied, slightly hurt that he would assume I was.

"Oh, okay," he said. "Well, have fun anyway."

He waggled his fingers at me and departed. An approaching baggage handler in a reflective vest cast a sidelong glance at him before addressing me.

"Two black Samsonites?" the man asked.

"Yeah," I replied, fearing the worst.

It was worse than I feared.

"You're going to have to come with me," the baggage handler said. "TSA wants to talk to you."

As it turns out, carrying an entire suitcase full of weird spy equipment raises some red flags with baggage screeners. In Chicago they had looked at me like I was insane as they pulled a wireless recording device and a concealable camera out of a padded case. Having two dozen bullet-shaped batteries in with them didn't help.

Miraculously, the screeners at O'Hare had let me on the plane as long as I checked both bags. I jumped through their hoops and got my spy gear to Pittsburgh, only to be detained by less trusting screeners at my destination.

The baggage handler showed me to a small windowless room with a folding table and three chairs. My cop show instincts told me to sit down on the far side of the table facing the door. The side with only one chair.

A TSA official arrived shortly along with the same baggage handler and my two black Samsonites. Exhibits A and B. The baggage handler set them down on the table and left the room.

The TSA official was a ruddy-faced guy with the bulbous nose of an alcoholic and the beetle brow of a man used to clubbing things to death. He had a thin ferrous mustache that resembled a crust of hair formed above his thin lip as part of a natural chemical process.

His name tag read LOU ASTOR. His accent suggested he was one of the Scranton Astors.

"Mr. Parsons," he said. "We are not normally in the business of detaining people leaving our fine airport, but for you I have made a special exception. You have some very interesting devices in your baggage."

"I don't—"

Lou wasn't finished. He pressed down with his fingers on the tops of both bags.

"Seven hundred fifty dildos a week come through here. Half of 'em vibrating dildos. Nine hundred knives. Fireworks, dangerous chemicals—people try to bring all sorts of dumb shit into my airport. Mr. Parsons, I have never had someone bring a bomb into my airport. So please, please, tell me that you are not my first bomb in the airport."

I was scared shitless by the word "bomb," but just smart enough to realize that if Lou had really thought there was a bomb in my luggage he would not be leaning on my suitcases and conducting the interview without FBI agents present.

"It's not a bomb," I said.

"Sure, sure." Lou waved a hand and sat down. "I'm sure it's just some sort of fancy dildo. A vibrating dildo. Lots of them this weekend."

"It's not a dildo," I said. "One of them is an audio recorder in a, ah, cigarette box. A wireless transmitter. Ah, there's a, hidden camera—"

"Hidden camera?"

"Right."

"Like the nanny cam?" he asked. "Like on Maury when the nanny used to pick up that little baby and just swing it around by its fat little arms and yell 'shut up!' I loved that thing."

"It's, yeah, it's a hidden camera," I said.

"Hidden, huh? So tell me, why do you have all of this hidden camera and sound equipment? What are you, some sort of terror spy or something? An al Qaeda spy?"

Lou was obviously getting a kick out of scaring me.

"Are you part of a plot?" he asked. "Who are your conspirators? What are you hiding your cameras from, Mr. Parsons?"

"The furries," I replied. "They hate us."

"The furries," Lou repeated bitterly. "Those motherfuckers."

Furries: Those Motherfuckers

The furry subculture is so large and long-lived that it has become an inseparable part of the blighted tapestry of the Internet. Furries are not just popular compared to weird or fetish subcultures, they stand out as popular among all Internet subcultures. A search for "furries" in Google returns almost 1.5 million results, including artwork, videos, and links to real articles in real magazines like *Vanity Fair*.

So what are furries? You really don't know?

Sorry, I don't mean to be condescending, it's just that they're everywhere. If you have used the Internet for more than a few hours you have probably run into someone or something associated with furries.

Furries represent a diverse subculture that includes many offshoots, but at the core all furries have an interest in anthropomorphic animals or animals with human characteristics. Think Disney characters like the bipedal chipmunks from *Chip 'n Dale's Rescue Rangers* or the ducks of *DuckTales*. Ducks so human-like they built a city and fly in time machines just like humans.

The iconic image of a furry is of a man inside a sports mascot–like suit with big furry paws and a cartoony face. This is actually just one of many types of furry called a fursuiter. Fursuiters dress the part of their furry persona or fursona.

Yes. Fursona. Get used to it; most terminology related to furries is a portmanteau of fur and some other word.

One notable exception to this rule is the term "yiff" or "yiffing." *Yiff* is supposedly the sound foxes make during mating. It has been around in the furry community since the early 1990s and has become a multipurpose term for furries having sex (yiffing), furries feeling horny (yiffy), or furry erotic art (yiff).

One key objection of furries to their portrayal in the media is that being a furry is treated like having a fetish. Furries view it as a lifestyle, more akin to lifestyles like homosexuality or being transgendered. They live as furries, not as normal people who sometimes put on mascot animal suits for kinky sex.

The upshot of this is that furries have come to demand the same degree of respect and understanding afforded to homosexuals or the transgendered. They view being a furry as a legitimate lifestyle that should be protected from hate crimes. When mocked, furries will often react in the same way as the victims of bigotry and racism.

In other words, it is impossible to convince a furry that their lifestyle is insane. They are nearly immune to mockery.

A Wildly Incomplete List of Furry Offshoots

I mentioned that so-called fursuiters, the classic archetypical furry, represent only one of many subcategories or sub-subcultures inhabited by furries. Just as "gamer" describes a person who plays games, but not the sort of games they play, "furry" is the biggest possible tent for a group of folks with diverse tastes and interests in the lifestyle.

To truly understand furries you have to have an appreciation of, or at least a passing familiarity with, the many furry subcultures.

Confurvatives Confurvatives take a bizarre psychosexual obsession completely discounted by the majority of the world and combine that with being a furry. Imagine the worst thing ever and then multiply it by the next-worst thing ever. Your end result should be anthropomorphic cartoon foxes that believe it is liberty-ending communism to adjust the tax rate upward by 2 percent on people with enough money to own more than one NFL team.

Zoophiles Furries and non-furries who "take it to the limit" and yiff the real deal. Sometimes this limit is exceeded, leading to yiff-related tragedies like the colon-shattering Mr. Hands incident in which a full-size stallion dealt mortal harm to a man's tract during the act of sweet lovemaking. Contrary to popular opinion, most furries are not zoophiles.

Plushies Plushies or plushophiles are furries who take out their sexual frustrations on innocent stuffed animals. This can involve cutting holes in existing stuffed animals, making stuffed animals specifically for intercourse, or simply rubbing up against the stuffed animal. Like zoophiles, there is some animosity toward plushies from "normal" furries. In other words, the dudes who dress up in big wolf suits or think they're a cartoon fox look down on these guys.

Furry Gamers Much like marijuana is said to lead to heroin, furries arrive at the conclusion that they are a furry through a combination of anthropomorphic cartoons and video games that are geared toward furries. One of the oldest and most popular of these games is Furcadia. More a graphical chat room than a real game, Furcadia allows players to create and customize a wide variety of furry characters to "role-play" and interact with other furries.

Baby Furs Furries that pretend to be baby anthropomorphic animals. This involves role-playing them in furry games, furry artwork with a diaper theme, and eventually dressing up as a furry in a diaper. It seems ridiculous to imagine a mascot-like anthropomorphic wolf wearing a diaper, but really, what is one more layer of mind-bending insanity once you're at that point?

Christian Furs Self-described "furries for Christ" believe in the primacy of the Lord Our God and his holy yiff. It is only a matter of time before the "born furry" believers collide with the Christian furries and there is a camp where people can pray away the fur.

Macro Furs Remember *Attack of the 50-Foot Woman*? Think *Attack of the 50-foot Anthropomorphic Horse Woman with Giant*

Boobs. Macrofurries are furries interested in giant versions of anthropomorphic animals. In furry artwork these giant versions often exaggerate sexual characteristics to an even greater degree. The rare reverse, Micro Furs, are titillated by tiny furries.

Fan Furs Not an actual furry term, fan furs is my term for the thousands of furries who involve their pop culture interests in their furry lifestyle. *Star Trek* fan furs are particularly prolific, reimagining *Star Trek* characters as furries in art, fanfic, creating mods for video games, and much more.

Nazi Furs Similar to confurvatives, but with snazzier uniforms and better branding. According to the Nazi Furs they seek "to further the understanding of Hitler's Germany through study and discussion." And also erotic artwork and dressing up in costumes and having sex while pretending to be furry Nazis.

Scalies Furries who are not furry at all! Anthropomorphic reptiles and amphibians are more popular in furry artwork than with fursuiters, but there are some. Scalies include dragons and dinosaurs, which is totally outrageous and must really make it difficult to suspend your disbelief when you're trying to immerse yourself in the reality of a furry convention.

Anthroids Furry robots or androids. As if being an anthropomorphic animal was not enough, anthroids are artificial anthropomorphic animals. Think ShowBiz Pizza's Rock-afire Explosion band with tits and dicks. Not to be mistaken with mechies, which are anthropomorphic inanimate machines and are for whatever reason not considered a part of the furry fandom.

That is just a sample of the ever-evolving furry fandom. In the time it took me to write this section of the chapter, three new niche offshoots of the furry fandom formed.

Metamorphosis

Lou Astor, convinced of my general ill-will toward furries, sent me on my way with nothing but a "godspeed." Not wanting to bother trying to educate Mr. Astor on the wonderful ways of Super God, I waved good-bye and hopped into a waiting taxi. My suitcases full of spy gear were stuffed safely in the trunk.

Yeah, about the spy gear . . .

I mentioned earlier in the book my intent to attempt honest and straightforward communication with as many of the featured subcultures as possible. Unfortunately, it was simply impossible for furries to be one of those subcultures. Something Awful, my employer and home for nearly a decade, had somehow developed quite a reputation among the furry fandom.

I say "somehow" when I know exactly how. Over the years, a number of Something Awful's members and readers have, sadly, engaged in harassment of furries both on and off the Internet. These activities have included spamming their websites with harassing messages and going to their conventions to mock and insult them. These regrettable actions sadly resulted in Something Awful being branded as a "hate site" in the furry community.

I planned to travel into the heart of darkness, Anthrocon 2008. My shady dealings with Something Awful made me seem to be a hatemonger and even if I was not ejected from the convention, my identity could be a disruption that spoiled any chance at objective observation.

A firsthand investigation of furries meant going incognito. It meant spy gear and surreptitious recording during my interviews. It meant becoming a furry.

The first step in that transformation involved meeting with a costume supplier in Pittsburgh by the name of Maopaws. Costume supplier was the way he described himself in his e-mails to me, but Maopaws' Costumed Amusements had no signage, no shop windows, and no stock available to buy off the shelf. He didn't supply costumes to Las Vegas showgirls or movie sets, he custom made fur suits for furries. Period. No other business that I could discern.

The taxi dropped me off in a Pittsburgh neighborhood that looked like it had been built during the height of the Great Depression and had just continued to get sadder from there. One look at the destitution and I knew I wouldn't be getting another cab here. I handed the cabbie an extra twenty to keep the motor running.

Forlorn brick apartments slumped against one another. Liquor stores and convenience stores were encased in bars and wired glass. The address Maopaws gave me was just another walk-down basement apartment waiting for the wrecking ball. The stairwell smelled like piss, and broken glass crunched underfoot.

Maopaws answered the door after three buzzes of the doorbell. He was a sniffling, pale man with the high cheekbones of the Prussian aristocracy and the drooping chin, watery eyes, and slumped posture of the Prussian children confined under the stairs.

"Yes?" he asked.

"Maopaws," I said. "I ordered the costume."

"Come in, come in," he said, and showed me into his dark studio.

Shelves and workbenches and piles of felt, like a mad-tinkerer's workshop, collided with the reality of a man living in his workspace. A huge purple dog's head was balanced on the tank of a mildew-stained toilet. A white cat slept on the deflated body of a fox. Barely any light made it through the stained, leaded windows, and the walls were covered with sewing patterns.

The ceiling was low enough that I had to stoop on my way through each doorway. It was like the lair of an evil hobbit.

"Which one was it?" Maopaws asked, stepping nimbly around a stack of furry comics.

"The ah, the special," I said.

"With the holsters?" He laughed and began to lead me deeper into the grim bowels of his workshop. "You must be into some weird shit, my friend. I do front and back flaps. Holes for butt plug tails. I've even done some . . ."

He pushed aside purple beads hanging in long strands over a doorway before continuing.

"Even done some tear-away pieces up top for titty play." He snorted up a wad of phlegm and spit it into a sink as we passed. "But holsters in the head and tentacles? What is that? Dildos?"

"Don't worry about . . . wait . . . did you say tentacles?"

"Oh, yeah," he grinned, his teeth yellowing and uneven. "I had to go with an unusual design. You said you didn't care what the animal was."

He pulled aside another curtain of beads and revealed my costume.

"Five hundred," he said and began to pick at a scab on his arm.

"A squid?"

"Cuttlefish," he corrected. "It's cuter."

Two fist-size plastic eyes bulged from either side of an enormous white headpiece mottled with gray airbrushing. The suit's tentacles served as the body, extending downward from the head and covering the grayish tube of fur. Two smaller tentacles were flexible and not pinned down, allowing me to use them as arms, while the two larger hunting appendages were for my legs.

That was how Maopaws explained it all to me. He even tried to convince me to let him dress me in the costume. When I refused to reveal my naked flesh to his black-nailed claws he sighed and pushed a set of crumpled instructions into my hands.

"Follow them exactly," he warned, "or the whole thing might fall apart."

I emerged from the basement workshop and ascended the stairs, struggling with the awkward bundle of the white furry costume. When I approached the cab, I saw the irritation explode from the driver. He was a large Jamaican man with dreadlocks drooping out of a beanie beret like the tentacles sticking out of my roll of butcher's paper.

He hopped out of his cab and said, "Gwan go maas! Aint a ting gwan in there."

He was right, there was no way the costume was fitting in his trunk, but with a little cajoling I managed to convince him to let me put it in the backseat while I rode next to him in the front.

"Ya crezzy ya bumbaclot, wit da ting. You an yours is!"

I was staying at the Westin Hotel, which turned out to be the hotel of Anthrocon and the hotel of the New York Yankees, in town to play the Pittsburgh Pirates. A similar coincidence happened at 2007's Anthrocon, when the Milwaukee Brewers ended up in the hotel with the furries. Bob Uecker posed for photos, but the Brewers Radio Network's host Jim Powell was less kind.

"At first it was kind of funny to see these people wandering around the downtown streets and filing into the hotel," Powell wrote in his blog, "but after the novelty wore off it just made everyone feel creepy."

The Yankees were not hanging out in the lobby when I arrived at the Westin with my parcel of cuttlefish costume, but I still got the creepy vibe. There were furries everywhere. Even when they weren't in costume, you could detect them by their excited conversations and use of Internet catchphrases. I just kept my head down and borrowed a luggage cart as I wheeled my suitcases and my new fursuit into the hotel.

It was a relief to be back behind closed doors with the cuttlefish suit. Carrying it around was enough of a horror. The idea of putting it on was downright terrifying. I felt sure I would be identified immediately as an impostor.

The next morning, I left myself about an hour to get dressed in the costume to make it to the convention on time for the opening ceremonies. A lot of furry activities were taking place in the Westin, but the majority of official convention events were being held across the skywalk at the David L. Lawrence Convention Center.

I was not able to get dressed in an hour. The cuttlefish costume was as elaborate as a model airplane, but the instructions provided by Maopaws were nearly illegible. His illustrations were done in an intentionally cute anime style that did not correspond very well to the anatomy or dimensions of the costume. He also drew me, or whoever the person was donning the costume in his instructions, as a spiky-haired Japanese student with a persistent erection.

I appreciated his gratis inclusion of "front and back yiff flaps," but since he had no idea why I ordered a costume with a bunch of holsters and straps, his interpretation was a bit off. I had requested the holsters for my spy gear, but Maopaws's illustrations accompanying the instructions assumed the direst possible purpose. Dildos abounded, as well as anal beads, a bottle of lube, and some sort of V-shaped object that I still do not fully understand.

I rolled around on the bed, crushing tentacles and pulling on sleeves with my teeth. The suspenders and straps securing the body to my shoulders and midsection were the hardest part, forcing Houdini-like feats of stretching to fasten one-handed from inside the suit. The whole time I was thrashing around and struggling to get myself and my spy gear into the costume, I had a clear view of myself in a nearly floor-to-ceiling mirror.

I looked disgusting. Red-faced and sweating, I collapsed on the bed like a dying man growing out of a giant alien asparagus. The head portion of the costume looked back at me from the paired bed.

One huge and blue eye, glassy and lifeless as a doll's, stared at me unblinking. It was a reminder of my shame and the lengths to which I would go to write a book.

Journalists captured by al Qaeda should have to awkwardly shuffle a mile in my shoes. Furry tentacles.

I rode the elevator down with two guys in Yankees caps wearing street clothes. They had the schlubby looks of support staff, not players. They gawked at me, but said nothing until I stepped out of the elevator.

"Calamari comin' through!" one of them shouted.

The one with the beard.

I'll make him pay for that one day, I thought.

The walk through the lobby to the skyway could not have been more humiliating. It was like that part in *To Catch a Predator* on TV where the child molester sits down on the stool and has to pretend like he isn't a child molester while Chris Hanson reads his child molester chat logs. Only worse than that. Worse than being revealed as a pederast on national television.

There was much worse to come.

Losers and Outsiders

In the first minute I spent inside the David L. Lawrence Convention Center, I saw more signs of the apocalypse than are described in the entire Super Revelation of Super John. I saw Darth Vader as a fox with breasts. I saw a man selling artwork of giant anthropomorphic horses and tigers crushing buildings with their immense genitalia. I saw a dolphin furry flapping his fins with annoyance at a booth owner charging too much for a homemade comic book.

There were hundreds of attendees, dozens of booths, and many dozens of people dressed in full fursuits. There was a hormonal buzz in the air, from the graphic artwork on display, the costumes, and the raw nerdy hookups being arranged around the edges.

Here was a place where the man dressed as a lion had no problem lying down with the man dressed as the lamb and would even be willing to splurge for the quarter that makes the motel bed vibrate.

I realized quickly what a fool I had been to allow Maopaws to choose whatever animal he wanted. There were no other cuttlefish in attendance. As far as I could tell, there were no other cephalopods at all. The reality of this was a steady stream of furries, in and out of their fursuits, walking up and demanding a picture.

The weirdest pictures were the ones with the kids. There weren't a ton of kids and they weren't allowed into certain areas, but when a parent walked up with a kid and wanted me to a take a picture it was a really weird feeling.

There I was in my cuttlefish suit with a visible front and back flap for furry sex and standing next to me were two kids in *Lion King* face paint. There was something perverse even though there was nothing explicitly sexual. It was like leaving a closed box full of dildos on your coffee table or letting your kids ride in your sex swing.

One thing you never really think about until you are in a fursuit is how difficult it is to carry on a conversation with someone else in a fursuit. It was difficult to be heard through my fursuit and it was difficult to hear others through my fursuit. Two fursuits meant double difficulty.

"Mmmmph mmmmhmm oh mamam Redcat," went a normal fursuit introduction.

To which I would answer, "Thanks! I made it myself!"

Occasionally the fursuiter said something else to me like, "Mmmmph mmmmmhm mmphmmhmm yiff?"

My stock answer to that one was, "Not now, I'm feeling tired."

This usually convinced them to take their picture and be on their way, but a few continued to hang around and even rub their stinking paws on my costume. Literally, they had paws that smelled like they had spent the last six months marinating in a jug of body fluids.

On a camping trip I would have brought out a pot and a ladle and banged them together until I scared the animals away from the garbage cans. Sprinkles the Panda and Took (pronounced like mook) the Tanooki were a little more persistent. They stopped short of grinding on my tentacles like I was the catch of the day, but only just. They hugged and rubbed my back and there was little I could do to stop them other than flap my tentacles around ineffectually.

The conditions were appalling inside my cuttlefish fursuit. It was smoldering hot, at least 100 degrees. I was drenched in sweat in a matter of minutes. The suit was not quite properly ventilated and as time passed the air became heavy and unpleasant. And then there was trying to walk.

Moving anywhere involved performing the constrained hobble of the man searching for a fresh roll of toilet paper with his pants around his ankles. I had almost no leg movement, so I couldn't escape from the likes of Sprinkles and Tanooki no matter how badly I wanted my freedom. If I moved any faster than a very slow walk, I felt as if I would fall at any moment, a terrifying prospect considering the limited range of movement I had in my arms and legs.

And then there was Peter Two-Tails. He was a ridiculous white rabbit fursuiter with an oversized head and red blushing circles painted onto the fur of his cheeks. He had, get this, two-tails. I know, didn't see that one coming, did you?

Peter was not as grabby as Sprinkles or Tanooki, but he stood very close when he talked and he refused to back away. On the plus side, this meant I was at least able to hear him. On the minus side, I was able to hear him.

He pressed in close and I could see the moving shadows of his face behind the dark mesh of the vision screen on his suit's neck.

"What's your name?" Peter asked.

His breathless words were redolent with the caked-molar stench of Cool Ranch Dorito and chocolate milk.

"Otto," I replied, slapping a tentacle tip on my name tag.

"Otto," he repeated. "You like to party?"

"Having fun," I answered, trying to move away a little.

"Good, good, man. Good. Wanna yiff?" he asked, a tuberculoid wheeze at the trailing end of the fricative.

"Not now, I'm feeling tired." I dropped my stock response.

"Mmm," he said, and rubbed a white paw up his bulbous torso.

"If I take a little hop around the convention, come back, will you be ready then?"

"I don't think so," I said.

Just then, a family of three approached. The children were fat and wearing cat ears; the mother resembled one of the chirruping blobs from *The Herculoids*, but they were a welcome sight.

"Mmmmm," Peter said, adding m's and beginning to worry me. "I see, I see. Well, Peter Two-Tails will make two laps around and see you when he sees you."

Peter attempted to make a shooter with the fingers of his paw, but the inarticulate mitten produced something that looked like a gang sign.

"Awww," the woman said with apparent disappointment, "I wanted to get a picture of you two together."

The product of my awkward day bumbling around the convention center was an invitation to an after-hours party at a suite in the Westin. Normally I would have been apprehensive about attending such an event, but the invitation was given by a very fetching girl in a cat suit that was more Catwoman from *Batman* than Paws from the Detroit Tigers.

"It would be purrrrrfect if you could make it," she said, and winked her long lashes at me.

Don't get the wrong idea; I'm a happily married man, but this woman tendering the invitation automatically made the party seem safer. After all, if a beautiful girl in a skintight cat suit was going to be there, didn't that lower the odds of some implausible nightmare scenario?

Don't answer that question just yet.

Some Implausible Nightmare Scenario

I never expected to make it through the writing of this book completely unscathed, but it wasn't supposed to go down like it did. I figured being put in some psychedelic torture chamber by a fake researcher in Chicago and run off the road in Missouri was bad enough. What happened in Pittsburgh, well, that was just unfair.

Super God had another surprise up his all-encompassing sleeve.

I showed up at the party fashionably late and with a six-pack of Rolling Rock tucked into the awkwardly folded tip of my arm-tentacle. I desperately needed to interview some furries in a more personal setting. The convention center had been too bewildering and, I will admit, intimidating. Maybe a little alcohol and a more relaxed atmosphere would loosen up some tongues.

"Heyyyyyy!" a skinny guy with leopard face paint exclaimed as I walked in through the door.

The suite party was packed. They had opened the doors between adjoining rooms and it still seemed cramped and claustrophobic. It didn't help that I could barely walk and when I sat down I had to either roll back up to my feet or be helped up by someone else. I also realized that I was one of the only ones wearing a full fursuit at the party. The other one I could see was Peter Two-Tails.

"What the fuck is up, nigger!?" he shouted, and gave me a giant hug.

People cheered at the sight and cheered more when he pretended to hump me.

"Get the fuck off!" I said, and shoved him roughly away.

Or that was the idea, but no one heard me over the cheering, and a "rough shove" from inside a squid suit looked suspiciously like I was trying to hump back. This produced even more cheering. When it eventually died down, I collapsed awkwardly into one of the hotel chairs, sweating and panting inside the suit and already regretting showing up at the party.

The pretty girl who had lured me to the party showed with a cool drink at my moment of greatest weakness. She was wearing an even more revealing costume than her skintight cat suit. This one had a diamond cut in the stretchy fabric just below her neck and I could see two buckets full of cleavage. She swished her tail and showed off her butt to everyone as she handed me the drink.

The cheering became so loud at the sight of her shaking booty that one of my spy gear microphones squealed with feedback. By the time I yanked my arm out of the tentacle and was able to pull the earpiece out, I was completely deaf in my left ear.

I opened the mouth slot on my costume and gulped the sweet alcoholic beverage through a straw. It tasted like a whiskey sour.

Cat girl jumped up on one of the dressers in the suite and began to dance like a stripper, swaying her hips and running her hands up and down her shapely body. People were cheering and clapping. I was pouring sweat inside the furnace of my suit, drinking the whiskey as quickly as possible to keep from overheating. My ear was ringing.

Colors began to run together. Faces and bodies stretched and distorting like animals in a Salvador Dali painting. I leaned forward in the chair; cat girl seemed to vibrate.

Peter Two-Tails loomed out of the crowd, more bulbous than ever; his rabbit head was a nightmare mask with grinning buckteeth.

"I'm hallucinating," I said, but no one seemed to hear me.

"My hands are snakes," I thought I heard Peter Two-Tails say, and when my gooey eyes looked over, his hands were bundles of snakes.

I looked down through the grid at my own body and I could see I was made up of white worms as thick as elephant trunks. The plush suckers on each limb became tiny mouths snapping open and closed.

My mind was just working well enough for me to realize that I was drugged. The whiskey slipped from my fingers and the glass bounced on the carpet.

"Fuck," was the last thing I said as I slumped forward out of the chair.

When I woke up I was moving. Shaking from side to side. There was a rumble. My whole body ached and I was nearly naked. My head felt like someone had shit fire into my ear and deafened me in the process. My temples were throbbing with pain.

The movement stopped and my head collided with a hard surface. There were voices. Clicks like latches being unlocked. What was happening?

Light exploded around me. The entire wall seemed to fall away and I tumbled through it, falling and landing on another hard surface. Heavy objects landed around and on top of me.

"What the fuck?" The question was asked by a shadow looming over me. A voice I recognized.

"There's shit written all over him," said another voice.

"Owned at Anthrocon 2008," said the first person. "Something Awful hatemongers will pay."

My eyes began to adjust to the light.

"Yo," said a third voice. "They want . . . what the hell? Is that a dick drawn on that dude?"

"Yeah, I think he's one of those furries from the hotel."

"What's he doing in our luggage compartment?" asked the newcomer.

My eyes finally adjusted. My embarrassment was complete as a small uniformed crowd gathered around my nearly naked, graffiti-covered body.

And that was how I briefly met the equipment managers for the New York Yankees.

CHAPTER EIGHT

Old Friends and New Enemies

No fate but what we make.
—Sarah Connor

This is the story of how my journey writing this book and a little help from the Internet reunited me with the woman named Lindsay Dawn Riley. Sort of.

During the course of my lifetime I have met many fascinating, wonderful, and terrible people. No one quite manages to juggle all three qualities like Lindsay Dawn Riley. She is the mean, redneck, disaster of a human being who has haunted me for a full decade. I have written many articles about her, some more embellished than others, but I have always remained faithful to the woman and the story at its heart.

To get to that story I need to begin with the story of Todd. Todd Glenn. Like John Glenn, only Todd. Todd the Ron Paul supporter. He was my gateway to Lindsay.

I have known Todd Glenn since the weekend *Terminator 2: Judgment Day* opened in theaters.

I was thirteen years old and I wanted to see *Terminator 2* so badly that in the car on the way from Ohio to Georgia I read the novelization. I loved it! Now I know that the only form of literature lower than a movie novelization is a video game novelization, but at the time I gave the book high marks for the vivid descriptions of assault shotguns.

Our first day in Georgia, we visited one of the overcrowded tourist beaches and I swam in the ocean for nearly five hours. I realized something was wrong on the drive back to my family's rental house. Hideous liquid-filled blisters began sprouting from my shoulders and back. My carelessness with sunscreen resulted in a biblical plague version of sunburn.

It was epic sunburn. Heroic sunburn. The sort of sunburn where doing anything hurts. Laying down? Hurts. Sitting? Hurts. Turning your head? Yeah, it hurts. Hurting itself somehow hurt.

After two days of suffering in the darkened rental house, we moved on to a family reunion in Tucson, Arizona. The reunion barbecue at my great uncle's house happened to coincide with the release of *Terminator 2: Judgment Day.*

At the barbecue two dozen or so relatives I never met before and have never met since were cavorting around a pool, playing volleyball, and generally having a good time. While they were doing this, I sat beneath an awning looking like the white devil from a Joseph Conrad story and feeling like a rasher of bacon degreasing in a paper towel.

The Arizona heat was bad enough, so bad that you had to run on asphalt or the rubber soles of your shoes would begin to melt, but add in the sunburn and I was basically paralyzed. It was the agony of dying without the sweet release of death.

I longed to be in a cool, dark theater watching the impossible things described in the novelization of *Terminator 2: Judgment Day.*

A man made from liquid metal with knife hands! He grows extra arms to fly a helicopter and shoot guns at the same time! This was the sort of cinematic masterpiece that had to be seen on opening day, a film as epic as my sunburn.

Relief came from an unlikely source on that scorching July day. From my shaded position in one corner of the patio, isolated and suppurating sullenly, I caught a glimpse of someone lurking on the other side of the nearby fence.

A soft voice emerged from the shadows on the other side of the wooden fence and asked, "What happened to you?"

"Flamethrower mishap," was my answer.

The nosey interloper turned out to be Todd Glenn. He was staying with his divorced father and had been told to "go outside and play." Todd was a shy, frail kid a month or so younger than me. His mother lived with her new husband in California and sent Todd to stay with his father in Tucson during the summer.

He invited me over to his dad's house to hang out in the air-conditioned darkness of the basement rec center and play Sega Genesis on the big screen TV. After two hours of Alien Storm and E-SWAT, we had exhausted all feeling in our thumbs.

Todd's dad, who looked like an extra from the movie *Wall Street* with his slicked-back hair and suspenders, suggested we go see a movie and get pizza. I suggested *Terminator 2* and Todd literally gave me a high five.

Our trip for dinner and movie turned out to be just for me and Todd. His dad shoved cash into Todd's hand and deposited us in the long line waiting to get tickets to see *Terminator* while he drove down the block for a massage. At the time I didn't really think a whole lot about what his dad was doing for the more than two hours we were watching the movie. In hindsight it was probably pretty dire and Todd's dad was one of the worst dads ever.

At least he might have been, except for the simple fact that he dropped us off to see *Terminator 2*. With me and Todd stuffing our faces full of candy and popcorn and witnessing one of the cinematic masterpieces of our lifetime in an air-conditioned theater it was hard to come to any other conclusion: Todd's dad was the greatest man on earth.

After the movie, we sat out on the curb as afternoon faded into evening. Todd's dad was very late, but we didn't care. I was bonding with Todd, nearly giddy from watching *Terminator 2*. We were like two ecstatics discovering Christ together in the same faith-healing tent.

"The best part was the way the T-1000 shot his guns super fast like faster than a normal person!" Todd enthused.

"And he ran with his arms like this," I said, and I ran down the sidewalk flailing my arms like an idiot.

When Todd's dad arrived and took us out for pizza it was just icing on the Judgment Day cake.

"It was good?" he asked, and laughed when we cheered our approval.

The evening did not have a happy ending. When the car pulled up outside Todd's house and I hauled my pizza- and candy-stuffed carcass from the backseat, I was greeted by the particular rage of a mom who has spent most of the day searching for you.

Meeting Todd and seeing *Terminator 2* with him was the one thing that kept that vacation from becoming the worst of my life. The spring break trip to New Orleans where my friend got hookworm walking barefoot at a Zydeco festival is probably number one on that list. That was the same vacation where I got stabbed in the arm with a broken bottle by a French Quarter prostitute named Vantressa.

Almost every summer since then I have seen Todd Glenn. When family vacations didn't bring me to Tucson, I would find an excuse to take a bus or a plane by myself and hang out with my buddy Todd.

We spoke regularly on the phone. I don't think I would call Todd my best friend, but I have a deep suspicion that I was and maybe still am Todd Glenn's best friend. There was a certain desperation to him. Like he was constantly afraid I would disappear from his life.

Todd's father died in 1996 only a couple weeks after Todd's eighteenth birthday. His father left Todd half of his money and all of his car. The house in Tucson went to a woman Todd had never met, but who was named in the will as "Sweet Melissa." She had two kids of her own and little time for Todd. She wanted to get the house on the market as soon as possible so she could take the money and move to Michigan.

There was never any doubt that I would fly down to Tucson and help Todd, but when I called to confirm my plans he was inconsolable. I love Todd like a brother, but if I had known then what I know now, I might have bailed on him. Like a boyfriend abandoning his girlfriend after a car accident turns her into a paraplegic. I was too young and free to be tied down by Todd and his deep depression.

A black cloud hung over my trip to Tucson. Todd wasn't laughing; he wasn't the animated guy I remembered. As we boxed up Todd's things I kept catching him crying. He would wipe tears from his eyes as I looked away and shuffled past him with another box full of old toys or books.

There was nothing funny about the job of emptying his dad's house. Nothing amusing at all, other than the hundreds of porno tapes Todd's dad kept in a locked series of filing cabinets.

"I thought it was his office stuff," Todd said as we pried open another drawer.

The tapes were all, thankfully, professionally produced. I don't know if Todd could have handled discovering a home movie of his dad sticking the old Glenn sausage to Sweet Melissa.

Later that night, after we had driven all of the boxes of stuff over to Todd's apartment in Tucson, we filled the back of the rental truck with porno and we drove it out into the desert. A case of warm Budweiser fueled us through the cold desert night as we heaped the porno into a pile and drenched it with gasoline.

The mushroom cloud of fire that erupted from the heap of pornos singed off Todd's eyebrows and the hair on one of my arms. We didn't care; we were both laughing hysterically as the cloud of incendiary smut blotted out the stars above. We danced around like mad Indians, hooting and swigging cheap bourbon until we both collapsed on the hard dirt.

I watched Asia Carrera's face bubble and burn in the heat at the edge of the fire and I remember thinking to myself that this was the cathartic moment Todd needed to get past his father's death. He deeply resented Sweet Melissa. After all, she was the woman evicting him from his father's house. But Todd really blamed his father for the betrayal, for allowing Sweet Melissa into his house.

I was wrong about the catharsis, of course. Our pyro for pornos adventure in the desert did nothing for Todd emotionally. Life is never as neat and literary as that.

The Arizona Highway Patrol found us sprawled next to a smoldering fire in the early hours of the morning. It might have been easier for us to go undetected setting fire to the pornos on the steps of the police station in Tucson. Out in the desert the smoke of a fire is visible well beyond the horizon, and burning VHS tapes create a particularly dense black smoke.

"All right, you fruits," a square-jawed patrolman said as he nudged me awake with his shoe. "You get this shit cleaned up and get moving."

He and his partner roused us from our uncomfortable sleep and set us to work burying the remains of the fire and collecting our empty beer cans. Once he was satisfied we had cleaned our impromptu campsite he handed over a ticket. Todd snatched it from my hands, but I had just enough time to see it was in the low three figures.

"You two have a nice day," the patrolman said.

His partner spit on the ground. It was a classic cowboy gesture of disrespect and a clear message that they were not about to countenance some sissified argument over the ticket. We loaded into the rented truck and drove away with the pair of patrolmen watching us from the side of the road.

They say you have to hit rock bottom before you can begin to recover, but after his father's death Todd hit rock bottom fairly quickly and then just stayed there. He was never able to hold a job, aspire to higher education, or really do much of anything. He lived on public assistance and some pittance of money from family members and he increasingly relied on me for all contact with the outside world. As someone who can be antisocial at times, I can only begin to relate what a terrible mistake that was for him.

As the years wore on and I entered the professional workforce, Todd continued to languish alone and miserable in Tucson. He drank constantly and his health deteriorated as he suffered from a series of bizarre ailments and unusual injuries.

In 1997 Todd suffered for two months with croup, a disease that usually afflicts infants and small children. I spent the last two weeks of those two months nursing him back to health, sleeping on his couch in his roach-motel of a hovel and waking up in the middle of the night to his barking cough.

In early 1998 he suffered a stress-related blackout and was hit in the shins when he wandered in front of a miniature trolley. The trolley derailed and several children were slightly injured. Todd blamed himself and became suicidal while recovering from micro fractures to his shin bones. During this recovery, he called me at all hours to complain about every imaginable topic.

Later that year, Todd was drinking at one of the only bars that still allowed him in the door. After downing multiple beers and shots of cheap tequila, Todd wandered out into the quiet streets and encountered a coyote. He then attempted to wrestle the coyote and was badly bitten on his arm. When the ambulance arrived, Todd refused treatment and attempted to stagger home. He confessed that he never made it, instead passing out inside a Dumpster full of rancid meat next to a butcher's.

The open wound became infected and Todd developed gangrene. He called me and told me that his arm smelled funny and I insisted he go to the hospital. They cut away part of his arm and attached a hideous compress of live maggots to chew off the dead skin while a megadose of antibiotics did battle with the infection. Todd didn't do himself any favors as he recovered.

I had made friends in Tucson during a few of my earlier visits with Todd, and I begged them to check in on him. The news was not good. Todd was drinking more than ever, suicidal again, and the house call nurse who was changing his horrible maggot bandage was on the verge of giving up on him.

Todd had stretched our friendship past the breaking point. I had no reason to go help him out again. And yet, I could not sit by as he literally rotted to death.

Against my better judgment, I caught the earliest possible flight to Tucson. Unbeknownst, I was on a collision course with Lindsay Dawn Riley.

The Whirlwind, Reaped

Most of the windows were broken out and covered over with cardboard. Todd had randomly ripped up carpet and smashed or punched about twenty holes through the drywall in every single room. His house smelled like cat piss and he had never owned a cat in his life.

Every day a nurse and a big Mexican guy in an Ocean Pacific tank top came and applied the maggots to Todd's arm. This involved the Mexican guy chasing Todd around his house, tackling him, and then holding him still while the nurse swabbed writhing white maggots under his bandages.

"Why you got to be so crazy?" the nurse asked rhetorically every day as Todd struggled against the headlock being applied by the Mexican.

I couldn't take hanging out with the guy so I had adopted the strategy of all truly caring and nurturing human beings; I made him drink until he passed out. Every afternoon at about three I would cruise over to the liquor store a couple of blocks away and buy the cheapest plastic bottle of vodka I could find.

At four dollars for a fifth, "Yuri's Special" had more in common with kerosene than Ketel One. I would pretend to do shots with him until his head sagged down onto his bent-legged kitchen table. I'd check his pulse, suppress a gag at the way his bandage was moving, and then I'd head out for a night of drinking away my own sorrows at a much safer pace.

I had two options within walking distance of my friend's squalor; an all-Mexican blue-collar bar and a biker bar called Pete's Junction that usually had at least one fight every hour, on the hour.

Race fear kept me out of the Mexican bar the first few nights, but on my third night at the biker bar I got hit in the jaw with a thrown billiard ball that took a chunk out of one of my teeth. The guy who hit me claimed the ball was intended for the woman sitting next to me and I was too busy spitting blood and trying not to black out to really argue the matter.

From that point on, I spent my time in the Mexican bar, a lone gringo ordering cerveza after cerveza until I would stagger out at last call. I can't really pretend to have bonded with anyone at the bar, but when they realized that white people are immune to racial epithets they stopped calling me "stupid fucking gringo" and just shortened it to "gringo."

During the second week of my visit with my maggot-eaten friend,

I stomped out for the night only to discover that my beloved casa de la intoxicación had been closed due to a grease fire. By "closed" I mean that it had "burned down" due to "insurance fraud." I wiped a solitary tear from my gringo eye and bid a fond farewell to the bar. I realized as I trudged away that it was time to permanently throw in my lot with the rowdy bikers at the other watering hole.

A night that began inauspiciously continued in much the same fashion when I arrived at Pete's Junction. Whimsy struck me as I approached Pete's, and I decided to take out my frustration by kicking a rock down the road. My boot struck the stone, it sailed through the cooling night air, bounced off the curb, and smacked directly into the skull painted on the side of a low-rider motorcycle.

The owner was not present, but a hulking biker in a leather vest that looked like something an S&M organ grinder monkey might wear decided to play patriarch to the parked motorcycles. He charged at me, the beaded braids of his beard swaying like wind chimes, and shoved me to the gravel.

"Oooo fukken didems! Buke gonzer kibbuhew!!" he shouted down at me.

I wasn't quite sure what he was yelling, but I was reasonably certain that I could rule out helpful affirmations of my life choices. He produced what looked—in the dim light outside Pete's—to be an axe handle.

It turned out later that what my lying eyes had really seen was him holding a shovel handle. I'll never make that mistake again.

I scrambled to my feet as he brandished it menacingly and he plowed forward, unconcerned with my invisible bubble of personal space. I backed away again and he raised the axe handle as if to strike me. I closed my eyes and awaited the inevitable, but when I opened them again it was to see that the meaty hand of Lindsay Dawn Riley held the business end of the axe handle.

"He's with me you sack of shit hammers," she said.

Her elocution left something to be desired, but I could at least understand what she was saying.

"Ohm eh fukken fukkd upda byesal." The biker lowered his weapon. "If hewa ooo fuggetit."

Lindsay nodded to the man, smiled, and punched him square in the nose. The bigger they are, the more damage they do to the bike they land on. Lindsay laughed and slapped her thighs at the sight of the man tangled in a Harley with blood streaming out of his nose. Then her bright red lips turned down into a frown and she stared at me like I was a kebab.

"You owe me, nigger," she pointed out, and then clapped her hands on my cheeks hard and gave me a friendly head butt that left my vision dazed.

That night marked the beginning of a brief, but intense and fascinating symbiotic relationship with Lindsay Dawn Riley. Even in the dim light of Pete's I could see that she had applied her makeup like she was painting a billboard that said FUCK ME. Unfortunately, no amount of base or concealer could hide her jagged half-rotten teeth or the dozens of extra pounds that ran amok on her six-foot frame.

To say that she was not attractive would be entirely missing the point of her composure. Lindsay knew that she was repellent and she liked it. She was a voracious omnisexual predator who would grab a woman's ass as she walked by the bar and then turn and plant an open mouthed kiss on me that reeked of wing sauce and beer. She rarely went beyond groping and occasionally lifting up her shirt to reveal enormous, uneven, and well-veined breasts to an unsuspecting public. All the same, I never quite got used to her randomly grabbing my testicles and squeezing them like she thought she could make lemonade with enough pressure.

After pouring two and a half pitchers of draft down her gullet and chasing that with three shots of Jaeger, Lindsay propositioned me.

"Nigger," she began eloquently, "want to go out back and fucker in the Dumpster? I just got my period, so put on a cow catcher."

I politely declined and told her that I had previous arrangements. She nodded sagely and threw up down her shirt. She reached for my testicles again but by then she was so drunk I easily dodged her pawing hands and made for the door.

"See you tomorrow, sunshine," she threatened, a greasy film of puke shimmering on her fingers as she waved.

The next night Lindsay was waiting for me outside Pete's with her prominent backside resting on a windowsill. Her face was caked with powdered sugar and she was holding a half-eaten funnel cake folded inside a paper plate.

"Hey, faggot!" she beamed, and hopped up from her perch. "I saved you some."

I took the saliva-soaked funnel cake and took a wary bite from it.

"Want to shoot a machine gun?" she asked.

Who doesn't? Maybe people with tinnitus.

"Sure," I said noncommittally, although the idea of firing a machine gun was thrilling.

With that one word I sealed my fate.

Lindsay drove us out to a junkyard outside of Tucson in her decaying Chevy Cavalier. She claimed that her brother ran the junkyard yet insisted that we climb up a pile of oil drums over the security fence. We used a disconcerting rubber mat she had in the trunk of the car to shield us from (most) injury as we rolled over the razor wire at the top of the chain link. She took me on a brief whispering tour of the haphazard heaps of smashed automobiles that included rummaging through several abandoned RVs, her prying the alternator out of a Cavalier of the same model year as her own, and her taking a pit stop at an old ice cream truck to urinate in its freezer.

Then she took me to the area she called "Sang Gillar," which I think was her trying to say "Shangri-La" and failing miserably. Ordered ranks of aircraft extended as far as I could see in the dark of night. Civilian planes first, ranging from dozens of rusty single-engine prop planes to huge jetliners missing their engines and frequently their wings. Beyond these was an even larger field of military aircraft. There were helicopters, fighter planes dating back to the Second World War, and more than a hundred decrepit bombers that I didn't even recognize.

The wing attached to the front two-thirds of a B-52 provided the shelter beneath which someone had set up a card table, rust-scarred boxes of machine-gun ammunition, and a Browning .30 machine gun. It was wrapped in a powder-blue blanket that Lindsay kicked to unfurl. Lindsay was already drunk when we got there and it took her half an hour to set the machine gun up on the card table. She instructed me to feed a belt of ammunition into the weapon while she dragged a cooler full of sun-hot beers out from inside the airplane. When she realized I was having trouble getting the machine gun loaded, she ran toward me.

"Got you all distracted?" she shouted, pulling up her shirt to reveal her terrifying bosom.

I ran away from her, laughing at first, and then I realized that she was actually trying to catch me for Lord knows what reason. Her face was serious, her eyes wild, and with her shirt still held up, the position of her arms and her waddling gait made her resemble a silverback gorilla. I managed to conceal myself inside a cavernous jet engine resting alone on the desert ground until she grew tired of my antics and returned to the machine gun.

"All right, Gabby!" she crooned. "Camptown racetrack . . . five . . ."

Her voice slurred and I could hear the crick-crack of a beer opening.

"Get over here, nigger!" she shouted.

189

I reluctantly complied, afraid that I would be confronted with her bare breasts again. Instead I found her sitting contently on the bucket seat of a minivan, the Browning resting on her lap, a bent cigarette between her pursed lips, and three empty beer bottles next to her. She motioned me over with a drunken swing of her head.

"This thing is all lubed up and ready to squirt." Lindsay extended it toward me. "Ladies first."

She launched into a profanity-laced lecture on how to set up and fire the machine gun at a series of paint cans lined up roughly a hundred feet away. Whenever I did something she didn't approve of she would squeeze my testicles. The third time she did it, I slapped her hand away and told her to "fucking knock it off."

"Oh, ho, ho!" Lindsay exclaimed. "Piss and vinegar from the round eye. Let me show you how it's done."

With one meaty hand she grabbed the machine gun and pulled. With the other she covered my face and pushed. The result was that I fell onto my back and overturned the cooler full of hot beers and she claimed the machine gun for her own amusement. I hadn't even fired a shot yet.

"Watch and learn." Lindsay laughed, spitting her cigarette onto the ground.

It's pretty clichéd to say that time seemed to switch into slow motion, but it's true. I was acutely aware of every detail in that moment as Lindsay pulled the trigger of the machine gun. The way the gun was awkwardly cradled in her arms. The way a thin strand of tea-colored saliva was running from her open mouth down her chin. The way her left foot was resting precariously on an overturned beer bottle. The machine gun fired.

The gun's receiver returned again and again and bright tongues of fire emerged from the barrel. I could see the smoke curling away from each ejected shell casing as they arced over Lindsay's arm.

I wasn't even paying attention to what was happening to the paint cans down range; I was too concerned with the deadly weapon being fired by this terrifying and half-crazy woman only a few feet away. It was the sixth or seventh shot when things started to go wrong.

By that point, the recoil of the weapon had completely unsteadied Lindsay, and as she stepped to brace herself—still firing, mind you— the arch of her foot came down on that beer bottle. She began to fall, still in slow motion, still firing, and the barrel of the gun swung in my direction. I was still on the ground propped up with my hands behind me when the barrel started to slowly turn down toward my head.

I felt a sharp pain in my thumb and knew with certainty that one of the hundreds of scorpions I had seen during my stay in Tucson had chosen that ironic moment to sting me. I couldn't worry about it yet. I scrambled away as bullets from the machine gun ricocheted loudly off the B-52 at my back. I rolled, hopefully crushing that goddamn scorpion, all the while expecting to feel bullets cutting through me at any instant. Mercifully, Lindsay lost her grip on the machine gun entirely and the shooting stopped.

The air stank of cordite and my eyes were stinging.

"Something fucking bit me," I gasped, sitting up.

Lindsay was unshaken. She kicked the machine gun out of the way and staggered over to me.

"Show me, you big baby."

I held up my hand and pointed to my thumb. Then I looked down at it for the first time.

The tip of my thumb, nail and all, were gone. Blood was running down past my wrist. I felt queasy. Lindsay laughed and gave my mutilated hand a high five. She did a weird spin on her heel that showered me with loose sand. She stomped back over to where I had originally fallen and picked up a bloody hunk of meat and a three inch long shard of metal.

"Looks like the airplane bit you," she joked. "Put it in your mouth to keep it warm."

She shoved the tip of my thumb into my mouth and laughed again, then helped me to my feet. An hour later at the hospital the now black tip of my thumb had been reattached. I felt an intense throbbing pain there and I looked over at Lindsay, who was eating peanut M&M's in the emergency room in violation of probably eight or nine health regulations.

"I can't believe you put it in your mouth," the doctor chastised. "It's maybe the worst thing you could have done next to shoving it into your anus. You've increased your risk of a serious infection."

"She told—" I began, but the doctor wasn't about to hear it.

"I don't care who told you to do it. Your entire thumb may become gangrenous and you know how we treat gangrene?"

"Maggots."

"Maggots." The doctor nodded.

Lindsay smiled at me, her rotten teeth studded with M&M's and pieces of peanut.

"Maggots, nigger!" she exclaimed.

Separation and Reunification

Over the years I had many more uniformly unpleasant adventures involving Lindsay Dawn Riley. I was injured multiple times, sexually assaulted, and I drank bleach to escape from her house during one particularly dark period in my life.

It seemed impossible for me to escape her clutches, until an incident in September 1999 that involved a faked death, being chased through a graveyard, and having my skull fractured by a malfunctioning model rocket. The incident, of course, involved Lindsay Dawn Riley, yet in the aftermath of the incident she disappeared.

I remained in contact with Todd, but when I called him even he admitted he had neither seen nor heard from Lindsay Dawn Riley. It was a real surprise considering Todd's hobby was listening to the police scanner and Lindsay's hobby was being the main character of whatever story the police scanner was telling.

After eight years and no sign of Lindsay, I had written her off. I was still in contact with Todd, so I still visited Tucson occasionally, yet neither of us had any information about Lindsay or her whereabouts.

Lindsay had certainly changed me. I was more willing to get drunk in strange places and bite people in a fistfight. I no longer feared death, because whatever primordial rudeness Lindsay Dawn Riley embodied was much worse than the reaper.

There's no pretending I could forget her. You don't forget someone like Lindsay. But I had just about lost track of the way she smelled. Sort of a hot garbage smell, only half drowned in a perfume discontinued in the '90s because it contained radium. That rotting meat rubbed with orange peels smell of Lindsay Dawn Riley was just about gone.

I was in Tucson in October 2007 for a possible wedding. There was an engagement, there were reservations made at a chapel, there were dresses, and tuxes, and invitations. Unfortunately, the bride and groom had never met. At the last minute the groom mysteriously grew some balls and decided he had to meet his dream girl before the wedding. Just to be sure.

"You have to meet her before you go through with this," I shouted at Todd over the phone. "If you're not going to then I want you to do me a different favor. Think of all the stupid, fucked up things you have done in your life. Go through them all. Make a nice list. Then get ready to add marrying your fucking women's prison pen pal without meeting her in advance to that list."

Todd hung up the phone on me, but he came around. He always does.

"You've gotta be here for it," he said. "I need the moral support."

"You're such a fucking little baby girl," I complained, but I knew I would be there for him.

I'm always there for little baby Toddina in her little baby dress.

I hopped a red eye from Chicago to Tucson. I packed light, like they teach you in the SAS handbook. Who needs a suitcase full of a bunch of bullshit when you can kill a deer with your bare hands and turn its skin into an all-weather shelter? Not me, that's for sure.

"Open your luggage . . . whoa, holy shit that's empty," the TSA screeners would no doubt declare upon seeing four articles of clothing and a toothbrush.

And I never even bothered to tell those simpletons that I could have killed them all in ten seconds with that toothbrush. Luckily, terrorists don't have the SAS handbook. That's reserved for SAS dudes and also bad-asses who use the Internet to download the PDF from the right website.

My flight was uneventful. Tucson was hot, dry, and ugly like a lopsided coffee mug fresh out of a grade school kiln. I didn't even need to improvise an SAS sextant to find Todd's apartment. I knew the way.

"What the fuck is up!?" I shouted when Todd answered his door.

He looked older, less hairy. Like David Bowie if David Bowie had a bunch of scars from weird skin infections and suicide attempts.

"Rita is getting out in two hours," Todd said. "I am nervous as fuck."

"Don't be, bro," I said. "What do you have to be nervous about? You totally know how to live on the outside without resorting to cutting up a bitch's face with a razor in the shower. You even buy some of your own clothes. Think about Rita. She's more afraid of us than we are of her."

"That's what they say about tigers, and tigers fuck people up all the time," Todd countered.

"Sometimes," I agreed, "but overall, who is winning? Us or tigers?"

"Us." Todd had to agree.

"Exactly," I replied.

"Hey, come in," he said, finally realizing that he left me standing on his doorstep like some asshole kid trying to sell tins of popcorn you don't even get until like six weeks later because everybody loves to plan more than a month in advance for a snack food.

I mean shit, what the hell are the Boy Scouts thinking still pushing all that crappy popcorn? The Girl Scouts at least have a product with those cookies. Something to look forward to when you make an order. Some Samoans and Thin Mints.

But in this day and age of instant gratification and a shitload of food that tastes better than air-popped bullshit, what kind of lame dickhead is going to be all excited about getting that tin of popcorn? Who even notices a qualitative difference in popcorn? I eat it like once a year outside of a movie theater and it's always worse than the popcorn at the movie theater. Always.

Boy Scouts are bitches. Tell them I said that shit; I don't give any fuck. What are they going to do, be cheerful and thrifty? Slit my throat with citizenship badges?

Todd allowed me into his surprisingly well-stacked and non-death-smelling domicile. It appeared he finally plucked all of the dead June bugs out that were tangled up in his shag carpet the last time I was there. I still saw a few wing casings, but you had to really be looking for dead June bug parts to spot them.

"So let's see the pictures," I said.

Todd grinned and I followed him to his computer. The first picture was just the lame poorly lit Polaroid from the prison pen pals website. Rita looked okay, but the flash made her look extra pale and evil. Although she might have been pale and evil anyway on account of her being in prison for nineteen years charged with nine counts of felony arson. She burned down a bunch of schools and churches at night.

"Oh, damn," I exclaimed when he brought up the next picture. "That is crazy."

The rest of the pictures were photographs of Rita shoving various objects into her vagina. Nearly all of them were extreme close-ups of said vagina being stuffed full of the aforementioned various objects.

"Holy shit, that girl is crazy," I remarked at her scandalous poses with huge ass telephones betwixt her nether-loins and also up her bootyhole.

"Is that her bootyhole?" I inquired.

"That's her vagina, too," Todd explained. "Just a different part."

"I am really looking forward to meeting her," I said. "Yo, do you think she will want to be into some crazy prison scene? Like will she want to choke you and stick pens up your dickhole?"

Todd just stared at me.

"Hey, I'm sorry, I don't mean to besmirch the name of yon maiden fair, but I just looked at seventy-five pictures of that bitch's crazy-ass hooch."

"I knew I shouldn't have opened up to you," Todd complained, and turned the computer off.

He was right, he shouldn't have, but that was no excuse for my bad behavior. Something had come over me. Some rude strain had infested my brain. It was almost as if I was being haunted by . . . no . . . it couldn't be.

"Yo, I think I am possessed by Lindsay Dawn Riley," I said. "Before we do shit, I need to get an exorcism."

"Why do you keep saying 'yo'?"

"Yo, I don't know, I think there are some specters or some shit up inside my mind."

"You are not possessed," Todd said. "You'll be fine. It's just jet lag. Or something. Take a nap."

Against my better judgment I drank half a bottle of Nyquil and stretched out on Todd's couch that made crunching sounds and smelled like a birthday cake. I fell asleep almost instantly and dreamed of Lindsay Dawn Riley. Her rough features were beautiful, her bulging grotesquery was like the rapturous curves of that one broad with the ass from the Internet.

You know who I mean. The one who for a long time she was just pictures of an ass and then *Playboy* got her to pose and her face looked like an old goat with highlights in its hair. Vitamin Guerrero or some shit.

In my dream Lindsay was like an angel. And she was calling to me, saying, "I'm in the jail. You've got to save me. Save me, you're my only hope."

And then I woke up and Todd was in a tuxedo poking me in the face.

"Yo, I just had the craziest dream," I shouted.

"You're still doing it," he observed.

"Man, fuck you and your noticing things bullshit. I am talking about some important shit here. Not some trivial shit like a wedding to some crazy broad that burns churches."

"Hey!"

"Hay is for horses, motherfucker. Let's roll."

And roll we did, once we were able to find a taxi willing to drive us out to the prison. We arrived at the prison and Todd was allowed in right away because of some shit about scheduling a conjugal visit for marriage or something. Yet, due to a snafu and red tapes I was not being permitted inside the premises.

"Let me see the warden," I told the guard dude who was hassling my shit.

"I'm afraid I can't do that," he said.

"This is bullshit," I informed him. "I am an Iraqi Freedom veteran. I didn't die face down in the sands of Iraq just so some dude in a brown shirt could tell me I wasn't allowed to exercise my Constitutional rights inside a prison."

"What unit were you with?" the guard asked. "I was stationed in Baqubah."

"Oh, yeah," I said. "I heard about you guys. Bunch of chodepullers. I was part of Commando Alpha One. Yep. We were the guys who captured Saddam. You know that picture of Saddam? I'm the dude. That's me with the swirly face."

"Oh shit, let me put you through to the warden." He pressed a bunch of buttons while staring at me like a dickhead because he was just faking pressing buttons.

"Real funny, why don't you station yourself back the fuck up out of my way so I can get in there and help my number one dude with his wedding. Or if you want I can make a sextant out of some pipe cleaners and rip your ass up with it. Got a preference?"

This dude wasn't budging. I thought about using some of my moves to disarm and disable him, but there were a bunch of other guard dudes with shotguns walking around. Somehow they knew my weakness to shotguns, the one type of bullet that is impossible for me to dodge.

I waited for the next fifteen minutes, desperately wondering what was going on with Todd and Rita in the prison. Knowing Todd, he was getting mauled by some skinks or some sort of weird shit that crawled up out of a drainpipe.

I was about to bust out those SAS moves anyway when suddenly in walks the warden.

"Warden," I shouted. "Can I talk with you for a minute?"

"Sure, what the fuck is up?" He said something like that.

"Hey, look, bro. I know your job is to lock up all these ladies, but check this out. I had this really vivid dream last night and there was this woman I knew in the dream and she was begging me to come bust her out of prison. Do you think I could come in and bust her out?"

"Well, we don't normally allow breakouts," the warden said, and my heart sank. "But your story has moved me deeply so come with me."

I pumped my fist in excitement and flipped a super hard bird at the guard guy as I walked past him with the warden. He couldn't even begin to comprehend the degrees of ownage I was bestowing, so he looked away. I am pretty sure I saw some tears. At least some of them welling up.

Me and the warden walked along a walkway that went over the deep pit where all the women prisoners were kept in triple-max security and we entered the warden's control room. He had all these monitors showing all parts of the prison, including the cells and even the showers.

"Oh, hell yes," I said, noticing some women showering. "You can just watch them shower whenever?"

"Rules, don't it?" the warden said, and then he busted out this big computer keyboard. "Okay, so what the fuck sort of name is it?"

"Lindsay Dawn Riley," I said.

The warden punched in the buttons on the keyboard and her name came up and then it said SEARCHING . . . and there was a magnifying glass looking at folders on the screen. Suddenly, Lindsay's picture popped up on the screen. She was an inmate!

"Yo, she's here!" I exclaimed. "I gotta bust her out."

The warden shook his head sadly.

"I'm afraid not, my friend," he said. "Look at what it says right here."

He pointed at the big screen.

"Yo, she is diseased?" I asked.

"No, deceased," the warden corrected. "She is dead."

I felt the "yo" die before it left my lips. I had no rational response to the realization that this woman who I thought was invincible, was eternal, died of liver cancer in a shitty Tucson jail.

"How long ago?" I asked.

"She died in the infirmary about three months back," said the warden. "I'm so sorry."

"She was supposed to be alive," I said.

The warden tried to comfort me as best as he could, but it was no use. Dejected, I followed a guard out and back to the main entrance. Todd was waiting there, a ring on his finger and a smile on his face.

"I'm married!" he shouted.

"Congratulations, man." I gave him a heartfelt hug, my gloved hand clicking as I squeezed the nape of his neck.

I couldn't feign being fine.

"Did you find Lindsay?" he asked, rubbing the back of his neck.

"Yeah," I replied.

"Is she still here?" He looked around as if he would see her trundling around a corner. "Are we going to get her out?"

"She got out about three months ago," I replied.

"Lindsay on the loose." Todd laughed, not understanding. "It's only right. You can't cage a beast like her."

CHAPTER NINE

Vores

15 So they took up Jonah, and cast him forth into the sea: and the sea ceased from her raging.

16 Then the men feared the LORD exceedingly, and offered a sacrifice unto the LORD, and made vows.

17 Now the LORD had prepared a great fish to swallow up Jonah. And Jonah was in the belly of the fish three days and three nights.

—Book of Jonah, The Bible

15 And lo, motherfuckers, for Jonah did karate-chop the last of the sailors and burp and say LATER BITCHES and just went ahead and threw his own ass into the sea: and the sea was like DAAAAAMN.

16 And the sailors were all messed up with broke clavicles and dislocated wrists and shit and they were all NUH-UH NO WAY at Jonah.

17 Now the frigging **SUPER LORD** had prepared **WHAT ELSE** God-fucking-zilla to swallow up Super Jonah. And Godzilla ate his ass and Jonah was in the belly of that dude for three days and three nights.

—Book of Super Jonah, The Super Bible

"It's not about being killed," said Ruby Dupuis. "I'd say it's about not being killed. About being eaten and then being alive."

Ruby and I were sitting on the front porch of her dad's North Texas ranch in old, creaky rocking chairs. We were looking out across her father's two hundred plus acres of inhospitable pasture. There was as much red dust and rock as grass for the skinny-looking cows. It was a hot day and Ruby's stepmom provided us with tall glasses of iced tea and a plug-in fan blowing air across our legs.

"Being inside the snake?" I asked.

"Or whatever." She slapped her meaty thighs. "It doesn't have to be a snake."

Ruby was a vore, short for vorarephile, and she wanted to be eaten.

"Not just eaten either," she said. "Digested."

I looked at Ruby and thought that might take some time. She was a big-boned gal in her early twenties, largely made in every sense.

Her tree-trunk legs barely crammed into her denim shorts and she had an upper body that was all bulges, good and bad. She was like an R. Crumb character come to life, but the results weren't necessarily working together very well as a cohesive whole.

It was a cliché, but Ruby did have a pretty face. It was heart-shaped and her features were perfectly scaled to the size of her head. She had sparkling green eyes and a full-lipped smile that was warm and honest. She smiled a lot, but her smile was self-conscious, her lip held awkwardly to cover her small top teeth and big gums.

And she smelled like baby powder. Quite strongly.

"Dissolved," she said, her mind far away. "Slowly dissolved by the digestive juices and moving through the digestive tract . . . until you're nothing but some bones."

"And you're alive as a skeleton?" I asked.

"No." She laughed. "No. I guess death does factor into it somewhere, it's just not about death, if you see what I mean. It's about . . . the process."

"Can I see your artwork?" I asked.

She nodded, but was in no hurry. She sipped her tea and rocked slowly, watching the cows out in the pasture picking languidly at the forlorn patch of the Texas Panhandle.

Ruby's room was a shrine to her vore artwork.

Vorarephilia is the technical term. Everyone comes at the fetish differently, contributes to the subculture differently. Some people like to fantasize about being a monster devouring tiny men and women. Others like to imagine themselves being consumed by a creature or person, often swallowed whole. Furries in particular cast themselves in a predator/prey relationship with an anthropomorphic version of their predators or preferred prey.

The concepts are usually sexualized, involving nudity and pain or pleasure, or a mixture of both.

Ruby was the sort of vore who liked to imagine herself as the object of consumption. Her bedroom walls were covered in drawings depicting her being swallowed by various animals and monsters.

"These are the tame ones," she said.

Most of them were fairly tame, even comical. In many, the Ruby character was dressed as a princess in a pink frilly dress and she wore a pink conical cap and veil. The drawings were childlike in their style, obviously influenced by Japanese anime or manga, but they all demonstrated a substantial degree of artistic talent.

In some of the drawings she or another woman was a morsel about to be devoured by a giant. Several featured her held between chopsticks or in a raised spoon and looking straight across a giant man's tongue and down his throat.

In other drawings she was running from monsters chasing her with open mouths. Dragons and giant trolls opened their mouths to swallow the princess as the dainty character fled or, in many cases, had tripped or fallen.

"Please, don't eat me!" read the speech bubble in one.

"Is it about the chase? The fear of being eaten?" I asked.

"That can be part of it," she said. "Yeah. I like the idea of being pursued."

"Overpowered?" I asked.

"Swallowed," she said.

"But not chewed up?"

She showed me a drawing of a crocodile swallowing a character that resembled Lara Croft from *Tomb Raider*. The image was like the others, except in this version Lara Croft had been pierced by several of the crocodile's teeth. These had created red dots of blood on her stomach, but Lara Croft appeared to be alive and still struggling halfway into the crocodile's mouth.

"I don't do those like that much," Ruby confessed. "Only when people request it now."

"Do a lot of people request it?"

She shook her head.

"No, mostly they want the digestion drawings," she said.

These she kept tucked into one of several binders, well out of sight of her parents or sisters. She closed and locked the door before sliding them out from the bottom of a box of tamer sketches.

She placed the binders on her bed. We knelt down together and she began to open the binders and show me her graphic vore artwork.

"These are the more realistic ones," Ruby explained, and pointed a chubby finger at several sketches that were quite detailed and graphic.

Her "realistic" style revealed her technical inadequacies: poor shading and shadows, poor perspective, and occasionally poor anatomy. These faults only made the drawings more disturbing.

Grim-faced and tortured women dissolved in the cavernous bellies of monsters, their flesh sloughing away to reveal muscle and bone and organs. She drew all of the breasts the same style, quite large areolas and freakishly long nipples that usually were catching droplets of steaming digestive liquids.

These sketches lacked the cartoonish speech bubbles. A few were labeled beneath the image.

"Off with Her Head!" was scrawled beneath the image of a headless princess in a torn dress toppling over. Blood and viscera connected the stump of her neck to the crooked beak of some avian monster.

"A Bubble Bath," was written beneath another, depicting a cutaway of a man's stomach. Inside the stomach, a nude woman, partially dissolved in a pool of stomach acids, her face frozen in an expression somewhere between pleasure and pain.

"And this sort of stuff, it, what? Is it erotic to you?"

"Yes," she said quietly.

Images of dismemberment, unbelievable violence, and cannibalism followed. The multipanel digestion comics done in the childlike fairy princess style of the art on her walls were probably the worst of it. The comics depicted, sequentially, the cute princess version of herself being overpowered and consumed by wolves, snakes, and dragons. Then, in the following panels, the princess writhed in the bellies of the creatures as first her clothing and then her flesh dissolved.

"Do you ever worry about drawing this stuff?" I asked.

I closed the third of the binders and opened the fourth.

"I know I'm not right," Ruby said. "I know it's crazy."

I withheld judgment or comment. It was definitely weird.

"When did you start thinking like this?" I asked her as I pored over the fourth binder. "When did the drawings start?"

"I don't know." She shrugged, almost nonchalant. "I guess I've just always been like this."

I paged through several more drawings. Pictures of more normal erotic art, but still with an undercurrent of lurking violence. Two women embraced at the foot of a demon with a huge fanged mouth. A man and woman had sex in the palm of an immense dragon.

"We had some chicks," Ruby blurted.

"What?"

"We had some chicks," she said. "My dad bought them at the feed store. Little yellow ones. They were soft as could be. He put them in a pen in the barn."

"Did something happen to them?" I asked.

"No," she said. "No, well, some of them. Some died. And when they grew up some wild dogs killed a few of them before Dad shot one of the dogs. But no, that's not what it was. It isn't that."

She seemed to grapple with revealing this to me. She spoke as if she was working through her thoughts as she spoke them aloud.

"I used to go out into the barn—I was only about five or six—and I used to reach in and pick them up." She held out her palm as if she had a tiny chick in it. "And I would pet them. And then I started thinking about squeezing. Just squeezing my hand around it. And smooshing it."

She made a fist.

"So I stopped going out to hold them, but I didn't stop thinking about it. And I thought about swallowing them whole and hearing them peep inside my belly at night. I guess, I don't know, at some point I started to think about being the chick. Being in a belly."

"And it became sexual?"

"Yeah, I guess," she said, and embarrassment showed on her face for the first time. "I mean it did. And, I did normal things too, you know. It wasn't just this stuff. But, yeah, I . . . well, you know what I'm saying."

I stood up and thanked her for showing me her art. Beneath the strange drawings plastered to the walls of Ruby's room there were the pink and white traces of a little girl's bedroom.

A Sloppy Joe Dinner

If you search the Internet for vore videos you will eventually come across a number of graphic 3D-rendered clips of monsters and aliens devouring naked women. You may also encounter clips taken from a series of grotesque Japanese live-action videos that include a woman being swallowed by a snake monster. As the helpless warrior woman struggles, her clothing gradually dissolves.

Narrowing the search for the word "vore" on the popular video-sharing website YouTube turns up thousands of clips. These videos are mostly culled from various horror and science fiction movies and cartoons and feature non-erotic clips of monsters devouring people. Half of this list is devoted to clips taken from weird, no-budget SciFi channel original movies about giant sea serpents and giant snakes. Clips from less obscure movies like *Deep Rising*, *Little Shop of Horrors*, and *Termors* are joined by dozens of videos taken from children's cartoons like *Pokémon* and *The Wild Thornberrys*.

There are also a surprising number of original vore productions. The Internet original Bugmen series features an attractive woman, the use of a fiber-optic camera that can be placed in the mouth, and a number of tiny plastic figurines.

The trailer for *Bugmen 2—A Vore Movie* begins with a series of green text messages displayed on a black background.

It's a nice day for a picknick.[sic]

The sun is shining—the birds are singing . . .

. . . and there's only one little problem . . .

A lid is lifted away from the camera and you can see a pretty woman looking into the camera, her hand reaching forward and seeming enormous in the frame.

. . . you are part of the lunch!

The hand pinches closed in front of the camera and . . . cut to the woman picking up one of the tiny man figurines, examining it, and then dropping it into a container of yogurt. Subsequent footage uses the fiber-optic camera to simulate the perspective of the tiny yogurt swimmer disappearing down her gullet.

One of the most prolific of the Internet vore video makers is a man who goes by the name of Redd. He is better known by the names of his two comical characters: Chompps and Sloppy Joe. Chompps is an alligator and Sloppy Joe is described by his creator as, "basically a strange creature from parts unknown."

What distinguishes the work of Redd from that of other vore video makers is that Redd works purely in live action and he has a sense of humor about his work. No grim bloodshed or dismemberment. No gory digestion sequences.

Redd sticks to the basics. An attractive woman caught unaware by a monster that slowly swallows her whole.

Redd's monsters aren't exactly the scary sort of creature, either. They resemble two giant sock puppets, with huge cartoonish eyes and an awkward movement that would seem to be easily escaped. The two clumsy monsters are often responsible for dealing out some sort of comeuppance to the women in the videos. They may sneer at the idea of being eaten by the monsters or they might take unnecessary to taunting risks.

Redd was a difficult man to track down, but I located him through his now-defunct spinoff of an adult pay website. He was happy to get in touch with me through instant messenger and discuss his creations.

When describing his videos, he admitted that they were erotic in nature, but was very clear that the videos were playful rather than violent. He insisted that the female characters didn't necessarily like being eaten, but it was more like a prank. A little joke played on them.

"Imagine the Roadrunner and Coyote," he said. "The Coyote creates a plan, it backfires, and he is blown up."

Finding attractive women willing to play the victim for vore videos has limited the number of live-action videos on the Internet. I don't know, something about going down into a strange man's basement, putting on nylons, and climbing into the mouth of an alligator must not appeal to most women. Redd has bypassed this impediment by hiring professional models to portray the hapless morsels in his video vignettes.

"When you hire the women, do you tell them you're making a monster movie?" I asked. "Or do you explain vore to them?"

"I explain vore to them," Redd answered. "Certain aspects need to be captured in the images. For example . . . good leg struggling."

Many of his videos include the classic vore image of a woman's legs in stockings and high heels sticking out of the mouth of one of his monsters and kicking impotently in an effort to escape. Sometimes they kick for a while and then stop moving and disappear into the fabric mouth of Chompps or Sloppy Joe. In other videos, Redd spends a great deal of time focused on the legs as the women kick until they are completely swallowed.

"At what age did you become interested in vore?" I asked.

"Young!" Redd replied. "Maybe age ten. I didn't know it had a name, I just thought it was cool."

"Was your interest triggered by some event or memory or TV show? Was there something that served as a gateway?"

"Yes," Redd replied after a bit of hesitation. "*The Muppet Show.* I saw a human guest being eaten. I think it was Carol Burnett, but I'm not sure."

After my conversation with Redd, I went through an episode listing for *The Muppet Show* and discovered that Carol Burnett guest-starred on a single episode in the show's fifth season. I tracked down a copy of the episode with relative ease and watched for the fetish-forming moment Redd mentioned to me.

About ten minutes into the episode there is a "Pigs in Space" sketch. The pigs have brought aboard a very large and shaggy space monster with wandering eyes. Miss Piggy is trying to communicate with the alien. Link and Dr. Strangepork are competing in the dance contest that is the episode's theme. Miss Piggy asks them for their help and they are distracted dancing with each other, but Dr. Strangepork suggests Miss Piggy try dancing with the alien.

"Dance is the universal language," Dr. Strangepork observes.

She demurs haughtily, as she is wont to do, but before she can continue the monster grabs her and pulls her to its enormous face. Miss Piggy screams. The other two pigs seem unconcerned with her safety.

"What's he saying?" wonders Dr. Strangepork.

"Hungry!" declares the monster.

It grabs Miss Piggy and pulls her into its huge maw. For a few seconds her porcine legs stick straight up out of the monster's mouth. Hooves that resemble black high-heeled shoes kick ineffectually. The alien forces Miss Piggy's kicking feet into his mouth.

"Well, look on the bright side," notes Link. "She'll probably be happier in there."

"We'll probably be happier out here!" agrees Dr. Strangepork.

There is more to the sketch and the episode, including more with Miss Piggy who truly is unharmed by the alien.

No Carol Burnett, but the resemblance otherwise is uncanny. And like Redd said, it was all just a prank.

Last Chance to Make a First Impression

I was twenty miles out from Ruby and her family's farm, still thinking about the volume and luridness of the images in her secret binders. Her ranch was the first of three planned stops for me in the great state of Texas. All three were remote and all three were distant from each other.

I had another long drive ahead of me and in the Texas badlands I needed to do a little planning before I drove myself into an irreversible situation. I needed gas, a bathroom stop, and some refreshments before I attempted to tackle the 350 miles to the tiny town of Grundy.

The nearest town big enough to show up on the rental car's

GPS was a tiny town called Marigold. The GPS had the little gas pump icon. Unless they were siphoning gasoline straight out of the ground in Marigold I would be able to take a leak and stock up on caffeine and snacks. Junk food and Pepsi amounted to survival rations on the long, lonely Texas roads.

I turned the wheel and was just about to ease the car back onto the road when my phone rang. I dug through my man-purse full of notepads and recording equipment and managed to catch it just before it went into voice mail.

"Hello," I said into the receiver.

"Ah don't believe we have been acquainted fully." The voice on the other end was sweet as caramel poured on an apple. "Mr. Parsons, my name is Canyon Fish. My brother is Travis Fish."

I was all too familiar with the Fish family, or at least Travis Fish. The name sent a cold chill up my back.

"Uh, how did you get this number?" I asked.

"That is not important, Mr. Parsons," said Canyon. "I am given to understand you are attempting to contact and/or visit a member of our community. On our property."

Canyon Fish's younger brother Travis is an end-times prophet operating a reclusive Christian sect called the Fishes. They recruit their members from the Internet and enforce strange and strict rules on their Gideon Flats compound.

It took weeks, but I set up an interview with one of the cult members, an ex–massage therapist from California named Barney Winston. He never said he feared for his life, but he did seem to dread the wrath of the Fishes if they realized he was betraying their confidence. All of my conversations with Barney Winston were kept very secret. After our first few he insisted on contacting me. I wasn't even allowed to e-mail him.

"I can meet him somewhere else," I suggested.

213

"It might be better for just about everyone involved and especially Mr. Winston if you just went ahead and did not come to visit us at all."

"I—"

"There might be some safety issues," Canyon said coldly.

Before I could formulate a reply, the line went dead. I'd like to pretend I was worried about the safety of Mr. Winston.

CHAPTER TEN

Welcome to the New Hate

> I would watch Sports if the teams were not 90%
> Black. The NFL used to be White now it has been
> taken over. White people invented these Sports like
> Football Soccer and Basketball the Blacks would have
> never have invented these Sports. The Blacks should
> thank Whites for inventing Sports because now the
> Blacks are worshipped as heroes and are rich.
>
> —A disgruntled sports fan on Stormfront

Grundy was one of a handful of sand-blasted shitholes creaking in the corrosive winds of southwest Texas. It looked like the sort of town the Army Corps of Engineers would build to test the effects of an A-bomb blast on a populated area.

Their plans were foiled when a bunch of dusty vagrants and fat kids wandered in and started living there. No more A-bomb tests for Grundy.

Which was frankly too bad. There were lots of clapboard houses and aluminum trailers just sitting and waiting to get picked up and tossed around by a thousand-degree tornado. This doomscape was populated by plenty of ugly, low-wattage mutants doing ugly things in ugly shopping centers. Folks waiting to have their shadows seared into the curb outside a barbecue rib restaurant or liquefied as they walked out of the Dollar Store with a sack full of Chinese truck nutz.

My rental car looked like someone had taken a powder puff covered in chalk and smacked it from above. I spent the preceding two days traversing the staggeringly vast state of Texas to reach Grundy and my arranged meeting with Luther Kitchener, head of the American Protection Unit. Kitchener founded the APU in 2003 as an organization to protect against "Jews, negroes, homosexuals, and the tide of illegals threatening to drown white America."

Kitchener was a white-power militant, neo-Nazi, a singer-songwriter, and a video game enthusiast. More established hate groups pointed me to Kitchener as a sign of the future of white nationalism. In their view, Kitchener's use of the Internet to grow the movement and spread the word, "revolutionized white power."

"Not since Stormfront has a group used the Internet so effectively to broadcast our message and attract new members," wrote one delighted hater who wished to remain anonymous. "If you want to talk to one guy at the forefront of the twenty-first-century white pride movement then Luther is your man."

I really didn't want to talk to anyone at the forefront of the twenty-first-century white pride movement, but potentially violent hate movements like the APU represent one of the most troubling subcultures on the modern Internet.

Hate movements were a dying breed in the multicultural atmosphere of the 1990s. The younger generation, possibly due to the influence of corrupting pro-negro forces like MTV's *The Grind* and *Yo! MTV Raps* no longer found it "cool" and "hip" to hate people of other races. Old guard haters like David Duke were being publically humiliated by the liberal media. Big-city Americans rushed to embrace a wide range of evil agendas, including the Zionist agenda, the gay agenda, the black radical agenda, and the Mexican agenda.

White pride was at an all-time low. Whites could barely stand to look themselves in the mirror and think about their superiority.

Then, in its moment of defeat, the white nationalists were saved. It was as if Kampfgruppe Steiner broke through the ring of Soviet steel surrounding Berlin to rescue Der Fuhrer in his beleaguered bunker.

The Internet! It was the birth of a technological panzer for the neo-Nazi and white nationalist movement to regain their ability to recruit and reach out to a new audience. The Jew-controlled media and the Jew-controlled government could no longer suppress the voice of white pride in America. From 1999 to 2005 Internet hate sites grew in number by an average of 20 percent each year. By 2007 nearly a thousand hate groups were active in the United States, recruiting through the Internet and spreading their message through message boards and popular content aggregators like Digg and Fark.

This latter technique was one of the favorites of the APU. Luther Kitchener often penned hate-filled articles or collected "facts" that cast Israel or minorities in a poor light and then turned to his legion of online followers to promote these articles on sites like Digg.

Kitchener's article "ZOG Plans New 9-11 Attacks" received almost two thousand Diggs. Another article, detailing a mummy supposedly discovered in Iran with blue eyes, received almost three thousand positive ratings from users.

There was little doubt in white power circles that Kitchener had figured out new ways to harness technology and that his star was on the rise.

I followed the directions Kitchener gave me, winding my way through the windswept town of Grundy. There were a few signs of civilization. I passed the smallest Wal-mart I have ever seen and two half-full strip malls. There was a hardware and lumber store, but it looked closed down and its parking lot was empty except for a few overturned carts.

Even the main strip of the town, a series of folksy shops like Button's Sodas and Nancy & Joe's Diner, looked like it had been barricaded up to weather the zombie apocalypse. I turned off Main Street onto Sam Houston, passing through dilapidated residentials, a dusty trailer park, and into a newer subdivision that was nonetheless desolate.

The houses there were small, split town houses. Dead grass and bare dirt yards were present on nearly every other house, suggesting either a low occupancy rate or the worst homeowners' association north of the border.

There was nothing to distinguish Kitchener's town house from any of the others. I walked up a small ramp onto the concrete block of his porch and rang the doorbell.

My surprise must have been evident when he answered.

"Yes, I am *the* Luther Kitchener," he said.

Luther Kitchener was sitting in a wheelchair.

"Just because I can't walk don't mean I can't hate," he said. "I hate just as much as anybody else. I hate more, cuz the nigger can run and I am stuck in this chair with my superior white mind."

He was a skinny man in his late twenties or early thirties, with pale skin and a clean-shaven head. There were little red spots of razor rash on his scalp. He wore khaki shorts and sandals and the collar of his cream-colored polo shirt almost concealed the cross-and-circle tattoo of the white pride movement on his lower neck.

Kitchener extended his hand and I shook it.

He seemed about to invite me in when his neighbor poked his head around the wall.

He was an older African American man, dressed similarly to Kitchener. He waved and flashed us a white-toothed smile as he walked out onto the grass holding a hose in his other hand.

"Hey there, Jack," he called to Kitchener.

"How you doin' today, Reggie?" Luther called back.

There was not a trace of rancor evident between the two neighbors. They smiled and waved to one another. Reggie offered to water "Jack's" lawn.

"I would be mighty grateful," Kitchener said. "It's a pain in the ass gettin' the hose out in my chair."

"I hear ya," Reggie said. "Well, I'll let you and your friend get back to it."

The inside of Kitchener's town house was painted in adobe colors. The walls were a darker terracotta color and the faux tiles were lighter brushed sandstone. It was cheaply furnished with modern fixtures and cabinets. The whole house was a straight shot down a hall leading to the back bedroom, with living room, office, and kitchen off to the right side.

I was surprised how clean it was and the air-conditioning was doing a great job of keeping the Texas summer heat down to a reasonable level. The decorating was sparse, but it seemed to have a Southwestern theme of tasteful wolf-and-Indian-on-mesas-bullshit.

"You were expecting a Nazi banner maybe?" Kitchener asked as he wheeled into the kitchen. "Something with the swastika?"

"I guess," I replied. "Honestly, I just didn't expect this. It seems so . . . average."

Kitchener chuckled.

"Then the ruse has worked," he said, and chuckled again, his laugh beginning to sound a bit more sinister.

He reached over to a large jar on the counter.

"Would you like some sun tea? It just finished brewing."

A Sit-Down with the Evil That Cannot Stand

"The Jews control the banks," Kitchener said as we settled into his living room. "Do you think they would give a home loan to someone that wanted to open up a Nazi bunker? They can't get their gelt from the mortgage of a survivalist compound."

"So you leased a town house?"

"That's right." Kitchener sipped the iced sun tea. "One of the advantages to doing the majority of my work on the Internet is that I am able to work out of almost any location. When I started this movement, I was using an old Pentium three in my mother's garage. I was literally sleeping sitting up in my chair."

"It sounds awful," I said.

The sun tea was good. There was a hint of lemon and the tea was not too sweet. It was a fine racist brew.

"No, it wasn't awful. It was difficult, but we all must struggle. That which doesn't kill us makes us stronger."

"Can I ask you a question about your neighbor?"

"You just did," Kitchener said. "But continue."

"Well, forgive me for stating the obvious, but he's an African American. Doesn't that fly in the face of your ideology?"

"Common misconception. That the white man wants to exterminate the nigger. It's a common thought. It's just not true."

I admit, hearing someone casually drop the "hard r" n-word into the middle of a conversation was bizarre. By the time I left Kitchener's house I was completely used to hearing it.

"The white race is interested in self-preservation and self-defense."

"You're talking about racial purity," I said.

"That's a part of it." He pointed a finger at me. "But make no mistake. Reggie over there is a monkey in a person suit. He's a trained ape. Trained to act and look like me. But when times get rough, you can bet your ass he will join in with the rest of them."

"The rest of who?"

"The niggers," Kitchener said. "Ain't you been payin' attention? Racial warfare is comin'. The niggers and the liberals are gonna elect them a coon president and when they do the holy war begins."

"You said a racial war and then you said a holy war. Which is it?"

"Ain't no difference. The war against the Zionists is behind it all. We been fighting them for thousands of years. Long before Hitler. But the race war is what people will see on the TV. Niggers enslaving the whites, raping in the streets, deflowering our white daughters. All because of the Jews."

"The Jews?" I asked incredulously.

"And the homosexuals," Kitchener added.

"Before I came here, I read several articles on the APU's website, your website, that said the Republicans were accelerating the racial holy war. How do you blame the liberals and the Republicans?"

"Make no mistake," Kitchener said. "I will vote for any white man over a dumb animal like the nigger. Any man but a Jew, which is a devil not even a man. But that don't mean the Republicans ain't acceleratin' the race wars."

He took a sip of his tea before continuing. "They invaded and killed Aryans in the Middle East. That John McCain is a white traitor. If he gets elected it'll be almost as bad, cuz he will invade Iran and the Persian is an Aryan people."

"So why not vote for Obama?" I asked sincerely. "You might consider him an animal, but he's not going to invade Iran."

"Maybe not," Kitchener granted me. "But he wants to raise the capital gains tax. I got a lot of money in the stock market right now."

He cocked an eyebrow and looked at me over the line of tea in his glass. "Beats havin' your money in a Jew bank."

We finished our drinks and Kitchener invited me to his office. Unlike the rest of his house, which I would describe as very neat and tidy, Kitchener's office was a mess of papers and books. He had two computers and a microphone stand.

"That's where I record my podcast," he said, pointing to the computer with the microphone. "White America Truthcast. They took it off iTunes."

"Do the Jews run iTunes?" I asked.

"Nah." He shook his head. "The Jew doesn't understand the computer, which is why we done so well on the Internet. But the faggot, now he is a clever one. He works for the devil Jew and uses his white craftiness against us to destroy us."

222

"So homosexuals run iTunes?"

"Obviously," Kitchener said.

I looked around Kitchener's office. In this room there were some examples of the racist regalia I had expected from the outset. A framed portrait of Adolf Hitler hung above the computer. Another framed photograph of David Duke standing next to Kitchener shared shelf space with a number of other photographs. I stepped over a stack of old computer game boxes—*The Sims 2* was on top of the stack—and looked at the framed photos a bit more closely.

There was Kitchener on stage at a rally, yelling into a microphone. There was Kitchener doing a Nazi salute with a swastika armband around his arm. A number of chubby and bald white guys with goatees stood around him in various simulations of Nazi uniforms, also saluting in the direction of the camera.

Then I noticed the other pictures. Pictures of Kitchener with an attractive woman with brown skin and dark hair. I picked one of the pictures up and turned to ask him, but he already knew what was coming.

"Teresa," Kitchener said. "We were engaged."

"She's Mexican," I observed.

"She is from Mexico, but she is as Aryan as you or me." He reached up and took the picture from me. "We dated for over a year before we got engaged. I traced her genealogy back over three hundred years. She has never once bred with a lesser race. She is pure Spanish blood."

"I didn't know that the Spanish were Aryan," I said.

"Not all of them are, but her grandfather fought on the side of the fascists in Spain. He helped to defeat the communists."

"That made him Aryan?"

Kitchener nodded.

I had never considered that Aryan was like a religion that someone could adopt or lose through some terrible act of race treason. I felt certain some of the Aryan race scientists at the racist science institute might have a few problems with Kitchener's theory.

Kitchener showed me the backend of his website and the system he used to create updates for his site. It was not too different from our system at Something Awful, reminding me that according to some corners of the Internet our mockery of furries and Otherkin makes us as much a hate site as Kitchener's APU.

He then fired up his copy of The Sims 2 to show me how he had created a house filled with "apelike niggers," which he trained to "service his needs as the white master." "I love this game," he confessed. "I love any game where you can sorta like, play God with people. Make them do stuff or build up the world."

Kitchener also confessed that neighbors in The Sims that appeared "Jewy" or "tried to be gay around him" found themselves trapped in rooms without doors or in pools without ladders.

"If only it was that easy in real life," he said.

I thought back to Reggie watering Kitchener's lawn.

"People will be arriving any time now," Kitchener said as he closed the game. "I gotta get the barbecue goin'."

"What do you mean?" I asked.

"You said you wanted to know how I used the Internet to be successful," he said. "In y'all's e-mails. You said that. Well, anyway, I invited a bunch of people from the APU. You can ask them about it."

Frankfurters und Schadenfreude

The cognitive dissonance of Kitchener and his entire movement was on full display once the guests began arriving at his barbecue. They came in every shape, size, and beard type. Some wore suspenders and shorts and big chunky military boots. Others were dressed in polo shirts like Kitchener, young, professional, yuppie Nazis.

It was almost a diverse crowd, with one obvious area of homogeneity.

Kitchener and a stick-thin blond girl in an SS halter top were manning the barbecue. The privacy-fenced backyard was teeming with hateful conversation about a variety of hateful topics. Wagner was playing at a reasonable volume from speakers that looked like rocks.

I was talking with a young APU member next to the barbecue. The wind was steady, but an occasional breeze whipped smoke into my face and caused me to tear up.

"If the holocaust is real," said the young man with the faux-hawk, "why are they so afraid to investigate it?"

His name was Doug and he had facial piercings. He was wearing a faded shirt from Beck's *Odelay*. When he introduced himself he showed me a tattoo of a swastika made out of severed limbs on the inside of his left arm.

"I mean, maybe only a million Jews died, would that ruin their holocaust?" Doug asked. "Or what if it was ten million? I bet they'd love that."

"I don't know if 'love' is the right word," I suggested.

"But what if"—he prodded my chest with his index finger—"what if, man, they find out that only like ten thousand Jews got killed and it turns out they were all criminals anyway."

"That would be a pretty major revelation," I admitted.

"Exactly my point, man." Doug seemed pleased that I understood. "So why don't they investigate? What do they have to lose?"

Kitchener wheeled up and said, "The Jews would just tamper with the investigation. Ruin everything."

"I didn't mean—"

Kitchener held up a hand.

"Don't worry about it, Doug," he said. "Hey, I'm going to borrow Mr. Parsons here for a minute."

I felt uneasy about Kitchener using my name, as if simply by him speaking it aloud I would be added to some sort of government list. And I don't mean the Zionist Occupation Government.

"There's someone I want you to meet," Kitchener said. "Follow me."

I followed behind him as he navigated the concrete pathways of his crowded backyard. People moved out of Kitchener's way. Some fearfully, but most out of respect. A few even gave him a Sieg Heil gesture, which he returned with a perfunctory wave of his hand.

"Here we are," he said. "Chloe, come here."

Chloe was a short and quite young-looking girl. She had long black hair and she wore a black velvet dress, black-and-white-striped knee socks, and huge go-go boots. It must have been a sweltering costume in the afternoon heat, but she seemed to be coping with it.

"Nice to meet you," I said, offering her my hand.

She shook it unenthusiastically.

"Chloe," Kitchener said, "this is Mr. Parsons."

Her face brightened immediately.

"Luther told me you were coming to write about us," she said. "He calls me his protégé."

"Well, ah haha," Kitchener laughed. "I thought Mr. Parsons should meet you. After all, young lady, you are the future of the APU."

At Kitchener's insistence, I sat down with Chloe underneath a shade umbrella. We drank ice cold beers and she told me about her involvement in the party.

"They've taught me to use guns, bayonets, and knives." She ticked them off on her fingers. "They've taught me hand-to-hand combat and wilderness skills. I know how to set a snare for a jackrabbit and skin it now."

"Those are, uh, great skills to have," I noted.

"The APU are preparing me for the coming racial war. When

Obama takes over my virginity won't be safe from the niggers or the wetbacks."

"I . . . uh . . ."

"They taught me Mexican language listening, too," she said. "So I can watch from a hiding place and understand what they're saying. I can't speak Mexican, but I know what they're plotting about."

I tried to steer her away from descriptions of her syllabus at Hate University.

"Did you find the APU on the Internet?"

"Ohhhh." She grinned. "That's what Luther wanted me to talk to you about. I am the new head of the APU's Internet outreach program. He said he got the idea from a church group. They have attractive young women go onto dating websites and set up dates with single guys, then when they go out on the date the girls convince the single guys to join the church."

"Does that work?"

"I don't know, but we're going to try. I've got six girls lined up and we're going to start going on all the dating websites and try to find Aryans who should be aware of their duty to the white race."

"So is that how they got you to join?" I asked.

"No, no, no." Chloe shook her head. "Luther went around to all the Facebooks and MySpaces for Aryans he could find in the area. Then he messaged us and straight up explained our duty to the white race. I was really bored with high school so I dropped out and moved here."

"What exactly is your duty to the white race?" I asked.

"It's the white race," she said. "I mean, we spread it."

"You spread the white race?" I asked.

"Yeah, well, I'm gonna. When I find the right Aryan man I will spread the white race."

"But why?" I asked.

"Because it's our duty," she replied.

"Why is it your duty?"

"To the white race, it's our duty to the white race."

I sensed that we were entering some sort of Abbott and Costello nightmare vortex of repeating misunderstandings.

"I think I've got it," I said.

"Good." She looked over and squinted into the sun. "Is that . . . ?" She grinned.

"Hey, Bethany! Over here!"

She hopped up to greet her neo-Nazi friend and like that I was ditched beneath the umbrella. I was fine with that. I was a bit over-whelmed by all the hate. Hate stroke.

Towheaded children were chasing each other around the back-yard with cap guns blasting. Near the back door of the house a few of the skinheads were trying to set up some hate-core karaoke. A fat girl with a spiky purple Mohawk was pulling up the back of her shirt to show her huge iron cross tattoo to a guy who looked like a Mexican biker.

"We're just one big family," Kitchener remarked.

He was sitting at my elbow in that damn silent wheelchair of his.

"All of these people except for Prison Jim found out about the APU on the Internet," Kitchener said. "They all post on our forums. We're it, man."

He took a swig of his beer and cut his eyes at me.

"We're the future of the white race," he said.

Interdiction

I bid Kitchener farewell as the party was winding down. He tried to bribe me with a replica iron cross medallion. I was almost too tired to resist, but I knew if I accepted I would feel tainted by the exchange.

I thanked him for the hospitality and walked out to my car. On the way out, I saw Reggie working in his yard. We briefly made eye contact and I tried to somehow signal, with a wink and a slight shake of my head, that I wasn't one of these people.

It's a sad testament to race relations that Reggie couldn't see past the color of my skin. He thought I was just another white power racist because I am white.

And walking out of a white power party.

It's called reverse racism. Look it up.

Feeling chastened by Reggie's accusatory stare, I started up my rental and roared out of the cul-de-sac, headed for the distant interstate and my last stop in the state of Texas.

I stopped on the edge of Grundy and began to fill my tank. The Grundy part of West Texas was as barren as could be imagined and the last thing I wanted was to run out of gas and end up as a sunbleached skeleton by the side of a strip of woe-begotten Texas highway.

I think I was checking messages on my cell phone when they attacked. At first I thought they were skinheads from the party, but after the blow to the side of my head staggered me to the ground, I caught glimpses of dark suits and well-manicured fingers.

"You wasn't supposed to hit him," someone said.

"It was an accident," whined another unseen attacker.

"Hold 'em," shouted a third voice with more authority. "Get the bag on his head."

A heavy canvas bag dropped over my head and my vision went dark. I could feel myself being dragged across the asphalt. I kicked and tried to lash out, but it was useless. Strong hands lifted me up and onto a bench. A car door slammed shut.

"Mistuh Pahsuns." The person spoke with a heavily affected and heavily accented voice. "Y'all shoulda quit while you was able. That time has passed you by."

The atmosphere was thick with mingled odors of hairspray and lies. That was weird in hindsight, because I was pretty much breathing my own air in that canvas bag. Maybe before they put it over my head they were using it to carry around a bunch of wigs.

Tires screeched. I was on my way to meet with destiny.

And the Fishes.

CHAPTER ELEVEN

The End

6 You are going to hear of wars and rumors of wars. See to it that you are not alarmed. These things must take place, but the end hasn't come yet,

7 Because nation will rise up in arms against nation, and kingdom against kingdom. There will be famines and earthquakes in various places.

8 But all these things are only the beginning of the birth pains.

—Book of Matthew, The Bible

6 Your phone is gonna blow the fuck up with all kinds of crazy shit going down. Do not freak the fuck out. It's gotta happen and it is cool because it is gonna totally rule.

7 All the armies are gonna start blowing the ever-living shit out of each other. And the King of England is

gonna ride in on a motorcycle and chop the head off
the King of France with a huge sword with a skull on
the handle. And lo, blood hath sprayed all over his face,
and he did strike down some other dudes that ran in
with machineguns. And then there was a fucking
earthquake and a big fireball shot up out of the crack
that formed.

8 And that ain't the half of it . . .

—Book of Super Matthew, The Super Bible

"**W**e are living in the final age," announced a male voice, smooth
as margarine. "I am the visionary of the End Times. The prophet
of the Alpha and the Omega. And I have witnessed the coming judgment of the Lord upon his children."

A group of voices murmured in unison. Somewhere, off in the
darkness, a synthesizer was doing a poor job of imitating a pipe organ.
It sounded like the funeral for Tangerine Dream.

I was on my side on a hard surface, probably the floor. I tried
to move, but my hands were tied behind my back. My shoulders
ached from the awkward position. My head was still covered with
a bag and it was hot in there, swampy humid from my trapped per-
spiration.

I heard and felt an approaching thump of footsteps. Then I was
lifted up off the floor by my arms and manhandled upright into a
chair. Someone tore the canvas bag from my head and for a moment I was blinded. I gasped and drew in a deep breath of cool,
fresh air.

"Why did y'all come to Gideon Flats?" Canyon Fish asked me.

He looked like a bigger and slightly fatter version of his brother,
Travis Fish. Pictures of both were available on their website. Canyon

had lustrous black hair slicked back and arranged in neatly parted waves. There was a suggestion of jowls forming beneath his cheeks, on either side of his dimpled chin, but Canyon was not yet old enough to droop. He was an ox of a man, clad in a tight white T-shirt and a pair of work slacks. He had a pack of cigarettes crammed into the T-shirt's tiny front pocket, some strange brand with a picture of a turtle visible through the fabric of his shirt.

"Why did y'all come to Gideon Flat!?" he repeated.

"I didn't," I protested. "I mean, you brought me here. Tied up with a bag on my head."

Canyon was sitting across a coffee table from me, his beefy arms resting spread out along the back of a vomit-colored couch. Standing on either side of him were men in cheap suits and ties. They wore plastic-framed black sunglasses. They looked like dollar store Secret Service or the sort of Mormon missionary you might send into the Matrix.

"I haven't talked to Barney Winston since you called me," I protested. "I wasn't even going to come here."

"Aw, well that just is a funny story, Mistuh Pahsuns, but I don't believe ya on account of Barney ain't had one single call. And you was supposed to come visit today."

Canyon lifted his arms off the couch and then let them drop back down.

"And here ya are," he said. "Right here with us in the heart of Gideon. Here to witness the foretelling of the End of Days?"

"Peace be on you, brothers and sisters!" a voice cried through the thin, faux wood paneling. "And may we gird our loins and armor ourselves in faith for the coming battle. Amen!"

Synthesized organ music swelled and a chorus of voices began to sing a hymn. Something about battling angels and swords of fire. Very dramatic stuff.

A door banged open and a thinner, slightly younger version of Canyon Fish entered. This was Travis Fish, also known as Deacon Fish, leader of the Fishes. The Fish brothers were the sibling founders of a creepy extremist Christian sect that has grown through the Internet, attracting members from as far away as Iceland. Fish styled himself a revelator, capable of interpreting numeric codes buried in the Bible; he would use them to discern the specific events leading up to Judgment Day.

"Who is this, Canyon?" Travis asked.

He removed his scarlet vestments, draping them over a chair before sitting down at a metal teacher's desk. He poured a glass of water from a plastic pitcher and drank it all in one gulp.

"This is our curious friend," Canyon said. "The one who wanted to have a talk with Mr. Winston."

"Ah," Travis nodded. "Well then, I expect he'll want to have a look around. See what we're all about. Then take that information and twist every bit of it until we seem like lunatics and monsters. And then he will vomit his lies onto the Internet and defame our glorious works."

Travis propped his feet up on the desk and inclined his head toward one of the two men in sunglasses.

"Lyle," he said, "why don't you go get Mr. Winston. I think he might have something to say."

"Look," I said, "why don't you untie me? I'm not going to karate fight my way out of here."

Travis gave the slightest nod and the other guy in the cheap suit stepped up behind my chair and untied my hands. The rough twine fell to the floor. I massaged the raw flesh of my good wrist, my hand clicking slightly beneath the black leather glove.

"I apologize for the rough treatment," Travis said. "You understand, I'm sure, that we deal with enough harassment from your ilk on the Internet. We can ignore it easily enough. To think that you would dare come looking for trouble, well, that required some action."

"I don't know what sort of Branch Davidian bullshit you've got going here, Deacon Fish, and I really don't care. If you didn't want me here all you had to do was ask."

"But I did ask," Deacon Fish said. "Didn't you get my messages?"

"I have no clue what you're . . . ," I began, but stopped.

I did have a clue. Better than a clue. I knew exactly what Deacon Fish was talking about. That weird threatening letter from Anders was really from Fish. The threatening phone calls. There were even a few hang-up calls in the middle of the night that I had attributed to the usual Internet cranks.

Deacon Fish smiled. Not cruelly exactly, but it wasn't a friendly smile. All I could think was that he had one really brown tooth and it ruined his whole smile. Your eyes were drawn to it.

"We were very clear with our message, Mr. Parsons. Now that you're here, I think we can dispense with veiled threats. We didn't want you here and we were willing—"

I interjected.

"You spent weeks harassing me with cryptic packages and messages and then when you finally ask like normal human beings I comply and you kidnap me and bring me here anyway."

I shook my head. "This is dumb as hell. Just let me go. Drop me off back at my car."

"I'm afraid we can't do that," Canyon said. "Sadly, we had to drive y'all's automobile out to the desert and set it on fire to prevent any traces."

"What?" I was stunned. "You what? You burned my car? I didn't pay for the insurance!"

"I'm sure it's—"

"You assholes! Did you burn all of my stuff?"

"No," Canyon said. "We recovered some of your—"

"Jesus Christ," I cursed and the mood darkened immediately.

"You will not blaspheme in my presence again or I will have you water boarded," Travis said loudly.

I shut up. I had just bought one of those cardboard windshield panels to keep the seats from getting too hot. They were shaped like a pair of sunglasses.

"My iPod," I muttered, imagining it melting into the center console.

The Bernard Winston they brought in was a transformed man. He slouched next to his escort; his hair was hanging over his face and he had several days' growth of stubble on his cheeks. His suit was old, dusty, and too-big.

The man I had spoken to weeks earlier was a vibrant and excited man, looking forward to a life beyond the Gideon compound.

He had a young wife he met on the Internet, another former member. It was her initial e-mails to me that had put me onto Winston. And now he had apparently paid the price for that contact.

"I plan to stay here and fight as a member of the Lord's Army," Winston announced. "I love Gideon Falls and I look forward to the return of Our Savior to this earth."

His statement was stilted, rehearsed, and given to nobody in particular. He did not even look in my direction. Travis waved him out.

"There you have it," Travis said. "He is happy as can be to stay here."

"He looked delighted," I remarked. "Can I go now?"

Travis clucked his tongue against his teeth in a scolding manner.

"Mister Parsons, you still have to write that article," Travis said.

"It's for a book," I corrected.

"Even better," he replied. "Even better. I want to help you."

"I can't believe you set fire to my fucking car," I said. "What am I going to do? All of my notes. My phone. I'm going to have to pay for the car! I had just put gas in it!"

He got up and came around from behind his desk to stand beside me. He smelled like hair product. And lies.

"All your questions will be answered. I will show you around, give you a tour. Let you meet the family." He clapped a hand on my shoulder. "I think you'll come to see why Gideon Falls is such a special place."

The Grand Tour

Gideon Falls was much too large to easily walk in an afternoon, but the Fish family had a whole fleet of old Army jeeps painted institutional blue. Some were covered with tarps, but most of them were parked in rows and baking under the hot Texas sun.

The jeeps seemed so tiny compared to the sort of modern cars with air conditioning and windshields and cushioned seats and my iPod that I preferred and that the Fishes hated so much. These things were barely larger than a golf cart and didn't look very flammable. Each vehicle was numbered on the side and had a beveled cross icon on the hood. It was an ugly logo. It looked as if someone had just arbitrarily applied a Photoshop filter to a crucifix.

"We are almost completely independent from the outside world here at Gideon Falls," Travis remarked as he guided our jeep out of the garage building. "The Internet is about the only thing we can't produce ourselves."

The Gideon Falls compound sprawled across four hundred acres of fairly barren Texas land. It wasn't quite the cactuses and tumbleweeds of the desert, but it wasn't far off. The roads were all dirt and we raised a huge cloud of dust behind us as we made our way to what Travis called, "the Lord's Larder."

It was actually a pair of filthy and dank-smelling hothouses where they were growing fruits and vegetables to feed the people who lived on the compound.

"The Lord provides," Travis noted as he plucked a tomato from the vine.

He bit it and let the juices run down his chin. One of the slack-faced greenhouse workers offered him a handkerchief. Travis wiped his face and handed it back with a murmured blessing.

We left the sticky heat of the greenhouse and followed a dirt path to a large barn filled with cows.

"We do not eat meat," Travis said, "but we drink milk."

A woman in blue military-style coveralls approached carrying a silver bucket full almost to overflowing with milk.

"Would you like some?" Travis offered.

I was very thirsty, but raw milk from a creepy cult barn was not the sort of thirst quencher I had in mind.

"I had a bottle of water in my car," I said. "I don't suppose you saved that?"

Travis exaggerated his fixed smile into a sarcastic grin and dipped a cupped hand into the milk. He slurped the liquid out of his palm and then shook his hand in the air, shedding the remaining droplets on the dirty concrete floor.

"Delicious," he announced. "Thank you, Mistra."

The woman with the bucket walked away.

"It's always best fresh and warm from the teet."

Under normal circumstances I would be compelled to quip after hearing and seeing something like that. Something like, "At that moment I wanted to die."

However, at that moment all I could think about was my rented car. All of my travel belongings, my clothes, my shaving kit, my notebook of random ideas, my vacation porno, all of it was gone. Weeks of spotty hotel Internet access and I had built up some pretty solid vacation porno. Past tense.

The tour continued with a swing by the dormitories. These were where the newcomers lived. Institutional housing for those recruited through the website or through community outreach programs. They were segregated by sex into two immense three-story slabs lined with windows about the size of ship's portholes.

There was some attempt made to landscape around the entrances, but lack of care and the difficult environment had left the flower planters and rose bushes looking desiccated and feeble.

"We shan't disturb them," Travis noted as we zoomed past the women's dorm.

One of the inhabitants had taped a colored drawing of a heart in the cell-like window of her room. Written beneath the crude cartoon were the words PRAISE HIM in fat black letters.

"Hey, do you think I could call my car in stolen?" I asked. "I mean, I'll keep you guys out of it, but I can't afford to pay for the car. You know they would charge me blue book plus a profit on something like that."

"I don't know," Travis replied, although I could tell he didn't care.

"You know, you guys did that," I said. "You guys burned my car. Not me. Not me, I would have said 'Oh, let's park it in a parking lot somewhere and he can get it when we're done.' I wouldn't have torched it. I mean you could have at least emptied my stuff out of there."

"Hush," Travis said.

"I'm just saying," I muttered and looked away from him and at the ugly squalor of his stupid cult compound. "Torch this stupid place instead."

The upper echelons of Gideon Falls lived in individual housing units. These were obviously modeled after suburban housing. The crudely constructed houses used substandard materials and were arranged around dirt cul-de-sacs in a parody of suburbia. It was almost amusing to see asphalt driveways and green grassy lawns facing dusty roads of hardened dirt.

I could only imagine the sort of muddy hell the roads became in the rainy season. Of course, that was pretty much fine, since everyone drove the same blue jeeps.

As we passed by the houses I noticed a gathering of people. About a dozen men and women, standing in a circle, heads low and arms interlaced. It was almost like a football huddle, except every thirty seconds or so the whole group would leap in unison.

"What are they doing?" I asked.

Travis slowed the jeep so we could watch.

"Leaps of faith," Travis beamed. "Every day we all take leaps of faith to try to get us closer to the Lord. Some day when they do that they won't come back down to the ground, they'll just keep going up and up and up."

"Into space?" I asked.

Travis laughed and drove on.

We ended the tour at the rectory, a palatial structure that was obviously meant to resemble, if not outright copy, the White House. The White House if most of the windows had not been installed yet and there was a 20-foot crucifix on the front lawn. Several jeeps were parked outside in the circular drive. Travis bypassed this and parked next to a side entrance that required a magnetic key card.

"Here's where the real work happens," he said. "Downstairs in the basement. That is where we crack the code."

"Oh, is this the part where you hand me a check for the price of my car that you burned?" I asked, but he did not answer.

Decoding the Word

We descended into the cool depths beneath Travis's White House. This was a world of clicking PC towers and the steady hum of cooling fans. The construction work was done by professionals, not eager amateurs.

Old CRT monitors served the network of computers.

"I wrote all of the software myself," Travis noted.

We passed a row of monitors, each covered with rapidly scrolling text.

"Every word and phrase in the Bible has a numeric value and these computers are calculating every possible equation and result of every scrap of code contained in the Bible."

"Where do you get the results?" I asked.

"I don't," Travis said. "I am the revelator. I reveal the Lord's Plan. These machines just dump all of their data into a huge printout. The Lord guides me to find the proper information."

We approached a silent bank of printers and Travis picked up a thick stack of paper. He waved it at me as if to prove his point.

"Wait a second," I said. "You just randomly pick stuff out of a big stack."

"Not random," Travis objected. "It is the Lord at work. He guides my selection."

"Why is it always about the end of the world then? All of your sermons in the church and on your website, all of your podcasts and videos, they're all about the End Times."

"Two reasons," Travis said. "One, it's the Lord at work. He wants me to read about the End of Days. Reason number two is that we're in the End of Days. The signs are all around us."

"When did you pull out the prophecy about you guys lighting my fucking car on fire, man?"

His expression darkened and the pits of his eyes fell into shadow as he tilted his head forward.

"Now listen here." He pointed a finger in my face. "The signs are real. Do you think I made up the wars in the Middle East? That's where the Antichrist will arise. Just some coincidence? Did I make up 9-11 or the Mayan calendar? It's all interconnected and it's all leadin' to one thing. It's leadin' to the End of Days."

"So when is it?" I asked. "When is it coming?"

"There will be signs," Travis replied, affecting a theatrical manner of speaking in the process. "Each day it will become worse and the signs will grow more obvious. Great conflagrations will swallow up entire nations. Meteors will fall from the sky and crash into the earth. Terrible plagues will afflict mankind."

"That sounds like Super Bible," I observed.

"What?"

"Nothing." I waved my hand, "Just something else in my notes that you torched."

He scowled at my impudence, but could not resist continuing.

"Airplanes will crash from the sky, ships will be dashed upon the rocks. Cars will stop working—"

"Oh, they just stop working? Is that how it is? The cars don't, I don't know, driiive out to the desert and get doused with gasoline?"

He stared at me silently for a few seconds and then continued, "Computers will go silent. The great armies of the world will be swallowed up by the earth."

"What about trains and buses?"

"What do you mean?" Travis asked.

"You said airplanes will crash and cars will 'stop working,' but will we still have trains and buses available?"

"No," Travis replied. "Don't be contrary. They'll stop working, too."

"So you are going to take them out to the desert and set them on fire? That seems like it might be doable for buses, but trains? Good luck."

"At that moment, when we are isolated from one another and terrified, our greatest fears will be realized and the monsters and demons of hell will be unleashed upon the face of the earth."

"Whoa," I said. "What sorts of monsters and demons?"

"Horrible, bloodthirsty ones," Travis assured me.

"Not sex demons? The big titty demons? Or the Monsters of the Midway?"

"Absolutely not," Travis snapped. "These will not be fun demons. They will be horrible locusts with the faces of men and recurved talons that—"

"Recurved?"

"Yes, they will curve back, like this." Travis bent his fingers back toward his wrist to demonstrate.

"Those seem like some shitty talons," I noted. "Wouldn't it be better to have, say, knife hands or one of those spiked balls on a chain instead of a hand?"

"That's beside the point." Travis sighed. "They're going to rip off your flesh. And if you're a sinner they will carry your soul back to hell for eternal punishment. This isn't one of your jokes. It's not some game. This is the end of everything."

"Do the demons have any weaknesses?" I asked. "Like silver or something you could research in advance?"

Travis shook his head, obviously irritated by my attitude.

"We can fight these guys," I said. "Come on, Deacon. We can fight back. Mankind will unite against these invaders and the world can celebrate a new Independence—"

Deacon Fish held up a hand to silence me. His glare would have been enough.

A Singular Ending

We retired to Travis's game room on the rectory's ground floor. A few of the guys in sunglasses were playing pool. Canyon and an elderly fat woman with a beehive hairdo were playing Connect Four. I was expecting someone to sing Roy Orbison's "In Dreams" into a light fixture.

"Sit down." Travis gestured to a leather couch and I obeyed.

He was drawn and serious, exasperated by my fixation on his cult's automotive arson. In hindsight, I think that he wanted me to be afraid, but nothing was getting in the way of my outrage about the car. I'm still mad about that.

Travis took a moment to prepare us drinks before handing me a glass of Scotch on the rocks. I reached out for the tumbler with my gloved artificial hand. My fingers clicked slightly as I took hold of the glass. Travis cocked his head and gave me an odd look, like a chicken studying a piece of birdseed that just pecked back. Whatever he was thinking, he shook it off.

The Scotch was the good stuff, or at least that's what he said. All Scotch tastes like weather sealer for a deck to me.

"We try to find people without friends or family," Travis said. "People who don't belong in society. The outcasts. People nobody wants."

"You know that's the same profile most serial killers follow, right?" I asked.

Travis didn't seem to notice the jab.

"Last year we recruited almost thirty people from the Internet. That was more than half the number of our community outreach work at a tenth of the cost. This year we're hoping to double that number. We might even triple it."

It was impressive, I guess. I didn't tell him that a couple weeks earlier, ninety people showed up in San Francisco wearing Guy Fawkes masks and protesting Scientology for no reason other than it was fun.

"The more tools for recruitment there are, the more successful we become. The more successful we become the more people we can have working on outreach. On and off the Internet."

I leaned in conspiratorially and asked, "Do you really believe all this shit?"

"Absolutely," Travis answered. "I speak the Word of God and to believe that word flawed is to not believe that God is infallible."

"Come on, you've got to doubt some of it a little," I said. "Like the bugs with the human faces. When have you ever seen shit like that outside a science fiction movie or a bad dream?"

Travis glanced at the others and then leaned in close. "I think some of it is metaphor, naturally. You ever heard of a singularity event?"

"Rise of the robots? Man versus machines?" I asked.

"Yes, exactly. Sometimes when I watch the news I think maybe it'll be like that instead of all this other stuff. I mean, I believe it's all true, I just think the Bible maybe can't describe it right."

I knew what he meant.

"Like if we went back in time and ran over some dude with a

truck his family would think it was a great iron beast or a dragon or something."

"Exactly," Travis agreed. "I think the angels with their burning swords might just look a little more like a droid with a burning laser saber."

I laughed.

"What's so funny?" he asked.

"That definitely sounds like you're getting it from Super Bible."

"What's that?" Travis asked. "I heard you mention it earlier. Some kind of joke?"

"It's serious to me," I said. "We all worship our own way."

He raised an eyebrow.

"There are wrong ways to worship," Travis said, and sat next to me on the couch.

I thought he was about to lecture me and probe my religious beliefs. Instead, he seemed almost eager to stay away from the topic of religion. He directed the conversation toward a discussion of Texas college football. I'm better versed in weird religious sects.

Travis was intent on talking up the "Aggies" from Texas A&M. The name suggested medieval illness and I was only familiar with the school because several students managed to get themselves killed at a school bonfire and made national news. I just nodded along to whatever Travis was saying about a quarterback and imagined my car burning in the Aggie bonfire. At least there it might stand some small chance of exacting its revenge.

For all I knew, the football talk was Travis's version of the villain revealing the master plan right before attempting to kill the hero. The hero always escaped, deflecting a laser with a belt buckle or disarming the villain with kung fu. My plan wasn't nearly as fleshed out. At that point I had worked out that I could punch Travis in the chest and then bite Canyon on the hand if he tried to crush my head. After that, all I had was my instincts and an SAS field manual PDF I think I read once when I was drunk.

"Would you like a refill?" Travis asked, rising from the couch.

I must have given him a dumbfounded expression in reply, because he shook his empty glass of Scotch in my direction. I cast my gaze to the empty glass in my own hand and nodded. The last thing I needed was more Scotch, but I supposed if they were going to kill me I might as well be drunk.

He took my glass and turned to the small selection of booze to make a fresh pair of drinks.

"Science is more likely than anything to bring about the end," he said, returning to his original topic.

Travis twisted the top off the bottle of Scotch and the tea-colored liquid spilled out into my glass. He looked over his shoulder at me.

"Might not even be a battle, you know? Look how much computers run our lives now. Even we use them. It's not like one day we are all just robots, but it could happen gradually. Then after years and years we're just metal servants of Satan."

"How do you fight that?" I wondered.

"Faith," Travis answered, and turned back, "and maybe a little bit of napalm."

He held out the glass for me and I took it without thinking. There was a whir and a click as the fingers of my right hand closed around the tumbler. We froze like that, my hand clasping the glass, Travis refusing to let it go. His gaze narrowed; his brow furrowed.

Suddenly, his eyes went wide, and he snapped his hand out and yanked the edge of my leather glove up my hand almost an inch.

It exposed the workings of the hand Doctor Lian gave me all those months earlier. The red ring of my wrist stump was welded with surgical staples to the metal stump-clasp of the hand. My arm muscles controlled the grasping and neural impulses operated the individual fingers.

The hand came with a polyethylene cover that disguised it as a real hand, right down to painted freckles and tiny hairs. Unfortunately, I melted the hand's realistic cover on the electric burner of my friend's stove long before my trip to Texas. I was waiting for a replacement, but they had to be custom made to fit each hand and match your skin tone.

Without the polyethylene cover . . . well, it was more Terminator than Bionic Man. It looked like the hand of a robotic skeleton inside my glove. It looked, for lack of a better word, evil.

Travis Fish couldn't pull my glove completely off with the glass of Scotch in my hand, but he yanked it down to my knuckles. He stood frozen, dumbfounded, by the prosthetic device.

"Canyon," he whispered.

"Deacon Fish," I pleaded. "It's okay. I ruined my hand in a car door several months ago and—"

"Canyon!" Travis Fish shouted.

His brother stood up, scattering the Connect Four board and pieces on the table. His matronly opponent gasped with surprise.

"What is it!?" Canyon rushed to his brother's side.

I tried to jerk my hand away, but Travis had a death lock on it. His face was red now, his eyes hot with anger.

"It is The Beast!" he raged. "He brought this evil into our house. He is a, a, a robot hellion!"

No use pointing out that they brought me into their house. I attempted to shove Travis away and I got to my feet. In that process, I somehow contracted my forearm muscle too much, triggering a sympathetic response in my prosthetic hand. My grip tightened on the tumbler full of Scotch and it shattered in an explosion of glass and "the good stuff."

Slivers of glass stabbed Travis Fish's hand and he yowled in pain.

"Aaaahh!" He held up his blood-flecked fingers for his brother to see. "He's bit me bad!"

Tears wet his cheeks. He swooned.

Canyon caught his brother as he fainted and the larger Fish boy lifted the smaller up like a bride in his arms. I saw my opportunity and attempted to escape, but was headed off by the Sect Service dorks wearing sunglasses.

"Hold 'em!" Canyon bellowed as he settled his brother gently onto the couch. "Hold that devil."

"Come on." I shoved at the skinnier of the two. "Get the hell off me!"

They weren't big, but their fingers were like metal restraints snapping around my upper arms. I knew I could force my way past them with my desperate strength given a minute or two of struggle. I didn't have nearly that long.

I grunted and shoved the skinnier of the two men backward. His flat face registered exaggerated surprise, like a cartoon painted on the blade of a shovel. My push flung him back into the door, slamming it open and almost toppling him over in the process.

"Gaaaoohh!" he shouted.

His momentum dragged me with him and we spilled out into the entryway of the building. I had a flash of hope, but it was fleeting. He regained his footing and shoved back while his slightly larger friend pulled me into the recreation room from behind. I kicked behind me, but I failed to connect with anything more solid than a pant leg.

I twisted and jerked around, nearly managing to pry open the hands of the larger of the two men. I was so contorted in one direction that when he abruptly released me I nearly fell to the ground.

Then Canyon arrived to give me his full attention. The big Fish brother easily overpowered me and twisted my left arm painfully behind my back. He grabbed my right arm just behind the wrist and held it away from my body like a dangerous weapon. The metal prosthetic sparkled and reflected the lights.

"I weel banish you back ta hell, devil," Canyon roared. "In the name of Jesus!"

"I'm not a robot you hickory smoked moron!" I cried in protest.

Then Canyon turned me around, his face a sloppy stack of furrows, and I saw he was holding a machete. It was carbonized black with a silver edge and Canyon was holding it at face-chopping level, cocked back in one of his meaty paws.

"What the fuck, man?" It was a rhetorical question.

Canyon answered anyway, swinging the machete directly at my face. As razor-sharp death hurtled toward my head I could only think of one thing, *Who is going to call the car rental company and let them know that m—*

Epilogue

Being dead isn't so bad.

You just stop doing everything.

I guess it might depend on how and why you stop doing everything. Dying from cancer might be pretty bad because it takes so long. One of those heroic movie deaths where you have enough time to gasp out some last words might be painful. I can say from experience, getting machete chopped in the skull is all right.

Not bad.

Without much reference I'd go with a seven out of ten.

"What the shit is up, bro?" The voice was soothing, materializing out of the nothing.

The darkness of eternal slumber gave way to a soft white light. Above me, gigantic and leonine, was an elderly man with a flowing white beard and long white hair. Though I somehow knew he was ancient—as old as time—there was no trace of weariness or weakness. He seemed almost youthful. Maybe it was the sunglasses.

"Helllllooo," he boomed from on high. "Wake up, dude."

The soft light slowly resolved into a large and brightly lit room. I could hear music playing, laughter, all around me were people. Dancing. No . . .

"Are those people having sex?" I asked.

"No, they are fuckin'," the voice boomed. "So are those other people. And those two chicks there. What's up, babies?"

"Are the—"

"Ooooh!" He interrupted and slid his shades down to the tip of his nose. "Some sex demons in here. Big titty sex demons. Mmm, mmm, mmm, look at those girls go."

"Demons?" I pushed myself up. "Am I in hell?"

"Hell?"

I heard a roar like a trillion thunderclaps all at once. I realized the white-haired giant was astride a burning motorcycle. With a rumble of thunder he descended from the cottony clouds to the soft, cushiony ground next to me. He smelled like pussy and weed smoke. He was wearing a denim vest that showed off his big biceps. One bicep was tattooed with a gorgeous naked woman, on the other a tattoo of gothic script read FUCK YEAH in all capital letters.

"Is this Heaven?" I asked.

The man laughed.

"Better." He took off his shades and hooked them in his front pocket. "This is Super Heaven."

A cheer of delight went up from the orgying masses all around us. Even the big titty sex demons cheered.

"So that means you're . . . Super God?"

It was almost too much to hope.

"I wish, bro. I'm Super Saint Peter." He pointed to his crotch. "Peter, like a dick. Like that kind of peter. It's easy to remember."

"I won't forget it," I assured him.

He was already busy with a spiral bound notepad. He flipped it open and clicked a pen.

"So, bro, you got macheted in the frigging head. Pretty sweet way to go. Did it hurt?"

"No much," I shrugged.

"Really? Well, I've got you down for natural causes."

"What do you mean?" I had plainly died from a machete to the face.

"Could be anything just about." Super Saint Peter shrugged. "Cancer, stroke, fatness, titty sex, dinosaur bite, lung wiggles, rockets."

"Rockets?"

"Oh, shit, guess that is an accident," he snorted. "Whatever. Replace it with over-wailing on your guitar. I am high as fuck right now. If you want to just go back there or whatever, that's cool."

"I can go back?"

"Naw, you got to go back," he said. "I can't have any early arrivals. So, one wish."

"A wish?"

"Yeah, are you a retard or something? You keep asking all these retard questions. You get a wish since we effed up. Our way of saying sorry."

"I can wish for anything?"

"Not more wishes, you chode. Don't try to game the system."

"I want my rental car back."

Super Saint Peter stared at me, his face slack.

"I want my rental car back," I repeated.

"Anything except more wishes," he said, apparently deciding to pretend that I had not just made my wish. "You want your real hand back? Maybe you want to have two dicks or, oh, I know, you can fly. You want to fly?"

"Sure," I said, "but that's not my wish. I want my rental car back, unburned."

"A billion dollars?"

"I had a lot of important notes in my car," I said, starting to grow annoyed. "I had a bunch of CDs too. And my iPod. And I had just bought one of those window shades."

"Bro." Super Saint Peter rested one of his giant hands on my shoulder. "Listen, bro, I can give you any wish you want. You can have anything. You can *be* anything. The only limit is your imagination."

I looked him in his eyes which were constantly exploding with fire in a super awesome way behind the sunglasses.

"Dude, I'm starting to get pissed off. Fix my car."

"I'm just saying—"

"No," I shouted, startling a pair of nurses 69ing nearby. "I will fuck you up, dude. I will fuck you up if you don't send me back with my car."

"Dude, you are such an asshole," Super Saint Peter said.

"Exactly," I said to the barren Texas roadside.

I was alive.

More importantly, so was my car. I looked at the backseat and saw the sunshade neatly folded and sitting next to my backpack full of notebooks and recording gear.

With a smile on my face, I put the vehicle in drive and pulled back onto the road.

Two Weeks Later

"I'm not surprised," said Roger Malthus.

His voice was distant, distorted, the words echoing out from the cheap speaker phone. It sounded as though he were calling to me down the length of a stone tunnel.

"It's not possible, Roger," I replied. "I was dead. The Fishes killed my fucking face with a machete. How could I be here, talking to you?"

I was actually in my house and Roger was back in St. Louis, but that didn't detract from the improbability of the moment. I was alive.

"I'm alive!" I added.

"Are you?" Roger asked. "How can you be sure? Maybe you're dead and this is all something your brain is imagining to comfort you in your dying moments. It's like that movie."

"*Jacob's Ladder*," I said.

"No, I think it was *Donnie Darko*. It had the fat guy from *My Name Is Earl*. But that's just one possibility. You already know what I think it is."

I had my suspicions as to what Roger believed.

"Say it so I can tell you that you're wrong," I insisted.

"You're an Otherkin," Roger said.

"You're wrong."

"You say that, but a lot of us don't want to believe in our Otherkin side when it first reveals itself. You could be a dragon, or . . ."

"Or what?"

"Ghostkin," he said. "It's an offshoot of spiritkin. Very rare."

"So you're saying I'm a ghost?"

"Kin. It's like 'ish' in this case. Ghost-ish."

"But I'm alive," I asserted again. "And what about all that stuff in Super Heaven? Am I an angel?"

"Dude, you're whatever you want to be." I could hear the creak as Roger leaned back in his chair. "You want to be a ghost, be a ghost. You want to be alive, then be alive."

"What if I want to be an elf?"

Roger laughed.

"Your hands are way too hairy for that."

I looked at my right hand, flexing it carefully and examining the fingers. He was right, the dark hairs crept from my wrist up onto the back and side of my hand. Wait . . . my hand . . . was . . .

"What about *Robocop?*" I asked.

"Sweet movie," Roger said.

"No, I had a mechanical hand, when I was there. I . . . can I be Robocop? Is there a Robocopkin?"

Roger laughed loudly for several seconds before replying.

"No," he finally answered. "That would be ridiculous."

Acknowledgments

A great many people have made this book possible and in a fair world their names would sit beside mine on the cover of this book. Unfortunately, we don't live in a fair world at all; we live in a Boschian hellscape populated by fish-headed children and rat men living inside hollow pumpkins. In this world all of the wonderful people who have contributed so much are relegated to a few short words at the back of the book.

My thanks to them are no less heartfelt.

First and foremost, I have to thank Michelle, who for the final few weeks of this project came to know me as a living grievance. She indulged my complaints or told me to shut my stupid face and get back to work depending on the situation. She is an invaluable ally in all of my work and the love of my life.

Rich "Lowtax" Kyanka deserves to be thanked in more than a few sentences here. He has been a friend, mentor, and employer for most of a decade. Without him this book would be about wacky cat pictures, or Mr. T eating balls, or it might not exist at all.

Josh Hass and Dave "Shmorky" Kelly were both great to work with on this project. Josh is my art dude. He is always willing and enthusiastic whenever I need his help on a project big or small. When I ask him to do a cover he exceeds my expectations. Shmorky has

259

been a buddy of mine for years and I'm not exaggerating when I say that someday there will be a documentary crew making a movie about his weird genius.

David Thorpe is the smartest guy I know. I asked him to write the foreword to this book because someday people will be buying anything involving him. It's like getting Kurt Vonnegut or J. D. Salinger to write your foreword before the world has really heard of him. Dave is the sort of writer that would make me hatefully jealous if he wasn't such a genuine and nice guy.

Josh "Livestock" Boruff, Reid "Frolixo" Paskiewicz, Johnny "Doc-Evil" Titanium, Joseph "Maxnmona" Fink, Dennis "CTS" Farrell, and Bob "BobServo" Mackey are just some of the writers I have had the privilege to work with at Something Awful. If I were starting a magazine to make people laugh I would hire them all, but magazines are some twentieth-century bullshit.

Richard Ember was my patient and helpful editor at Kensington, despite anything I might have implied earlier in the book. Jeremie Ruby-Strauss advised me throughout the darker days of this project, and he has been someone I know I can trust when it comes to books.

I talked to a lot of people while writing this book, and my sources were invaluable to the creative process. Believe it or not, there are real people behind the words in this book. Some of them might not resemble the characters so much, some of them might prefer it that way, but they all deserve my thanks. You made this happen.

There are also the hundreds of people who helped out in small ways. These people might be overlooked in boring regular books, or at best thanked on the Internet. Instead, I want to take the time and paper to thank each of them individually. May their legends never die.

David Coburn, thank you for always being there when I needed a huge pair of tits to cry on. Kaydie, you brought me my dramatic spittoon for whenever I said the name of the cowboy I hate. Alex "MajorPain" Chiodo, we never saw eye-to-eye, but that was because you were always digging those fucking holes. What the hell were you looking for?

Nathan McKenzie, your name will live on in this book of magical mystery, but you will be dead by sundown. Karen, I will never look at sporks the same way again, because you stabbed yours into my eye. Myles, though you are Irish, you have been trained with whips and hot tar to act almost like a human man. Someday we will teach you about pants.

Erik Gilson, thanks for hiding the bodies, you made our scavenger hunts the best ever. Baron von Bytecode, your gigaflops used terawatts, so we had to mega shut you off for a while. Ali Malesick (a.k.a. MonsterBunna) has been putting right what once went wrong. I hope your next leap is the leap home, Ali!

Skellen gyred and gimbled in the wabe and would not shut the hell up about it, either. The Reverend Fellow gay-married us all and we gay-loved it! Yayyy! Reverend Ian Sanderson gay-divorced us all and we gay-hated it! Booo! Thank goodness Philosopher Rhimes was around to lead us out of Plato's Gay Cave.

There was only one set of footprints on the beach, because Matt Maxwell was carrying me. Kerk offered to help, but then he just stood there and watched. Adam "Nam Taf" Jones brought snacks, and his old buddy Corey S. brought a surfboard. What a jerk!

Scott Cray wore a hair shirt for charity. Chris "Wykkyd-tron" Adams has a fucking ridiculous nickname. Daniel Dellinger is treating the symptoms but not the disease. John Price doesn't want me to thank Congressman Phil Roe (Tennessee, 1st). Suck on it, John Price. Brandon Soliday is sorry about your holiday. Kate "TunaSplen" Sgouros is stuck in the Sargasso and she loves it.

My good buddy Danielle Hadaway owns three turtles and kisses them at night! That's okay—Jamal Ginsberg owns four turtles and makes them watch while he lifts weights. MrTim223 doesn't own any turtles . . . because he's only a figment of your imagination!

Right now Marietard is trying to operate her computer with her teeth. Reverend James prayed for my failure, but it was he who failed! I watched while Mathew Gallant threw an old lady into a puddle. BBBoris was going to be thanked, but I want to fucking vomit, thinking of that bloated pustule on the drooling anus of humanity.

Steve LaPorte [TMFC] killed you with the knife, noobler! Dr. K. Hopper will write you a prescription for anything as long as you give him a taste. Steven Long hosed blood off the sidewalk. Clayton R. Schuler is planning to blame Twinkies when he pleads not guilty.

I have to thank Sano, who raided Molten Core solo and brought me the Eye of Sulfuras, even though I just wanted a coffee. Chris "BooDoug187" Myers was going to be thanked, but he's a reverse racist, so I am omitting his name. Mark's cat Onyx is heavyweight and still undisputed. Stefano "pigthe" Belli is welterweight and faces challengers for the title every day.

Brian Jet James is not autistic, but he is John Travolta's son. Valrin Valishen is putting boners back on the menu, BYOB. Missy Willard was there whenever I needed her, as long as I only needed her to shout "No!" and storm out of a room. I caught Chris Forbes and John Earl stealing from the honor system snack bar, but it's not like I'm going to tell anyone. Oops!

Holly Brockwell may brock well; she is useless when it comes to installing cabinets. David Shirley was no help either, he just sat there eating chips and commenting on her ass. Samuel Birbeck volunteered to help but didn't even show up. SodiumChloride made me retain water throughout this ordeal.

When I asked Daniel Southern for help, he just hung up the phone. Andrew Coja wanted to talk about the rapping song he was working on and wouldn't commit to helping. RewardMan will have to await his reward in the Elysian Fields because he will not be receiving a stinking dime from me!

Robert Catt lives inside a green pipe and hates Italians. Mike Douglas ate all of the ice cream, and when I got mad at him, he just said, "Greed is good!" Tyler Stickney and Jessica Colantuono make a cute couple. A cute couple of deadbeat rats! Mathew Weilbacher is my speechwriter.

Dennis Hale ran with a toothpick in his mouth—now look at him! Sakana should've had that looked at by a doctor. Ryan "FutureBoy" Sosa came in peace; now he rests in pieces. David S. Gunter just googled "gunt" and he is really pissed. Gareth Evans doesn't know what gunt means, but he has one. MrMoose loves gunts and has an encyclopedic knowledge of them.

I never would have written this book without Kyle Brodzky, my chief Brodzkier. Dr. Gabriel Jennings consulted on the subject of boners and the popping of them. Darryl Gervis has a laugh exactly like Beavis, and he never wears a shirt. I'm not even sure who Josh Bailey is, he just showed up one day and wouldn't leave.

John "Reggie" Balsam's mortal enemy is the infamous Reggie "John" Maslab. James Melvin Bull hates this book and that suits me just fine. Richard Harvey had a date with destiny, but he was stood up. LaMae L is now following you on twitter. Frank Talbot is smoking a Lucky Strike and just waiting for a dame to walk through that door into his office.

Sylvester Prunewinkle has never seen a woman naked. Not a human woman, anyway. WhamoCramo is my favorite board game from Parker Brothers. Thanks, Will. Just Will, you're so much better than that rascal Dick Ricardo. Brian D. Sek doesn't want to sit down; he prefers to stand. Sparky doesn't deserve to be thanked—but does anyone really deserve anything, or are we just assigning arbitrary values based on our own prejudices?

I tried to heat up some food while I was working on the book, but I accidentally plugged in my Hootplate. The noise was so bad, I decided to have a sammich. Thanks, Sammich.

Choco was supposed to be thanked in this sentence. Sorry, Choco. Sexy Kid Toyoma was not supposed to be thanked in this sentence. Mission accomplished. Juha Koo and Michael Du will someday meet in Tha Rhyme Zone. Ben and Linnea Gurn's plane went down over the Andes, and all we found were a few gnawed bones.

Brandon Alan Abell wrestles under the name Avant Guard. His Titantron entrance music is John Cage's *4' 33"*, and his trademark technique is painting an American flag on the mat in period blood. Lauren Reed is his manager and she was in a Situationist evening gown match with SummerGlaucoma. Summer won when she turned into butterflies.

James Snowdon's guts spilled out in slippery loops, white blood! That was Snowdon's secret: he was an android! Tom-Erik Oveson roared his Northman's rage and split the goblin in twain with his mighty axe, Rognoor. Holly Bronson thinks you humans are a disease and she is the cure.

Richard Parkin was parallel parking in Peking's park when he developed Parkinson's. At least he didn't run into Wenjii, the woman Benji. Michael "serakyu" Lee did run into Wenjii, and to make a long story short, he wants his VHS copy of *Pretty in Pink* and his guitar back.

Allan Thomas wanted to be famous—now he's famous and dead! Evan Taylor just wanted tanks. Now he's thanked and dead! W. C. Landis 1467 is still sitting in his seat waiting for the twist ending. Tim Hollan prefers his French creamy, his Ranch tangy, and his women fat and sassy. Jeff Wallen is allergic to cats and totally not allergic to the *365 Adorable Kittens* calendar.

Cara Skelsey sounds like she might be Irish, but I'm including her anyway. Jimmsta is definitely Irish. I won't be thanking Jimmsta. SuperSlacker was born under a blue sun, but beneath the light of our yellow sun he can do the nothing of a hundred men. Boaz will one day discover SuperSlacker's weakness and force him to work around the clock, mending shoes. Pakelika Wellington III commands you to run out the guns and prepare for broadside.

I can't believe Charles Skeavington just ate that Band-Aid he found on the floor. Jess and Doug Mundy are so disgusted, they stopped licking each other's sores. Mike Hill dropped his spoonful of cholera vomit right back into warm bucket. Sara Utley is still gnawing on her rat carcass teeming with maggots, but she is doing so with much less enthusiasm.

Eletricsugar is my favorite soda additive. William Bailey is a dickhead and Irish, and there is no fucking way in hell I am thanking him in this book. I hope Mike Squitieri isn't angry right now, but who can tell with that guy? Good news, Katie Leyland is going to murder everyone named in this book. Everyone, that is, except Josh Milburn. Her alter ego.

Tom Berube? Don't mind if I do! Bapes? Yes, please! Michael Piazza? With mushrooms and onions! No, wait, Michael I'm sorry. A pizza joke right there is disgusting. How about: Michael Piazza? I barely knew him!

Jon "Jingleheimer" Britton is ironically making a Redguard character in *Morrowind*. Nutella and Burtshine are great on toast with a little Marshmallow Fluff. Bill Rickabaugh agrees, and he started the damn company! Jurend Nogiec can't believe how many people are being thanked, but that's why we call him El Disbelievo. Sam "Underwater Welder" Nalven isn't really an underwater welder. He's an underwater cowboy!

Ian Gobert is my least favorite flavor of Gobert. Hey, take it up with Michael Piazza! Robert Yoon doesn't give a fuck about you Ian Gobert. He hates you! J. J. Collier is our poet emeritus of not giving a fuck. Mike-o gives a little bit of a fuck, but not about you, Gobert. Christ, Wesley Mead, he's got problems all his own. Why are you bothering him with yours, Ian Gobert?

DJ Action, meet MC Inaction. Mike Hartman is throwing his hands in the air like he feels a great deal of concern. Chris Leis is waving his hands to indicate that he is choking. Chris Ludden knows the Heimlich, but he's a nihilist. Miss America would like to thank fat people for eating. TeJay Guilliams wants five more minutes, mom! Jake Lindsoe wants five minutes with your mom.

Carlos M. Teixeira is opening a little Teixeira right down the street from the Super Mariocado. Brett Layer is not all that complicated and is nothing like an onion. I asked Sean "HAYDEZ" Connolly for Jennifer's phone number, and I ended up on a date with Billy Connolly. Joey Stidd sold the pictures of our illicit tryst to Perez Hilton.

Thomas B. Forbis is checking Corbis for Forbes. Internet Jocelyn just touched Regular Jocelyn, and the resulting explosion destroyed the planet. Xavier Jauregui has the hardest name to spell outside of Poland and the ant people. Smokey seeks bandit for friendship and maybe more. Satchel is what we named the dog, Henry.

Dr. Chewbacca Hastings can complete the tracheotomy in under twelve parsecs. Lose that And0, and get with this, Andhero. If you are what you eat, then Anne Armstrong and her cat are probably popcorn. Dave "The Studyman" Muntean had better brush up on his werewolf lore, if he knows what's good for him.

Kronprins Haakon Magnus has just been dethroned by Yugadabe Fikin Kiddinme and Withat Naame. Jason Kolwoski knows what I'm talking about. Yeah. He knows. Krystle Sonnenberg helped me immensely by sliding down a fire pole and then reversing the film while I played a slide whistle. Jairus Montanye and Evelyn Kelly provided me with some wonderful carpet swatches. John Mietz got a poop stuck in his butt and dragged his ass all over them, completely ruining them. By "them," I mean Jairus and Evelyn.

Anthony Cruz is unrelated to Annie Cruz, but they both deserve an equal amount of my thanks. Manuel Fortier-Lanctot supplied me with fleur-de-lis au gratin. Rich Beischer offered to use his connections in the book business to manipulate the *New York Times* Best Seller list. Then he forgot. Sammyz didn't forget, which is why Rich is lying facedown in a puddle of blood!

Klaus Käyhkö said the umlauts were important. Far be it from me to ignore umlauts. Benjamin Cole hates himself so much that I just ruined this book for him by mentioning his name. Myron Bruce, meet my Ron: Reagan. I'm not sure what Ken Benjes did to help, but I think it involved handling live snakes. Kevin Martin handled the snakes as well. It wasn't Kevin Martin's job.

Jason Lyon chased Mike Horsepool right off the diving board and into the completely normal pool not intended for horses. Then Jason Lyon bit Mike Horsepool because he is a lion! Chris Creasy was too greasy to help me much, but he could escape from a bear hug.

Evan Adkins and Neil Amundson should not be thanked after midnight, and you definitely don't want to get either of them wet. Nicolai Olsen wanted to give a shout-out to YCS, but in ten years, no one will even know what that means. Thank Jesus instead, moron! Percival Ignatious Jr. sounds like he has a fake name, which causes him a lot of problems when crossing international borders. Von Dü's Buff Stricker took my beef sticker, and now I'm eating bad meat! Timony Cutwell plays metal guitar for a very popular Poison cover band in the Encino area.

Kit Farman has white friends, and they're clappin' like this, y'all. Craver plans to drop the "C" and invest in glow sticks. Tim Heylen was not named in the indictment, but he promised to thank me in his book. They say Seth Mayne was blown up by Spanish saboteurs; I say he has blown up because of all those donuts. Jared Larsen searched the cushions of my couch for change and came up with half a potato chip. Jackpot!

Ben "Moose" Boyd provided the radioactive elements for my dirty bomb. Jordan "TelevisedInsanity" Hass thinks he is no relation to cover artist Josh Hass, but he is really his father! Beefnoodle is the worst kind of noodle and the best kind of friend. Josef Metesh has been conducting pressure experiments on members of the band. Dann Holmes implores you to tear up the floorboards, there, and there, to silence the beating of that damnable heart!

Markoff Chaney is my go-to guy for hitting the snooze button on the alarm clock. A God Damned Hilarious Fake Name should try not to take the Lord's name in vain so much. MissileWaster is a lender of last resort. Agent "Mike P." Escalus runs a resort of last resort, and he needs to borrow some money. Jon "Asshole" West was a big—well, he was an asshole.

Siminu Wolfcöre has nominated himself for treasurer but plans to vote for someone else. Steven Rogers is running unopposed as county comptroller. Alex Zawacki was thinking about running for something, but he forgot to file his papers. Josh Levine has decided to step down as 13th Ward alderman following a sex-for-contracts scandal involving the garbage trucks union and a couple of hookers named Stephanie and Joseph Savino.

Booger has a dumb-ass call sign, and a dumber-ass CB handle. 10-4, Senorita Boogerfarts! Fuller9x is recording numbers stations and posting them on his blog. Johann Skulason wants to know what happened to Tower 7 and doesn't think he needs to wear pants just to get a goddamn answer. Karsh knows the answer and demands pants. Phillip Jacobi will be representing the families of everyone who lost a loved one to this book.

Magnar postponed his suicide to read this book. Now that it's through, he can go ahead and take care of some unfinished business. LB & BG are having a LGBT BBQ, BYOB. Ian Burns wants you to take a look at this gape! It's insane! Ipzie was once a little green ball of clay; now he's dead because he refused to wear a seatbelt. Thomas Story was voted worst Story of 2007 at the Story Family

Reunion in Bookville. Jonathan Floriani did nothing wrong in the eyes of the law, but the rest of us know what he did.

Jewish Pokémon is searching for a mohel for Snorlax. MrOpus is a pocket monster mohel, but he only works on Digimon. Alexander Mackenzie Parkes Kent divides into two complete individual people when threatened. Branden Miesemer had better not try that hypnotism shit with my girlfriend! Will Knox just learned a valuable lesson about negging a handicapped girl in front of her sister. Austin "Ulkhaul" Luton has never learned any lessons in his life and wanders around in a sensory fugue state.

Geraint Cheers was implicated in the theft of the royal jewels. Robert Watling was the mastermind of the caper, but he got off scot-free. Kristoffer "Daydream" Hofmann was supposed to disarm the security system, but he became distracted, thinking about roller coasters.

Gabe Constantine asked for me to dedicate this book to Sarah Palin. I refused, and I am instead dedicating this book to Ed Hamper. Thanks, Ed! The PrankDialer Guy was really just a computer we plugged into the phone line that would call restaurants, play a sound clip of laughter, and then hang up. Drew "Leovinus" Moffatt ate so much ice cream, he died and is now the second man ever to die from ice cream. 486 is cooler than Steph. I don't really believe that, Steph. You're wonderful.

Brian Pinkos can point to this sentence in this book and maybe a girl will touch his wiener. FictionSpoilers.com is the worst website ever, and you should never visit it unless you hate children and baby ducks. M. Simon Rouswell doesn't have a twist ending. He just dies and gets buried like everyone else. Sub-Actuality, on the other hand, turns into a computer program and sells beverages for America.

James Hunt plans to name his kid Mike, and he can't stop giggling. Shout-outs to Big P: we shared the good times and the bad times and the loot from that bank robbery. Don't worry, Big P, I will never snitch about the Substandard Saving and Loan in Wood Creek, New Jersey, that we robbed on March 15, 2006. I won't tell nobody about that security guard, David Dorr, we had to tie up in the trunk, and then you forgot to take the tape off and he died in there. I will not tell the authorities about André Spångberg, our accomplice that we murdered so we wouldn't have to share the loot with him. Nope, my lips are sealed, Big P.

Liquidator says everything must go, and who am I to argue? Some dude says barren sky & Manta = BFF, and I am fucking embarrassed as shit right now to even include that. Dude, this is in a book forever, and that is the best you could come up with? Brandon Sladey knows what I'm talking about. That dude has a tattoo of himself on his ass. Duncan Boland knows, too; he got the Chinese letters that spell out "I hate America" on his back.

Keyboard Fox lives to eat; he doesn't eat to live. Bart Holthuijsen is probably reading this book under blighted foreign skies. Corey Greenhawk shares the name of my wood elf wizard, and he was a pretty good D&D character. SLoW learned the hard lesson that if you have never played a fiddle before, you shouldn't enter a fiddler's duel with Lucifer. Allison Clark is losing her battle against the gum disease gingivitis, but she's winning the war. Simon "McSteve" Bailey has never brushed his teeth, mostly because he has a beak!

Extra Innings Lovin is only getting his name mentioned because he beat me in a staring contest. Liam Treasure marked an "X" on the map to my heart. Pete Hansen has never caught a predator, but he has entrapped several herbivores. Aaron Lopez thinks it's funny to impersonate Jesse "The Body" Ventura. How about taking your craft seriously, Aaron?

Bob Moulton is cooling to form a substrate on which this island will grow. I would like to thank Lobsterboy for being Lobsterboy, Richard Takacs for being a hot tub swinger, and Josh Vermast for following the distress beacon and playing right into my trap. Stephanie Chaplin is not going to regret this in the morning. Matt Kwis is still downloading the Internet onto his disk drive. Please insert new volume, Matt.

Boo. Who's terrifyingly linguistic. Dr. Charles Boulware III, esq., is a made-up fake name some jerk wanted me to put in this book. Yeah, real hilarious, Admiral Peabody Jerkington IV, D.D.S. Chris "Niggard Please" Buckey is going to get me in trouble with all sorts of people who can kick my ass. Gary Carver doesn't care if I live or die, as long as I enter his name into the public record. Matt Cruea died for my freedom, facedown in the muck of Panama.

Outlaws-Delight is not the sort of name you want for your law firm. The Chinese Connection is great, as long as you just want noodles or dragon-themed import furniture. JasTiger is going hull down for charity, and duggimon is just trying to evolve before the next commercial break. Jossoy is burning churches in Norway because I asked for a black metal Christmas.

Cameron David Pryor was an honorable foe, and I salute his doomed effort to defeat me in combat. George, Paul, Katie, and Partha, you fight like a girl. Ha Ha Ha. John Rhines is the 2009 recipient of the World's Greatest Dad award. Chris Manlow isn't a dad at all, but when he's alone, he puts on a big dad hat and pretends he is a dad. Catelyn Newman loves me more than *Twilight*, and that's saying a lot because she likes the Twilight books oodles!

Kreeblah ignored the warning sirens and paid the price. Stefi Pfeifer, some dude thinks you're hot and wanted me to include you in this book. He's going to eventually regret it, so you might as well make him really regret it. Marry him.

Vidmaster likes to watch dogs kissing each other. Sashi G. Alvarez is wishing his hard drive would hurry up and defrag so he could download some more pornography. Sergio Opperman is today's Worst Person in the World. Colin Creasy may or may not be related to Chris Creasy, but I hate them both equally! Nick Dunn has never left my side, even when I'm in the shower. Nick, it's starting to get a little weird. Can you at least wash my back if you're going to stand there?

Stephen Kinser doesn't read Sutter Cain, but he'll still throw an axe at your face. Qiyu Liu is just trying to work out all the bugs before this book enters beta. Manky is willing to eat anything, if the price is right. Teemu Pulkkinen had a look at what's in the bag, and yeah, it's a human ear, alright. Scienide is not a part of your recommended daily allowance. VeryVito is updating his dream journal with another scorcher about your mom.

Slightly Evil Overlord James Hunt has ordered his minions to climb under your car and make it so your brakes squeak loudly at each stoplight. Chris "Petey" Peterson is my coworker, so how can I not include him? Thanks, Petey! Enok "kjetting" Moe is opposed to the bailout money for fjord. Souha Azmeh has two to beam aboard, captain.

I hope Erika Lee Schneider-Thurston and Sean Ronald Thurston stay together long enough to appreciate being listed as a couple in my book. If not, Erika bought the books, so I hope she won everything in the divorce. Sorry, Sean.

Mark Winckle slept for twenty years, and when he woke up, I had written another book. Perfect timing, Mark! Kyle Kalkman's name is a killing word. Beto's name is just a regular word, and no amount of fancy-pants science is going to convince him it causes cancer. Videodrome wanted to be thanked, but the new flesh died, so we're going to cancel the celebration.

Rudi Endresen is from Norway. He was the first guy in the whole world to buy this book. That makes him cooler than you, unless you are Rudi Endresen reading this sentence. Thanks, Rudi! Sorry about Norway!

Love,
Zack Parsons
2009